THE SWORD IN THE STONE DEAD

The Sword in the Stone-Dead

A 1930S MURDER MYSTERY

PAUL TOMLINSON

ISBN: 978-1-5327-0785-8

First published May 2016
Publisher: Paul Tomlinson

www.paultomlinson.org

Cover image and design © 2016 by Paul Tomlinson

For my parents, who bought
me my first typewriter

The Lake

Summer House

To the Village

The Wood

Bridleway

The Orchard

Path

Terrace

The Tower

Dining Room

Library

Great Hall

Drawing Room

Courtyard

Gatehouse

Pond

To the Main Road

Chapter 1

Sunset and the clouds were lit pink like the inside of seashells.
Off the main road, two massive crumbling gateposts stood
like sentries: no gates between them and no walls beside them,
but still it seemed that they could refuse access. A weathered
sign: *Silberman's Keep*. The unpaved road wound through trees
that dusk had already turned into spiky shadows. Darkness
grew deeper under the canopy of leaves. Suddenly the road
broke out of the trees into ground. The surface changed to
pale crushed stone and it became a long, straight driveway,
running between regimented lines of poplars. At the top of the
drive stood the keep.

The crenellations of the tower were a medieval silhouette
against the rosy sky. The keep was a castle in miniature, its
walls rough-faced stone, the corners standing out in smoother
limestone, like mortise and tenon in a dresser drawer. Windows
in the upper floors were dark, but orange light flickered lower
down, as if the tower had been placed on a bonfire.

In front of the tower was a gatehouse: square turrets on
either side of an arched entrance, portcullis raised. The
diamond panes of mullioned windows above the gate caught
the evening light like dragon scales.

Before it reached the gatehouse, the driveway split and

curved around a circle of grass that contained an ornamental pond. In the centre, three monstrous bronze dolphins rose out of the water, mouths gaping, but the fountain they promised did not appear. The surface of the pond looked oily and dead, mottled with the leaves of last year's water-lilies.

Beyond the gateway was a courtyard, alive with activity. To one side, a huge cone-shaped pile of timber blazed, splashing a shifting orange light up against the tower. On the other, close to a line of rough wooden tables, was a glowing pile of coals over which a spit was being turned: the roasting hog glistened like brown toffee and its juices dripped and crackled on the embers. Servers carried platters and jugs and huge wooden bowls out of the main hall, and laid the banquet on the trestle tables. The men were dressed in simple smocks over tight leggings; the women in tightly-laced bodices and full skirts. A group of musicians occupied a corner of the courtyard, all in simple peasant dress, nursing fiddle, lute, drum or recorder, awaiting the arrival of the guests.

Mist rose over the open ground as the sun disappeared. The croaking of a horn came from somewhere in the woods, and then two glowing yellow discs appeared, like eyes peering through the rolling vapour. There was a throaty rattling and rumbling as something emerged from the trees, crunching over the gravel, and moved towards the gatehouse. Cries arose from within the courtyard.

"It's here!"

The rumbling and crunching drew closer, and again the horn croaked out a warning. The coach loomed out of the mist, gleaming red and cream paintwork, twin silver bumpers beneath the black radiator grill. People began spilling out of the side door before the wheels had stopped turning. The women wore full-length gowns—no serving wenches, these—and the men in white shirts, velvet doublets, and hose. They had all been brought here from the set of the motion picture *Arthur and Guinevere:* the medieval banquet was a 'thank you' from their director. Or perhaps he was doing it for the sake of publicity

As its passengers trooped in through the gateway, the coach rattled into life again, bluish smoke clouding the air behind it. It ground slowly around the pond. There was a violent honking of horns as a small bright blue sports car sped around the fountain in the opposite direction, directly towards the coach, swerving at the last minute to avoid a collision. The coach driver leaned out of his window to hurl words at the grinning young man who clambered out of the little MG, and who seemed to be dressed as an off-duty knight. A Rolls Royce Phantom drew up to a more statesman-like halt. But its apparent calm was short-lived, as a wild-haired, red-bearded giant threw open the rear door, bursting out: Leo Fulbright looked like a Viking stuffed into the costume of a medieval King. He bellowed at the drivers of the coach and sports car.

"Get them out of the bloody way! I said *no* vehicles!" He stomped back towards the Rolls, where the driver stood looking lost. "Why is it that no one can take bloody direction these days?" Fulbright fumed. *"You,"* he pointed at his driver, "I want all of these cars out of sight. I don't want to see a single one. This is meant to be medieval bloody England!"

Fulbright's driver, Malloy, moved towards the MG. He was a broad-shouldered young man with dark hair and bright blue eyes that were almost turquoise.

"Where are you going?" Fulbright bellowed at him. *"After* you've fetched Miss Trenton from the station, you idiot!"

Malloy shuffled back towards Fulbright's car: he walked with his eyes down and head turned in an attempt to hide what might have been a grease smudge on his chin, but was probably a bruise.

As the Rolls Royce was pulling away, another limousine purred up behind Fulbright. He harrumphed and strode towards the latest arrival. Standing with his hands on his hips, he tried to present a regal figure and assert his mastery.

A uniformed chauffeur opened the door of the Bentley and helped his passenger out. She wore a long black evening dress and a black shawl; leaning on a silver-topped walking cane, she stood aloof and erect, like a Victorian dowager.

"Leo," she said, by way of greeting. He looked her up and down, clearly displeased with what she was wearing.

"You might have made an *effort*, Margot."

"I did: I am here, aren't I?" Without sparing him another glance, she strode past him towards the gateway, limping slightly.

Leo Fulbright muttered something under his breath as her Bentley drove away. He turned and was startled to find someone standing beside him. The thin man wore evening dress, his hair was slicked back and parted on one side, and his pencil-thin moustache twitched as his lips formed a half-smile.

"Vickery," Fulbright said, still regaining his composure. "You came." Was there a hint of disappointment in his voice? "No costume?"

"I feel I am too old for dressing up," Vickery answered. "I shall leave that to you actors."

"I—" Fulbright missed his cue.

"Shall we go in?" Vickery smiled his half-smile again, and set off towards the gateway into the courtyard. After a moment, Fulbright blew air out through his moustache and stomped after him.

"Benjamin, darling, how lovely to see you," Margot McCrae said as Vickery entered the courtyard. She was standing on some stone steps looking down on the goings on in the courtyard with an expression of disdain. "You avoided the fancy dress too, thank you."

Vickery shrugged. "My armour is at the dry-cleaners, they're trying to get a rust spot out of it. What *is* that smell?"

"They're burning a pig on a spit–presumably because they couldn't find the *Standard* theatre critic."

"A wild boar in place of a vile boor?" Vickery said. "We're not dining *alfresco* one hopes?"

"Only the hoi polloi are eating at the outdoor trough," Margot said. "You and I will be joining the blue-bloods and gentlefolk for a banquet in the 'great' hall."

"I do feel *ever so* honoured," Vickery mock-gushed. "Are *all* these people working on Leo's motion picture? There are dozens of them."

Margot looked down on those milling around in the courtyard. "And they will all be shipped back to civilisation on the charabanc come midnight—lucky blighters." She looked up at the keep and shivered. "I can't believe we've agreed to stay in this dreadful place for the whole weekend."

"It is rather medieval," Vickery said. "Though it's all fake, of course, a folly built as the country home for a wealthy Victorian businessman. He put all of his money in a South African diamond mine and lost it. The money, not the mine. No diamonds, you see. Drowned himself in the lake behind the keep, though his family maintained it was a boating accident."

"Who drowned himself?" Margot asked.

"Ephram Zilberman—of Zilberman's Pickles: made his fortune bottling eggs and onions, and later tried herring and pig's feet, but they never really caught on. Rumours that he requested his body be preserved in vinegar before burial are entirely spurious."

"Why are you telling me this, Benjamin? I have almost no

interest in the living, never mind the dead."

"I want people to think we were deeply engaged in a fascinating conversation," Vickery said.

"Since when do you care what people think?"

"When I am seeking to deceive them," Vickery said.

Leo Fulbright stomped across the courtyard, looked out through the gateway, and then stomped back to the door into the keep, where he shouted over the heads of the servers.

"Where's that butler chap, Crawley? I said I wanted that bloody fountain working before nightfall. And did it happen," he muttered, "did it buggery."

"Tell me, how is your secret investigation progressing?" Margot asked.

Vickery sighed. "Does everyone know my purpose here?"

"Only the family, dear. Everyone else thinks you're here to teach that old drunk a few tricks to make him look like a master magician."

"Oh, to have my services rated so highly." Vickery rolled his eyes.

"Was King Arthur really medieval?" Margot asked, watching Fulbright progress around the courtyard and stir the musicians into life.

"No, earlier. Until the French adopted him: they were mad keen on tales of chivalrous knights."

"I was married to a knight. He wasn't at all chivalrous. Though he does have a castle, apparently."

"The keep belongs to—?"

"My ex-husband, yes."

"Sir Geoffrey?"

"I only have one ex-husband—*at the moment.*" She growled

this last as she watched Leo Fulbright trot across to the gateway to greet the latest arrival.

Eleanor Trenton was his Guinevere, here tonight, and in the motion picture that Fulbright was currently directing. She was dressed in a long, pale dress, with tightly laced bodice and a richly embroidered belt. She wore her hair in a single long plait, and it was topped with a plain metal coronet.

"What do you think of Leo's leading lady?" Margot asked.

"Everyone knows he has only one leading lady, Margot."

"*Insipid* isn't she? I have never seen such absence of colour in a woman. Even her eyelashes are pale—like a piglet's. I suppose you think she looks angelic, you men are all..." Margot caught herself and coughed. "I'm sorry, Ben, I didn't..."

"It is nothing."

"Do you know her? When I first met her I thought she seemed familiar," Margot said.

"I don't believe I have ever seen her before," Vickery said.

"Hmm, there's something about her..."

"Where do you think you're off to, Molly?" Fulbright yelled at the driver who had delivered Miss Trenton.

"To 'shift those bloody cars' like you asked," Malloy answered, his voice calm and with a hint of an Irish accent.

"Yes, well, be quick about it. And then come and find me inside. I want you to set up the screen and the projector, if it's not beyond your ability."

"Sire." Malloy bowed and exited.

"Why do people stay in his employ?" Vickery asked.

"They don't. Malloy is the third driver this year—and it's only May."

"Malloy, that's his name?"

"Jamie Malloy. You know him?"

"I—he used to work for someone—an acquaintance,"

Vickery said, staring after the departing figure.

"But his name wasn't Malloy?"

"I'm sure it was. I just forget these things."

"But you remembered his face. *Interesting...*"

"What is?"

"The fact that I can never guess what you're thinking."
Margot smiled and shook her head.

Fulbright took Eleanor Trenton's hand and led her around the
courtyard, like a young man on a high school date.

"Does your husband's behaviour embarrass you?" Vickery
asked.

"You know I was unfaithful to my first husband with Leo?"
She said.

"I had heard that," Vickery replied.

"Actors are flighty. We are not to be depended upon. You
know what it's like in the theatre, Benjamin. A lot of scurrying
around behind the scenes to make everything look effortless.
Then a few short hours of high emotion—that's the thing we
crave. Anything that occurs away from the limelight is only
ever half as bright. Real life never quite reaches the heady peak
of a first night performance."

"Even love?" Vickery asked.

"Even love. So it would be hypocritical of me to throw a
tantrum now, wouldn't it? And it's not as though I have any
great desire to share my bed with him anymore. Husbands are
like children, they stray if you're too strict with them. Or in
Geoffrey's case, not strict enough."

Vickery stifled a laugh. "I'm sorry," he said.

"Don't be: I think it was hilarious. Geoffrey loves dominant
women—not a word from you! He strayed because I wasn't...
strict enough with him. But when he was caught with his
trousers down in Madame's dungeon, well, I just *had* to divorce

him."

"It must have been a terrible shock when poor Geoffrey's secret was made public," Vickery said.

"Well, of course, one has to give that *impression,*" Margot said. "Though you have to be careful with the moral outrage—particularly when you're carrying another man's child. That's why I married Leo—for Linette's sake. It certainly wasn't for his money!" She seemed to think this particularly amusing. "Geoffrey saw to it that I would never be penniless. And I got to keep the London house. He withdrew from public life, as they say. The divorce, marriage to Leo, it was all sorted before Linette was born. As with all plots, timing is the key."

She and Vickery regarded each other for a moment.

"Did Sir Geoffrey ever come to suspect that Leo was behind his public disgrace?" Vickery asked.

"Leo had nothing to do with Geoffrey's exposure, far too subtle a plot for him," she said.

"I see. Sir Geoffrey is unlikely to be a suspect then?"

"Suspect?"

"The death threats that Leo has been receiving," Vickery said.

"You mustn't take those too seriously," Margot said. "I'm sure they are just an attempt to court publicity. That sort of melodrama Leo is *quite* capable of plotting himself."

"Will he be here this weekend, Sir Geoffrey?"

"I very much doubt it. He's rarely seen in public nowadays."

"You two are still on speaking terms?" Vickery asked.

"We weren't on speaking terms when we were married. I haven't seen him in years."

"Leo has obtained the use of Sir Geoffrey's folly, for the party tonight, and for the filming of some scenes for his motion picture. Does it not strike you as odd that your husband and your ex-husband should engage in any kind of business transaction."

"Should it?" Her tone suggested that it didn't

"If I were Sir Geoffrey, I'm sure I wouldn't even want to be in the same room as Leo Fulbright," Vickery said.

"Benjamin, dear, *nobody* wants to be in the same room as Leo, we do it because we have to."

Vickery spied Margot's daughter across the courtyard. She was wearing the long dress of a medieval lady in a rich green colour, the sleeves trailing almost to the ground. She had on a pillbox-like hat with her hair in gold crispinettes.

"Who's that young man with Linette?" Vickery asked. "I saw him arrive in a tiny sports car."

Margot raised her lorgnette and peered across the courtyard.

"He's a photographer—Oliver something. Fast car, easy smile—could charm the knickers off a nun, as they say."

"Linette seems rather taken with him."

"Hopefully she's doing it to spite her father. Leo has forbidden her seeing him."

"Why? They seem a charming couple."

"Leo needs Linnie to stay at home and tend to me, otherwise he might have to do it himself."

"Ah," said Vickery. "And yet I see..."

"What do you *see*?" Margot peered through her glasses again.

"It is probably nothing."

"Out with it. You always 'see' more than anyone else."

"Linette, I think, has gone beyond a mere desire to defy her father. Those two are engaged, I should say."

Margot laughed. "There you are wrong, I can tell you that. Oliver asked Leo's permission, and Leo refused."

"And yet the pair went ahead despite his forbidding. See how she touches her finger? There is a ring, I think, that she is just now not wearing."

"She wouldn't *dare*..." Margot breathed.

"You were quite daring yourself at her age, if I am not mistaken?" Vickery raised an eyebrow and smiled. Margot smiled too.

"Well, well, the little minx. She's coming this way: I shall speak to her and try to catch her in a lie."

"I am sure she is up to the challenge," Vickery said.

"Hello, mother. Daddy says you look like a 'bloody widow.'"

"You can tell your father that I live in hope," Margot said. "Walk with me and tell me what you've been up to, I haven't seen you for days..."

Vickery edged away from mother and daughter, and was stopped by a brisk tap on his shoulder.

"Are you the wizard?"

Vickery turned. The woman who had spoken was tall, broad-shouldered and dressed in trousers and a man's tweed jacket. Her cheeks were ruddy and her hair a bright carrot red frosted with white.

"Miss Fulbright?" Vickery said.

"Veronica. The hair's a dead give-away, isn't it? Glad to meet you." Her handshake was firm. "I just came down on the train—didn't have time to dip into the dressing up box. I'm so glad my brother has hired you—'The Great Vicari'—a *real* magician! You look exactly how a magician should."

"I am a 'technical advisor' only. Mr. Bannister is portraying Merlin," Vickery said. "I retired from performing some years ago."

"You really shouldn't do that."

"Do what, Miss Fulbright?"

"Make out that you're some sort of old fossil. You're not as old as my brother, and he's chasing after some woman half his age."

"My chasing days are over, I think. It is so undignified."

"What rot! You're just afraid."

"I am?"

"You suffered a personal tragedy and are determined not to allow anyone close enough to hurt you again." Veronica laughed. "Don't look so shocked: we had newspapers, even—where I have been."

"Indeed," said Vickery. "But not everyone is so adept at reading between the headlines."

"I do believe that was a compliment. But don't worry, I'm not going to tell anyone your little secret: we'll let them go on believing you are the enigmatic *Vicari, Man of Mystery!*"

"You are most kind." Vickery's attention was caught by Veronica Fulbright's shoes: they were highly polished men's brogues, glossy as horse chestnuts. Veronica Fulbright seemed amused by his interest them.

"They were daddy's," Veronica explained. "They're about all I have that belonged to him. It amuses me to wear them. My brother believes he walks in my father's footsteps—"

"—but it is you who wears your father's shoes," Vickery said.

"You get it, I am pleased." Vickery gave her a little mock-bow. "I have daddy's pipe too, but Leo doesn't like me to smoke in public."

"Your brother is watching us now," Vickery observed.

"Brothers do that, don't they? Even little ones."

"He's younger than you?"

"By three years, yes. But he's always felt a need to watch over me—make sure nothing terrible happens."

"It is natural that he doesn't want any harm to come to you."

"Yes, that as well. I was first-born—but daddy wanted a son. And my mother wanted a daughter. I disappointed them both!" She grinned, showing the same large, yellowish teeth that Fulbright had.

"I am sure that is not true. You hinted earlier that you had been away for a while," Vickery said. "Abroad?"

"Not abroad, no. And not in a convent. Do girls still do that?"

"Some do, I am sure."

"Leo knows we're talking about him." A note of concern had crept into her voice. "He's coming this way. He'll want to know what we were talking about."

"My sister behaving herself, Vickery?" Fulbright asked.

"Indeed, yes. We were just comparing notes on family history."

"Were you, indeed? Well, we were brought up to believe that nothing is more important than family, isn't that right, Veronica?"

"Yes, Leo." Veronica Fulbright seemed unusually subdued in her brother's presence.

Fulbright scowled at them both and turned away. She brightened the moment he was gone, like a cloud had passed from the sun.

"He's always checking if I am behaving myself. I have to do what he says: I'm dependent on him since daddy died. He doesn't let me forget."

"Your brother inherited the family estate?"

"He has all of it now." Her voice was curiously flat, as if she was resigned to her fate. "And I—Do you believe in love, Mr. Vickery?"

"I believe it exists."

"Some people spend their whole lives wondering if they will ever meet that one special person who is out there for them, don't they?"

"And others find that person, and then lose them," Vickery said.

"Yes, that happens to some of us, doesn't it? And when it does—I wonder if we can ever find happiness with someone else?"

"Widows remarry," Vickery suggested.

"But we are not widows, are we Mr. Vickery?"

They were both silent a moment then, until: "I still wonder what my life might have been like, if I hadn't—if Leo hadn't had to—to lock me away."

"Lock?"

"It was for my own good," she said, too quickly. "I wasn't ready to live by myself. And poor George—well, he wouldn't have been able to take care of me. He wasn't the right sort at all." It sounded as if she was repeating something she'd been told, probably more than once.

"But George loved you?"

"Oh, yes, he does," she said brightly. But then the cloud crossed in front of the sun again. "Or he *did* at least."

"Until—?"

"Until he—until my brother had to intervene."

"And lock you away?"

"For my own good, yes." Her face brightened again. "I'm sorry, you must find all this family stuff frightfully dull. It's not important now. After all, everyone has their secrets, don't they?"

"Indeed."

"Shall I tell you another one of yours?" She asked.

"I—"

"You're not *really* here as a magic advisor."

"I'm not?"

"You're here because my brother thinks someone wants to kill him. I know about the poison pen letters. And about your clandestine activities."

"My—?"

"You're a *detective*, Mr. Vickery," Veronica stage-whispered.

"Hardly a detective, Miss Fulbright. I have merely helped out an acquaintance on occasion."

"Solving mysteries."

"Something like that. Now, I think perhaps I ought to show you a little sleight of hand in order to demonstrate to any onlookers that I really am here as magician-in-residence." Vickery took a pack of cards from his pocket and fanned them out, faces towards Veronica Fulbright. "Think of a card."

"Don't I get to pick one?"

"You already have."

Veronica frowned.

"What was your card?" Vickery asked.

"Seven of clubs."

"As I thought. It's in your top pocket."

Veronica dipped her fingers into the jacket pocket behind her handkerchief. The card she extracted was the Seven of Clubs. She smiled.

"Do you investigate as well as you prestidigitate?"

"That remains to be seen," Vickery said.

"No clues so far?"

"The night is young."

"Yes it is," Veronica said. "I think you should go and talk to Malloy."

"Malloy?"

"Don't pretend you haven't noticed him. My brother's driver. Shoulders like a rugby player, eyes like a poet."

"And what should I talk to Mr. Malloy about?"

"You're the detective. But if I were you, I'd ask him how he got that bruise on his jaw."

"Not playing rugby?" Vickery asked.

"You'll have to ask *him* that—if you want to know." She turned her body away, but kept her eyes on him. Then she winked and was gone.

"I don't know what she was telling you," Fulbright said, looming over Vickery, "but she shouldn't—"

"She was telling me about George."

"What about him?" Suspicious.

"He was her one true love."

"*Pshaw!* She was infatuated with him. Schoolgirl crush. I don't think George felt the same way about her. Or he would have stuck around when—"

"When Veronica 'went away' for a while?"

"You know about that?"

"You did it for her own good," Vickery said flatly. "And that's also why you had to take control of your father's estate while she was away?"

"She wasn't fit to look after herself, not the state she was in."

"And George?" Vickery asked.

"No idea what happened to him. But I think I did him a favour too, in the long run."

"I'm sure he sees it the same way," Vickery said.

Fulbright *humphed.* "I had better go and look out for Eleanor."

"It must be quite a burden for you," Vickery said, as Fulbright turned away.

Fulbright stopped and cast him a quizzical look.

"—being surrounded by women who need you to take care of them," Vickery finished. "Veronica after her 'episode,' shall we call it? Your wife after her accident. Your daughter. And now Eleanor—"

Fulbright frowned. "We do what we have to, for the people we care about. Don't even question it, do we? Don't go looking for motives there—they all need me. They're not going to poison the golden goose, are they?"

"Interesting you should say 'poison.' That is typically seen as a woman's preferred method."

"What?"

"For murder. Men tend to prefer something that better

demonstrates their—power over the victim."

"That right?" Fulbright said. "In case you've forgotten, the idea is that you find out who has sent those blasted letters *before* I am murdered."

"I shall endeavour to oblige," Vickery said.

"Do that."

Seeing that Linette had gone to re-join her fiancé, Vickery returned to Margot's side. She was staring up at the walls of the tower.

"Is Leo thinking of buying Silberman's Keep?" Vickery asked.

"Good lord, no. He hasn't any money."

"I heard someone referring to 'Fulbright's Folly,' and thought they meant this place."

"They were probably talking about this dratted moving picture of his."

"Did you apply the thumbscrews to Linette?" Vickery asked.

"Couldn't get a thing out of her. She's hiding something, though. Walk with me, let's go and frighten the groundlings." Taking his arm, she led him down the steps and across the courtyard.

"Isn't it unusual to have a party like this *before* the shooting of the motion picture is complete?" Vickery asked.

"I think Leo's afraid none of them will be talking to each other by the time they get to the end. Assuming they even get to the end. This thing will probably bankrupt him. Again. Remember that Shakespeare tour of Belgium? That's why I insist on separate finances. He's only invited me down here because he wants me to stump up the cash to get his blasted picture finished."

"Is it going well?"

"I doubt it. A bunch of old Shakespearean hams bellowing

at the camera and gesticulating wildly, working without a prompt. It'll be like... well, we'll see, won't we? The highlight of this evening is going to be a screening of the first few days' filming. Every retake, missed cue, and fluffed line, I suppose. I intend to be well and truly sozzled before then. Come on, there must be drink here somewhere. I just hope it's not bloody mead."

"I distinctly heard the sound of champagne corks inside," Vickery reassured her. They headed through the open door into the keep.

Chapter 2

Margot and Vickery entered the great hall. People were standing by a wooden table to one side, drinking and chatting in twos and threes. Vickery collected glasses of champagne and returned to Margot's side.

"Look at that bloody table," Margot said. "There's no escape, is there?"

The table—a replica of King Arthur's round table that had been built for Fulbright's motion picture—looked vast, with a dozen places set around it. The centre was covered with plates of carved roast meat, dishes of steaming vegetables, jugs of wine, and platters of breads and fruits.

The great hall looked to have been painted recently, but already damp was beginning to discolour the walls in places, and cracks had reopened. Bare oak beams in the roof made the hall seem larger than it really was, and a fire in the inglenook fireplace cast a pleasant glow.

The keep was furnished in Victorian Gothic style, with dark wood panelling. Large oil paintings and various bits of medieval weaponry adorned the walls. Electric lighting had been installed, but that looked to be the limit of any attempted modernisation.

Silberman's Keep was built around the courtyard. The

gatehouse, with walls either side, made up the front. A large drawing room made up the left wing of the building, and the great hall the right. Both wings had an upper floor containing bedrooms. At the back, the tower dominated, with a library to its left and dining room to the right. Behind the keep, outside the dining room, was a terrace; outside the library was a small orchard. Beyond this, paths through the uneven gardens and lawns down to the lake, a summer house, and—away to the left—through a small wood.

The ground floor of the tower consisted of a stone-floored entrance hall, with a grand staircase facing the door. Half-a-dozen steps carpeted in a rich red led up to a wide first landing, on which a stately grandfather clock stood. The landing was almost big enough to serve as a stage. Stairs led off left and right to the bedrooms above. There was a small servants' staircase in one corner of the entrance hall, leading down to the kitchens and cellars, and up to the staff quarters in the middle floors of the tower.

Margot took a sip of her champagne and grimaced. "Perhaps Leo is broke already. Now, where's his flat-chested little queen?"

"Here I am!" Said a voice brightly. Margot turned and under her gaze the thin young man in the minstrel costume visibly wilted.

"Not *you*, half-wit," Margot growled. The man smiled weakly and scurried away. Margot watched him go. "If my legs looked that good in red stockings, I could have done better than Leo Fulbright." She saw that Vickery was frowning at her. "Was he a friend of yours?" She asked.

"No, but still—" Vickery said.

"Simpering idiot. Artie used to be Ted Kimball's dresser. How on earth he got Leo to cast him as a minstrel, I have no—"

"Perhaps on the strength of his singing voice?"

"He sings?"

"As a minstrel, one would hope so."

"You've heard him?"

"Not as a—minstrel, no."

"There's something you're not telling me."

"Why do you say that?" Vickery asked.

"Because there is *always* something you don't tell me."

"I have a reputation as an enigma to uphold," Vickery said. "Will you sit by me at the table? I'm going to have a word with one of the waiters, get him to serve us the good champagne for the rest of the evening."

"That will help ease the discomfort."

"Your back troubles you tonight?"

"That as well."

"Ah, and there is Excalibur!" Vickery said, as people moved away, allowing them to see the *papier-mâché* rock into which the sword had been plunged. "Aren't you going to try and draw the sword from the stone?"

"If I had a sword in my hand, I might be tempted to use it," Margot said.

They watched as several people tried and failed to pull the sword out of the rock.

"It's a trick rock," Artie Delancey said, appearing beside Vickery. "I can tell you how to draw Excalibur out."

"A disguised foot-pedal," Vickery said. "Used in stage magic for years."

The young minstrel looked disappointed, until Vickery told him that he himself had been 'in the trade.'

A camera that looked like it had been made from an accordion and a Meccano set had been mounted on a tripod, and the young man from the sports car could be seen ushering those in costume to stand before it to remain motionless for portraits, or to adopt frozen poses to give the impression that an action had been captured spontaneously. Even Leo

Fulbright struck a kingly pose for a photograph and hardly seemed annoyed when he was half-blinded by the flash bulb.

"Young Mr. Garvin has been hired to provide publicity photographs?" Vickery asked. "I thought Leo wanted to keep him away from your daughter?"

"Ollie offered to do it for nothing," Margot said. "He must be an idiot."

"The work he does tonight may lead to paid work in the future," Vickery suggested.

"As long as he doesn't have to pawn the camera to pay for whatever he'll need to print those photographs. He can't afford to be doing this."

"Perhaps he's hoping that Leo may look more favourably on him in future."

"If he thinks that, then he's definitely an idiot," Margot said.

"Places everyone!" Fulbright's voice echoed out, silencing everyone. They set down empty champagne glasses, and moved to their places around the table. Once they were seated, Fulbright leaned forward and clasped his hands in front of him. For a moment it looked as though he was about to say grace.

"Dear friends," he said. "I want to thank you all for coming here this weekend. And I also want to thank you for being part of *Arthur and Guinevere*—our first motion picture together! Like all productions, there will be a great deal of work put in before our performances are seen by an audience, but this time we are creating something that will not fade from memory after a handful of performances, it will entertain audiences for generations to come!" He got to his feet and raised his glass. "To *Arthur and Guinevere!*"

"To *Arthur and Guinevere!*" Everyone echoed.

"Let the feast begin!" Fulbright bellowed.

Silberman's Keep was not Sir Geoffrey Atterbury's main residence: when he had left London in disgrace, he had purchased a large house just outside Bath. The folly was a country retreat that was overseen by Crawley, who lived in the gatehouse and acted as butler and factotum when Sir Geoffrey was in residence. There was a cook, Mrs. Battison, and three maids who also lived permanently in the keep. The gardener, Grives, lived in a cottage in the village a mile or so away. It had the appearance of a country house in miniature, but at the same time there was something not quite real about it. A suitable back-drop for this round table of theatrical gentry.

After they had eaten their fill, people got up and lit cigars or cigarettes, and set about the cheap champagne again.

"You've read the photoplay," Margot said, "what do you make of it?"

"It's not exactly Shakespeare," Vickery said.

"Can't film Shakespeare, Vickery," Fulbright said, butting in and slapping Vickery heartily on the shoulder. "The hoi polloi get numb bums if they have to sit for much more than an hour. You've got to give them sword fights and dramatic death scenes. A villain to boo, a hero to cheer, a break halfway through to buy ice-cream, then a couple of gory corpses and a wedding at the end."

"You've just described half of Shakespeare's plays!" Margot said.

"Yes, but we'll do it in half the running time," Fulbright said. "The Yanks are making thousands doing it: don't see why we can't do the same."

"A draughty shed in Hertfordshire isn't exactly Hollywood, though, is it?" Margot said.

"Come through to the drawing room when you're ready. We've set up a projector to show the first scenes we shot."

Fulbright wandered away to perform more hearty back-slapping.

"Can they really do King Arthur justice in six reels?" Margot wondered.

"The script includes all the famous scenes. But it owes more to those school storybook retellings than to Mallory or Wordsworth," Vickery said. "And there seems to be a suggestion that Arthur stole Guinevere from Lancelot, perhaps they had to do that to make the love story seem slightly less adulterous."

"Or perhaps Leo put it in to make a point of his own. Do you think Teddy is a bit old for Lancelot? I always imagined him younger and more—virile."

"I imagined him as blond with a neat little beard," Vickery said. Margot looked at him and smiled.

"What do you think *that's* all about?" Margot asked. Across the room, Ted Kimball and Artie Delancey were having what appeared to be a heated discussion in hushed voices.

"Pretend that I'm listening to you, while I watch them, then I'll tell you what they're saying," Vickery said.

"How? You read lips?"

"And sign language. I was deaf for over a month after a stage explosion during my act was rather more vigorous than expected."

"Is that true?"

"No, but it sounds better than saying I learned so I could eavesdrop on other people's conversations."

"What are they arguing about?"

"Give me a few seconds to catch the rhythm and then I will repeat what I hear. Artie is saying something about not knowing 'he' would be there, but I'm not sure who *he* is..."

Vickery nodded as if attending to what Margot was saying, and kept watching the two actors. After a few moments he began repeating their dialogue.

Kimball: "Did you know what sort of club it was?"

Artie: "Of course I did."

Kimball: "Why the hell did you take me *there?*"

Artie: "It's the only place I know that serves gin to drunks after midnight. Well, that and the bar in the Houses of Parliament."

"You're awfully good at this," Margot said.

"How would you know?" Vickery asked. "I could be making all of it up."

"Are you?"

"I'm guessing at some of it."

"What about whispering?" Margot asked.

"We could," Vickery stage-whispered, "but I don't think they can hear us all the way over there."

Margot slapped him on the arm. "I mean, can you lip-read when they're whispering?"

"Sometimes—depends how stiffly they hold their lips. Or if they do it out of the corner of their mouths. Mr. Kimball is accusing Artie Delancey of having done it on purpose to ruin his reputation. He's just a jealous little queen."

"Kimball?"

"No, Delancey, according to Kimball. No, don't turn your head away."

"Who said that?"

"I did. Ah, he's back."

"He called my *name,* Artie. How did he know I was there?" Kimball asked.

"Perhaps somebody tipped him off," Artie suggested.

"I thought you people had a code. Aren't you supposed to be *discreet?*"

"We are, darling. We have to be because of the way *you people* behave towards us. No one in that bar called the photographer: it must have been someone else."

"You think somebody *followed* me there?"

"Possibly. Or somebody knew that I went in there sometimes and guessed I'd take you there."

"I'm still not sure you didn't set this up."

"Do you really think I would do that to you? Why would I?"

"Because you can't *have* me."

"Darling, I've already *got* you. I wouldn't jeopardise that: You're my friend."

"But you want more."

"I'm a grown-up, I know that isn't going to happen. I can't give you what Eleanor's got." Artie couldn't manage to keep the bitterness out of his voice.

"You are jealous then. That's why you had that photographer there. You wanted to break up what she and I have."

"If you want to believe that, then fine, believe it. Next time you can find someone else for your after-hours pub crawl."

"Admit that you are jealous of her," Kimball insisted. "You wish I was on top of you, not her."

"You're a drunken oaf. I feel sorry for her."

"You make me *sick*!" Kimball said.

"No, that's the whisky, love."

"I should bloody smack you."

Artie stood with his arms wide, presenting his chin. "If you really want to hit me, fucking do it. You won't be the first."

Kimball, too late, realised he'd gone too far.

"Artie, I didn't—"

"No, maybe you are right, Teddy. People like you and people like me can't just be fiends."

"Artie, please—"

But Artie was already striding away, resolute.

"Lover's tiff?" Fulbright, at Kimball's elbow, laughed.

"We're not—"

"Lovers? I know that, you idiot. I've seen you at work, remember? The hunter and the prey. Chasing down some poor unsuspecting doe-eyed bint."

"And you're so different?" Kimball asked.

"I'm the King of the Beasts, Teddy—*they* come to *me!*"

"How much longer will that last? How long before Leo the Lionheart is a toothless tabby?"

"I'm King Arthur, my boy, not Richard. My legend will last forever!"

"But has King Arthur's sword been in Guinevere's stone yet, that's what all the groundlings want to know."

"It doesn't matter if I have or I haven't—"

"*No* then."

"It's what they *believe* that matters."

"They believe you're an old goat. And every one of them has a reason to hate you. Does that make you feel like a king, Leo?"

"They're *supposed* to hate me, you fool: they're afraid of the King's power over them. Your problem is you think everyone should *love* you. That's why you keep dear old Artie around to fawn all over you, you love to be worshipped. But how much longer will *that* last? Keep at that bottle, my boy, and those matinee idol looks will fade quicker than a politician's smile."

"I should be more like you then?" Kimball sneered.

"There comes a time when you have to stop filling a role, and *become* a character. You will face that choice very, very soon. Better to be a bastard than to be a has-been. When the looks go, it's the forceful personality that gets the women wet."

"Artie said *I* was an oaf..."

"There you are then, there's hope for you yet. And try and lay off the booze. You know where it gets you." Fulbright roared as if this was the best joke he'd heard all night.

"Bastard!" Kimball hissed as Fulbright swaggered away.

"You shouldn't let my brother provoke you." Veronica Fulbright handed Kimball a half-glass of whisky, no ice, no water. "He hates it if you don't rise to the bait. He feeds on anger and tears, like a leech."

"Are you two not close, then?" Kimball favoured her with a smile over his glass—then took a good gulp of whisky.

"No one is close to Leo. How could they be?"

"Did you *really* try and shoot him?" Kimball asked, slyly.

"Did you *really* fuck his wife?" Veronica smiled. He grinned back at her.

"If he dies, do you inherit?" Kimball asked.

"Why, are you planning to kill him?"

"Haven't the guts—even with this." He held up the empty glass.

"Pity," Veronica said.

"Perhaps we should have a whip round and hire an assassin."

"Would you hurt him, if you could?" Veronica asked. "If you thought you would get away with it?"

"Would you?"

"I didn't get away with it. Had to pay the price."

Kimball gave her a quizzical look.

"Locked up for my own good," Veronica said.

"Why'd you try and kill him?"

"Because he's Leo."

"There must be more to it than that."

"We lived in the same house for twenty years, with my parents, then just me and him. One day I thought I'd found a way to escape. I was in love, Teddy, can you believe that? Someone *loved* me!"

"Leo didn't approve of him?"

"Leo didn't approve of the fact that I was older than him, and would inherit half of daddy's estate if I married."

"What did he do?"

"He did what Leo does. How do you think that photographer *happened* to be outside that backstreet bar the other night?"

"Not Leo?"

"Someone ought to give him a taste of his own medicine, don't you think?"

"I'll drink to that." Kimball raised his empty glass. Veronica produced the whisky bottle and provided a refill. "Not joining me?" Kimball asked.

"I don't drink. Don't want Leo thinking I'm not in control of myself."

"That man takes away all the pleasures in life."

"Not all of them," Veronica said.

A hand seized Leo Fulbright by the shoulder and spun him round.

"It was you!" Kimball's face was bright with anger.

Fulbright expression registered confusion, perhaps even fear, but then he recovered himself and grinned—triumphant.

"Did you figure it out yourself, or did someone have to explain it to you?" Fulbright gloated.

"*Why?*"

"For Eleanor's sake. You weren't the right man for her."

"And you are?" Kimball asked.

"Of course not. But then I'm not going to keep her. I'll go back to Margot, I always do. I just needed to rescue Eleanor first."

"Bollocks!"

Fulbright considered this, then nodded. "You're right: I didn't do it for Eleanor at all. I did it because I *wanted* to. Because of what you *did* to me—to Margot!"

"Leo, that was *one night, six years* ago!"

"You made me look like a fool!" He began stabbing Kimball in the chest with a pointing finger, in time with his words. "No one makes me look like a fool. *Ever!*"

Kimball took a step back, his own anger swept away in the onslaught: he was staring into the open jaws of the lion for the first time.

And then the storm passed, and Leo was smiling into his face.

"Consider it over. *I've* won." And then dismissively: "Go and get yourself another drink."

Kimball felt his cheeks redden.

"You didn't win. This is *not* over. You didn't get your wretched pictures. I stamped on his camera, ruined his film!" His eyes were bright with this small triumph.

"There is more than one photographer in my kingdom, Teddy." Fulbright's voice was quietly mocking. "I got my pictures. And you gave me so much more when you attacked that poor fellow."

"You're lying."

"I have a set of prints upstairs. They're a little dark, but you can make your face out plainly enough. I'll push the envelope under your door later."

"I don't—You haven't—Has Eleanor seen them?"

"I don't think she will need to. Do you?"

"No. I'd sooner she didn't."

"Now," Leo smiled magnanimously, "how about that drink?"

"I don't—" But Leo's look said he wasn't going to accept a refusal.

"Scotch, no ice," Kimball said quietly.

Edward Kimball didn't think it was possible for him to feel any smaller. Until he glanced up and saw that Veronica Fulbright had watched the whole exchange between him and her brother. He couldn't bear the look of disappointment on her face, and so turned to follow Leo Fulbright.

"Mr. Vickery? We weren't introduced properly earlier, I'm afraid."

"Miss Trenton, how delightful." He took her hand and bowed his head slightly before releasing it. "I feel I should say 'your majesty'!"

"Ridiculous, isn't it?" She took off the coronet and dropped it on a table. Her hair was white-blonde, as were her eyebrows, and her eyes a deep blue. She was coolly beautiful, and yet there was also something of the gamine about her. Vickery suspected that she had been quite the tomboy in her youth.

"That dress looks frightfully uncomfortable," Vickery said.

"It is. But no one can see my feet, so at least I escape having to wear heels."

"And can instead wear tennis shoes," Vickery said.

"You can *see?*" She sounded horrified that her secret was known.

"The merest glimpse earlier as you crossed the room. No one else witnessed it, I assure you." He smiled and, finally, so did she.

"You must be used to this sort of party," she said.

"One's tolerance increases as the years pass," Vickery said. "I avoid them as much as I am able."

"I hate it that everyone seems to be staring at me. Or am I being paranoid?"

"No, they are staring," Vickery confirmed. "After all, you are the star, and also the most beautiful woman in the room."

"Thank you, but—"

"A statement of fact based on observation, not merely flattery."

"You are very kind."

"And old fashioned and a little boring," Vickery said.

"To be truthful, that's quite a relief from—all this."

"Ah, then I am pleased to be of service, and shall continue to bore you!" He smiled.

"It is good to speak to someone who is not quite so—"

"Actorly?"

She laughed. "Yes. It is all rather insular. I feel a longing for *real* people. Is that terrible of me?"

"Perfectly wicked. I approve! Though I should, in the interests of honesty, point out that I am not entirely untainted: I too used to 'tread the boards.'"

"Yes, I thought there was that whiff about you." Eleanor Trenton mocked his mockery.

"It does not matter how often one's things are laundered, alas the smell seems to linger."

"But you are not an actor?"

"Didn't Shakespeare say that we are all actors?" Vickery asked.

"Did he?"

"He did."

"Does that mean that none of us are ever quite what we seem?" She asked.

"Perhaps. Or that we all have to play our parts in a larger story. We adopt different roles depending on where we are and who we are with. Sometimes you are the actress; sometimes a daughter; and sometimes a lover. But none of these roles are all that you are, or ever will be."

"Did Shakespeare say that?"

"He would have done, if he'd been here instead of me. Only he'd have made bits of it rhyme."

"All the same, I am glad it is you here, rather than he."

"Indeed, he was both an *actor* and a *writer*—terrible combination. Actors have enough pride without they become writers too."

"Or directors?" She asked.

"Since we are both currently in the employ of a director, I

shall refrain from expressing an opinion."

"But he is rather pompous?"

"I shall not say." Vickery shook his head.

"Overbearing?"

"Not a word."

"In love with the sound of his own voice?"

"That I might concede."

"Does he love Margot, do you think?"

"Without a doubt. Unfortunately he tends to stray occasionally."

"But he always goes back to her?"

"Thus far, yes."

Eleanor thought about this for a moment, then: "Do you think a person can *change,* Mr. Vickery?"

"That is a question poets and philosophers have pondered for centuries."

"With no hint of a conclusion?"

"Has Mr. Fulbright promised you that he will change?"

"Leo? I think that would be highly unlikely, don't you? Unless he were to become possessed by an evil spirit."

"Or dispossessed of one?"

"You said you wouldn't," she admonished.

"I do not always tell the truth."

"Who does?"

"I thought perhaps Leo had promised that he would leave Margot and marry you," Vickery said.

"I suppose everyone thinks that he and I are 'an item,'" she said. "Leo said they would."

"He is not exactly discouraging the idea," Vickery said.

"He is flattered that people believe he has a younger woman for a lover. It is only natural."

"For some men, perhaps," Vickery said.

"To share your life with a younger partner, that must make

you feel younger too, do you not think?"

"I do not know," Vickery said. "It does not concern you if people are mistaken in their thinking about the relationship between Mr. Fulbright and yourself?"

"Not presently. It gives the magazines something to write about, and keeps our motion picture in the spotlight."

"Or so Leo would have you believe?"

"My agent, actually."

"And he has your best interests at heart, I am sure."

"Hardly! He merely intends that he and I should profit from this as far as possible. It may be that this is my only motion picture. We need people to flock to the cinema to see the great Leo Fulbright and the mistress who is young enough to be his daughter." She paused then. "Does that sound frightfully cynical?"

"It is difficult, I know, when our business requires that we must peddle some version of ourselves to the public," Vickery said.

"Then you don't think it is wrong to exploit Leo's interest in me?"

"Leo Fulbright is old enough to look out for himself, Miss Trenton. But how does your Mr. Kimball feel about it?"

"He is no longer *my* Mr. Kimball," she said frostily. "I have no interest in how he feels."

"I think, perhaps, that is not quite the truth, if you would only admit—"

"I can assure you, Mr. Vickery, that the relationship between Teddy Kimball and myself is ended."

"And yet you use Leo Fulbright's infatuation with you to punish Mr. Kimball, which you would not do if you did not care about his feelings."

"He has behaved like an absolute fool!"

"Sometimes people do that when they are in love. And then

we must forgive them."

"Must we?" She asked. "I do not see why. There must be a line. And if they overstep it, well, they are beyond forgiveness. That is my view."

"No second chances?" Vickery asked.

"In this case—no."

"Then you must let him go, Miss Trenton. To do otherwise will only confuse both him and yourself."

"He knows how I feel. I have let him go."

"But *have* you?"

"I did not come to you to discuss my private life, Mr. Vickery," she said haughtily.

"Then why *did* you come to me, Miss Trenton?"

"I just came to ask you about—well, to see what you—"

"I am sorry that I wasn't able to help you. But if ever I can be of service—" He gave a little bow, and left her to her thoughts.

"What?" Fulbright roared so loudly that the room fell silent and everyone turned towards him.

Fulbright's driver, Malloy, was standing with an open film canister in his hands. It was empty, and it soon became clear that the footage from *Arthur and Guinevere* was missing.

For a moment it appeared that Fulbright was about to explode. Malloy took a step back, perhaps anticipating another blow from his employer's fist.

Then Fulbright let out a loud sigh, like steam leaking from a pipe, and stomped out.

Chapter 3

"Hello, Linette."

"Mr. Vickery, how are you?"

Linette Fulbright was leaning in the open doorway onto the terrace, looking out over the grounds at the back of the keep. She was smoking a cigarette, but didn't seem to be enjoying it. In the darkness, trees were black shadows and the moon was glimmering on the water beyond.

"I'm not interrupting, I hope?" Vickery said.

"Oh, no, I just needed some air." She threw away the half-smoked cigarette. "Did mother send you to find me? Does she want to go up to bed already?"

"No, no, she is currently enjoying the company of Mr. Bannister."

"*Enjoying?*" Linette smiled.

"You do not find theatrical anecdotes entertaining?" Vickery asked, also smiling.

"If I hear another story that begins 'I remember when we were playing *Much Ado* in Edinburgh,' I swear I shall scream," Linette said. "Is mummy being intolerably rude to everyone?"

"No, she seems almost cheerful since she learned that she would not have to sit through that reel of your father's film."

"It wouldn't surprise me if she was the one who took it, just to hack off my father. He's downing brandy by the bucketful in an attempt to drown his sorrows. I can't remember the last time I saw him this pissed," Linette said. "Does my language shock you?"

"I am told that a sailor once visited the theatre backstage, and was offended by what he heard," Vickery said.

Linette smiled, but her serious expression soon returned. "My old nurse used to say that actors are highly strung and need to unwind, though she wasn't a stranger to the gin bottle herself. 'You should avoid drink, dear,' she said, 'it makes grown-ups act like children.' But actors do that anyway, don't they? It's all dressing up and 'let's pretend.'"

She looked down at her hand as if expecting the cigarette to be there, but her prop was gone. Her eyes turned toward the dark again, and Vickery saw in her profile how like her mother she had become.

"Nothing is real for them," she said. "No wonder they all struggle to get on with their lives. They only really exist in that twilight world back stage. I want to have *adventures*—out in the real world. Have you ever flown in an aeroplane, Mr. Vickery?"

"Twice. It was very noisy. I imagine that airships are a much more peaceful way to travel."

"I want to fly an aeroplane—like Amelia Earhart. But daddy won't even let me drive a car. Perhaps I shall get a motorcycle— that must be like riding a bicycle, except that you have to start it and change gear and whatever. I'm sure Ollie would show me how."

"Ah, to be young and full of enthusiasm for life," Vickery said wistfully.

"You don't need to be young to have enthusiasm, Mr. Vickery. You just have to have something to live for."

"You are wise beyond your years, my dear."

"Ollie says I'm too grown up sometimes. He doesn't know what it was like growing up with parents like mine—the emotional ups and downs; the arguments; the need for attention..."

"Both you and Mr. Garvin had to grow up quickly, I think. He was without parents himself, and so you must make allowances for him."

"How do you know that?" Linette asked.

"His aunt and I are old friends."

"I see. Do you smoke?"

"No, I've seen what it does to kippers."

Linette laughed. "I suppose I shouldn't either; the smell gets in one's hair and stinks up one's clothes terribly. But at school we all thought it made us seem so much more sophisticated."

"A common misconception amongst the young," Vickery said.

Linette put her head on one side and stared at him, a half-smile on her lips.

"I think you do that on purpose," she said.

"Do what, Miss Fulbright?"

"Pretend to be an old fuddy-duddy. I don't believe it at all, you know. You do it so that people will underestimate you and let something slip. That's what Monsieur Poirot does, isn't it?"

"Mais oui, mon amie." Vickery smoothed his moustache and winked.

"Daddy's not very fond of Belgians. They didn't like his Henry Vee."

"Perhaps they would have taken to him more as Falstaff?" Vickery suggested.

"He has rather grown in stature in recent years, hasn't he? I have no idea what the Snow Queen sees in him."

"Some women are drawn to men they see as powerful and successful. Perhaps they feel such a man will protect and provide for them."

"Doesn't Mister Freud say that women seek to marry their own fathers? What an awful thought." Linette gave a fake shiver.

"We hear many things that Mister Freud says," Vickery said disapprovingly, "not all of them in context."

"You aren't interested in human psychology?"

"Not in the abstract. I much prefer empirical observation."

"Er—?"

"I watch what people do and compare this to what they *say* they will do. This reveals much about them, I think."

"So if I say that I want a life of adventure, but then fail to do anything daring..."

"But that is not so, is it, Miss Fulbright? Already you begin to spread your wings and prepare to fly the nest."

"Well, I dream of it."

"This young man of yours, do you love him? Or do you see him as a means of escaping from the shadow of your parents?"

"I love him, of course."

"Of course. But will being with him provide the freedom that your heart seeks?"

"I don't... He wants me to be happy, I know he does. To do what I want..."

"That is good. When a young person has their dreams, and discovers another who wishes to share those same dreams— that is a truly wonderful thing."

"We do share the same dreams, Mr. Vickery. We have things we want to do together. We've talked about them."

"And yet there are some things that each of you wish to accomplish that the other has no part in?"

"Oliver has ambitions for his career, all men do. And I— well, I—" She grew flustered. "Has my father put you up to this? Are you trying to discourage us? Is that what he's paying you to do?"

"Your father is paying me to discover who is threatening his life. To do this, I must ask questions. Forgive me if my enquiries have offended you."

"You were questioning me because... You don't think *I* want to kill him?" Linette seemed shocked by the idea.

"Until I know for sure the identity of the letter-writer, I must suspect everyone. Including you and young Mr. Garvin."

"*Ollie?* He wouldn't harm a fly!" The idea seemed ludicrous to her, and she couldn't help smiling.

"Your father *has* refused him permission to court you," Vickery said.

Linette snorted. "These are the 1930s, Mr. Vickery, not the 1830s. Ollie asked my father's permission out of courtesy, it's how his aunt raised him. But you don't think either of us has taken my father's objections seriously, do you?"

"As I say, I ask questions in order to uncover the truth. If you tell me that your father's opposition to your engagement does not provide a motive for wishing him ill—"

"Engagement? Who said anything about an engagement?" Linette asked.

"I listen to what people say, and I compare this with what they do," Vickery said. He stared at her ring finger, which she was just now massaging furiously. Linette stopped herself when she saw where he was looking.

"I said it was a mistake to underestimate you," she conceded. "It's awful having to take it off. I wish we could just let people know."

"Perhaps your father will accept the idea in time," Vickery said. "And then you will be able to have a proper engagement party, instead of this—"

"It's like a pantomime, isn't it?"

"Gilbert and Sullivan without the songs, perhaps," Vickery

conceded.

"Oh, there'll be singing later, without a doubt," Linette said.

"If you marry against your father's wishes, will he disinherit you?"

"Almost certainly," Linette said. "But he will have nothing to bestow on me anyway, this moving picture of his will see to that. It is my mother's wishes that I had better take heed of, she's the one with the money."

"She does not object to your Mr. Garvin?"

"Why should she?"

"Perhaps she would be unhappy to lose the person she relies on for her care?"

"Ha! My mother isn't nearly as frail as she pretends to be. She could manage quite well without me."

"But would she wish to? If you are her only companion..."

"Is that what she told you? She is a lonely invalid, and no one ever calls on her? I'm afraid you haven't been asking the right questions, Mr. Vickery. My mother has a staff of four in her house in London, and rarely a day passes when she does not receive calls. Some of them from gentlemen, and some very definitely not."

"I had been led to believe that, since her accident, your mother rather relied on you for companionship."

"That is what my father would prefer to believe. The alternative is to accept that my mother's eye wanders just as much as his own."

"You do not approve of your parents' behaviour?"

"I don't look to either of them for moral guidance, if that's what you mean."

"I'm sorry..."

"Don't be. I'm not. For most people it takes years for their illusions to be dispelled. I should be grateful."

"Your parents loved one another once, and I'm sure they still do in their way. And they both love you."

"My parents shared a passion for the theatre. And—very briefly—a passion for each other. I was the result of the latter. My mother was married to someone else at the time of my conception. Margot McCrae married Leo Fulbright because she wanted to avoid any hint of scandal surrounding my arrival. A calendar and some basic arithmetic provide the facts in the matter."

"If your father didn't care for you, he would not seek to meddle in your affairs of the heart, would he?" Vickery asked.

"My father prefers it when people take direction well. He must always be the one in control."

"And your mother?"

"He seeks to control her too. And he's a fool for trying."

"I meant, does your mother seek influence over your life? Does she object to your relationship with Oliver Garvin?"

"Of course she doesn't. She prefers that I make my own choices. I think she's just relieved I'm not engaged to an *actor.*"

"She knows of the engagement?"

"Her mother is usually the first person that a girl tells of such things," Linette said.

"Forgive me, I had formed the impression that your mother did not know."

"Then again, you have asked the wrong questions, Mr. Vickery. My mother gave Ollie the ring, it belonged to my grandmother."

"Indeed?"

"I don't claim that her actions were entirely altruistic. I'm sure she encouraged us because she knew it would seriously vex my father."

Margot took Artie Delancey by the arm, startling him, and turned him to face her.

"Mr. Vicary thinks I was rude to you earlier. He wants me to apologise," she said.

"Oh, that really isn't—"

"I know," Margot said. "But try and look as if I'm being nice to you, seeing as it means so much to him."

Artie smiled weakly and tried to look grateful.

"Eleanor, wait! Please..."

Eleanor Trenton looked around, for a means of escape, or a saviour, but for the moment she was beyond rescue.

"Teddy, I said I didn't want to speak to you."

"But you didn't give me a chance to explain."

"What is there to explain?"

"It was all a silly mistake. Artie and I were just there for a drink. We weren't, you know..." He made a pumping moment with his elbow. When Eleanor laughed, he thought for a moment she was laughing *with* him.

"Is that why you think I was upset?"

"I thought that—"

"Teddy, you *hit* someone. You were drunk. You knocked them down. Kicked them..."

"It was just some lousy photographer."

"And who will it be next time? What happens when you're drunk and angry at *me?*"

"Eleanor, I would never want to hurt—"

"*Don't!* Don't say that! Not ever. That's what my father used to say."

"Eleanor—"

"You're just like him." Her voice was barely more than a whisper.

"Eleanor, that's not fair. I—"

"No, it isn't. It's not fair, Teddy. I *trusted* you. You told me you would stop. Said that you would find someone to help you."

"I *did.* Artie was—"

"Artie?" She laughed bitterly. "What sort of help was he?"

"He told me about a place—somewhere they help people like me. But you have to stop. Forever. Not even one drink after that."

"I know all about it, Teddy. My father, remember?"

"But I was going to do it. I *was.* I wanted to do it. For us. That night, with Artie, that was going to be my last night. One final binge, from dusk until dawn, then *never* again. You *believe* me, don't you?"

Eleanor was silent for a moment. Looking into his eyes, as if she hoped to find the answer there.

"I *want* to believe you, Teddy."

"Then you should. I would do whatever—"

She placed a hand on his chest to hold him back.

"Teddy, I can't. I'm sorry. If you knew what it was like for me growing up, you would understand."

"Eleanor, I *want* to understand. Help me—"

She shook her head sadly.

"It's too late, I'm sorry."

She turned away from him. He stared after her. For a moment anger burned in him, and he bared his teeth in a grimace. Then he caught himself, and his expression changed to something between loss and self-pity.

Chapter 4

There was a handful of apple trees growing in a patch of grass to one side at the back of the keep, making up what was grandly referred to as 'the orchard.' In the ethereal glow of the full moon, it looked like a painted backdrop done in shades of blue. Vickery found Dickie Bannister sitting on the bench under one of the trees: his face was ruddy, and he seemed to be trying to catch his breath. He was wearing a light brown robe, and his white beard was at least waist-length.

"Merlin, how wonderful you look!" Vickery smiled.

"I'm not sure about this frock. I thought Merlin would have worn something darker," Bannister said.

"I think it's meant to be druidic," Vickery said. "The beard is very impressive—and real too."

"I had a beard for *Uncle Vanya*—figured I may as well just let it keep growing. Besides, with those clockwork cameras getting in so close, I thought a false beard might look—well, false."

"It makes you look statesman-like, and wise."

"Well, if you don't tell 'em the truth, Mr. Vick'ry, I won't." He gave a theatrical wink.

"We shall just have to be careful not to set it alight," Vickery said.

"Shall we?" The old man looked about him, fearing sources of ignition.

"With the magic," Vickery said, "on the motion picture."

"Oh," Bannister nodded, but his watery blue eyes still said he had no idea what Vickery meant.

"Fulbright wants some bright flashes and clouds of smoke. We're going to test a few samples, see what the film will register. I've promised him a smoke ring, if I can manage it."

"Ah, Merlin's magic, excellent! Knew you'd be perfect for the job. Though I was quite surprised when Leo mentioned your name—you being retired and all."

"I still dabble," Vickery said. "Private parties only. Sleight of hand, nothing mechanical."

"That's understandable, of course..."

The two men looked at each other, neither wanting to pursue that line of conversation, but also not wanting to draw attention to it by too rapid a change of tack.

"I remember the day you closed," Bannister said. "We were touring up in Huddersfield, but we heard about it before the evening performance was through. Shocked us it did. It was silent back stage. Like we were all saying prayers for him. He was a lovely bloke, Terry was, lovely."

"Yes." Vickery's voice was a whisper. "Yes, he was."

"I couldn't believe it when we heard that the police thought you might have done it on purpose. I mean, how could anyone even *think* that. It was awful what happened to him. No man could do that on purpose. To suggest such a thing. With you and Terry being so wonderful together, and all. No wonder you never wanted to set foot on the stage again. To have put you through that, when you were *grieving*. We never doubted you were innocent, Mr. Vickery, never for a minute. We sent flowers, from all of us, but I don't suppose you'd remember now."

"White carnations," Vickery said. "Terry would have approved."

"He hated lilies, said—"

"—he said they reminded him of funerals. It was good of you to think of him."

"We thought of you both." Bannister reached forward and squeezed Vickery's arm gently.

"Margot is looking much improved since I saw her last," Vickery said.

"It's lovely to see her out again," Bannister said. "It's been over a year since..."

"The riding accident," Vickery said.

Bannister gave a non-committal grunt.

"What?" Vickery asked.

"There are some people that aren't sure it was an accident," Bannister said.

"Is that so?"

"You don't think it's odd, her horse getting spooked like that by some mad old woman who jumps up out of the undergrowth and then disappears, never to be seen again?" Bannister asked.

"When Margot told me about it, she did not suggest that it was anything but an unfortunate accident," Vickery said.

"Yes, well, there are things that Margot doesn't know," Bannister said.

"There are? Do tell."

"I shouldn't have said anything," Bannister said. "It's not my place to interfere."

"But if there are circumstances that should be investigated..." Vickery said.

"The truth will come out in the end," Bannister said. "I'm sure of that."

They were silent again for a few minutes.

"Margot isn't the same," Bannister said. "Since the accident."

"It's always a shock to be reminded of one's mortality," Vickery said.

"You should have seen her *Medea,* Vickery. Hair dishevelled, face gleaming with sweat, eyes wild! You could believe she helped Jason slay the dragon. And could kill his wife when Jason betrayed her. And the scene where she considers murdering their children..." Bannister shivered. "Chilling! Leo was Jason, of course, but the stage was hers. He refused to appear opposite her in *Macbeth* after that: didn't work with her again for three years, until *Taming of the Shrew.*"

"But he never did tame her, did he?" Vickery said.

"Who could?"

"We should probably go back inside. Don't want you catching a chill out here," Vickery said, as much to change the subject as from concern for the old man. He helped Bannister to his feet and they walked across the damp lawn back to the keep.

"If I may," Bannister said, "I should like to ask a favour."

"Yes?"

"Is there something you can show me? A trick that I can impress them with here? They're used to thinking of me as their clown. I need something that will help them to accept me as their Merlin."

"My dear friend, your performance will convince them of that, I am sure."

"But in the meanwhile..." Bannister said hopefully.

"In the meanwhile, I think I have just the thing."

"Something suitably medieval?"

"This trick is probably older than that! Hold out your hand."

"I won't have to keep goldfish in my underwear, will I?"

"That's never advisable when there's a chill in the air," Vickery said. "What you *will* need is an empty bottle. If you can find one anywhere..."

Bannister gave a little giggle: the grass near the keep seemed to be littered with champagne bottles. "Finding a full bottle would be a better trick," he said.

Vickery picked up one of the bottles. "What we're going to do is take a shilling and push it through the opening, down the neck, and into the bottle. Like that." He rattled the coin in the bottle.

"How? The neck is too narrow for a sixpence, never mind a shilling!"

"That's the trick."

Bannister took the bottle and tipped it upside down, tried to empty out the trapped coin. But without success.

"How do I do it?" His eyes were bright, eager like a child's.

"Ordinary bottle, magic coins," Vickery said. "Here's a coin, examine it closely."

Bannister did so, squeezing and rubbing and twisting it. "There's nothing magic about it." He sounded disappointed.

"That's right. *That* is the coin you will give people to examine. *These* are the coins you can put in the bottle."

Bannister took one of the coins from Vickery's palm, and subjected it to the same analysis. "I still don't..."

Vickery held up another of the coins between his thumb and finger. With a little pressure, the coin seemed to split down the middle, the two halves shifting by perhaps a sixteenth of an inch. Bannister did the same with his coin.

"Now fold it," Vickery said.

Bannister complied. "It's hinged!"

"Fold a shilling in half, and it will slide down the neck of the bottle. That's it. Do it quickly, let the coin hit the bottom of the bottle, the impact will restore the coin to its original shape. No one will know."

Bannister shook the bottle which now had two shillings rattling inside it. "How do I get them out?"

"You break the bottle," Vickery said.

Bannister looked at him, expecting him to be joking. "Do you know how hard these things are to break?"

"I've been hit with one, I know they don't break." Vickery held out his hand: there were more magic shillings in his palm. "Three more coins. One coin in three bottles, or three coins in one bottle, whichever you think will be most dramatic."

Bannister took the coins, holding them tightly in his fist. He was about to hurry through the door, back into the hall and his first performance, when a thought struck him.

"Did they have shillings in King Arthur's day?"

"Tell them it's a silver groat."

"Groat." Bannister nodded.

"In return, I want you to bring me back some gossip," Vickery said.

"Gossip?"

"I want to know what's going on between Artie Delancey and Edward Kimball."

"Is there anything going one between Artie and Teddy?"

"*That* is what I want you to find out."

Bannister wandered back inside muttering: "Groat, gossip. Gossip, groat."

Vickery followed him back inside.

"You're the Great Vicari, the magician! I've seen a poster of you somewhere, I just can't remember where."

Vickery turned and smiled.

"And you are Oliver Garvin, the—"

"I'm a journalist. Or rather, that's what I aim to be."

"But that makes you not quite respectable, I fear," Vickery said, smiling approval.

Garvin grinned. "I thought my aunt would object to my ambition, but she has been entirely supportive."

"She has been known to thumb her nose at convention, on

occasion," Vickery said. "She's a remarkable woman."

"You know her?"

"Our paths have crossed, once or twice."

"Wait, you were the one who—"

Vicary put a finger to his lips. "One must be careful what anecdotes one shares when one is surrounded by actors. Not to mention a *journalist,*" he said, with mock distaste.

"Or a *detective,*" Garvin said.

Vicary winced.

"Is it meant to be a secret?" Garvin asked. "I shan't tell."

"There cannot be many people here who do not already know," Vickery said. "It is not a place in which to try and keep a secret."

"Lucky for me that I don't have any," Garvin said. He looked around the hall, not wanting to meet Vickery's eye.

"It is not much of an engagement party, is it?"

Garvin's head whipped round. "Linnie told you? She wasn't supposed—"

"She didn't."

"Her old man has forbidden it, and she's only nineteen, so—" He shrugged.

"At your age, two years seems like a lifetime, I'm sure."

"Seventeen months—but yes, it does. You're not so old, you must remember how it feels."

"I came to love rather later in life."

"Is there a Mrs. Vickery?"

"No. No, there isn't."

"I don't intend to miss *my* chance. There *is* going to be a Mrs. Garvin. A Mrs. Linette Garvin. If I have to—"

"If you have to what, Mr. Garvin?"

"Not murder old man Fulbright, if that's what you're asking," he said. "I saw one of those letters. Linnie showed it to me."

Vicary raised an eyebrow. "And what did you make of it? In

your professional opinion as a journalist?"

"It was typewritten. With a fresh ribbon. But the typewriter isn't new: a couple of the open characters were filled in where the keys were clogged. I would say it was typed on something small, the sort of machine a writer would use, someone who travels."

"A journalist, perhaps?" Vickery asked.

"Possibly. But probably not someone who regularly earns his crust by writing: they would keep their typewriter in better order."

"Not a photoplay writer then?"

"I should say not. All writers procrastinate, and one of the things we do to avoid working is to clean things: our shoes; our cars; our front doors; our gramophones; and our—"

"Typewriters," Vicary finished. "I can see how this would be true. We are perhaps looking for an older typewriter, then? One that has been brought out of a closet and given a new ribbon."

"That sounds plausible. And we know it has a ribbon that is black and red: the bottoms of the descenders were just picking up the red colour, I noticed."

"A small, dirty typewriter with a black and red ribbon."

"That doesn't narrow it down much, does it?" Garvin said.

"No, but there are other characteristics that can help determine whether a particular machine typed a particular document. After a period of use, the keys become misaligned. One letter may always strike the paper slightly above its fellows, for example. Or one half of a letter may be less strong than the rest. Or one might be turned slightly to the left or the right. Given a handful of these characteristics, we will find that *all* are common to only one machine, like a fingerprint, and then we have them!"

"The murderer?"

"Well, the typewritist at least."

Garvin seemed to be giving this serious thought, but it turned out he was distracted by other things.

"My aunt only ever referred to you as 'a foreign gentleman,'" Garvin said. "But I have to say, your accent—I find it very difficult to place."

"That is another of my little secrets, Mr. Garvin. I used an accent on stage for so long that I am afraid it is stuck. In truth, my origins are really quite humble: the place of my birth was actually 'Alifax.'"

"Is that right?" Garvin obviously didn't believe this.

"But let that, too, remain our little secret," Vickery said.

"I shall not breathe a word to a soul," Garvin said. "You are quite adept at the art of deflection, aren't you?"

"I have some experience in avoiding the questions of people who want to know things that I do not want known."

"Journalists?" Garvin asked.

"*Journalists,*" Vickery confirmed, "and *detectives.*" He treated both words with equal distaste.

Garvin looked as if he was considering pursuing this, but he must have thought better of it.

"Is it terrible that journalism is what I aspire to?" He asked.

"Not at all."

"In the meantime, I get to lug a camera along to awful events like this to take photographs for the society pages. My aunt's reputation is enough to get me an invite to most of them. I hope one day that I shall chance to be on hand when something newsworthy takes place, and I shall get to write the story, rather than describe who wore what, and who they turned up with."

"Perhaps you shall get to report how the writer of Mr. Fulbright's threatening letters was apprehended."

"It would be better if I could report that old Fulbright was murdered."

Vickery gave him a dark look.

"It would be a better *story,* I mean," Garvin said. "Not that I would wish it upon him, obviously."

"Obviously," Vickery said.

Garvin coughed and thought it appropriate then for another change of subject.

"If you were in my position, what would you do, Mr. Vickery?"

"Elope."

Garvin laughed. "I do believe you are serious," he said. "Aren't you supposed to apply the benefit of your wisdom and suggest that I bide my time until Miss Fulbright gains her majority?"

"Why on earth would I suggest that? Age brings with it no guarantee of wisdom, Mr. Garvin. And prudence no guarantee of future happiness. Look around you this weekend and you will see older heads than yours behaving as if they're experiencing their first infatuation. If you and Miss Fulbright believe you can see future happiness together, then seize the moment!"

"The only things a man regrets in his life are the things he *didn't* do, is that how it is, Mr. Vickery?"

"I am sure that is true for many men. But that is not my story. Sadly, I very much regret something that I *did* do."

Garvin frowned.

"I killed the one person I ever truly loved. Good evening to you, Mr. Garvin."

* * *

"Have you seen Dickie Bannister?" Vickery asked.

Fulbright answered before anyone else could. "He's in the orchard with Artie—where else would you find a pair of bitter fruits!"

"They're not bitter, those two, they're both quite ripe," Margot said.

"How ripe are they?" Vickery asked.

"Let's just say that Artie will be singing *A Little of What You Fancy* before very much longer," Margot replied.

* * *

"What did you make of her, then," Artie asked, "our *Queen Guinevere?*"

"Well, I wouldn't go so far as to say she was a natural," Bannister said.

"What, blonde?"

"No, actress, you nitwit. She's not a natural actress."

"There's not much natural about the two of us, dear," Artie said.

"I mean that she didn't seem entirely comfortable before the camera."

"Before, during, or afterwards," Artie said. "I thought she was going to start blubbing."

"Fulbright was rather harsh. And loud."

"Not until the fifth take. I mean, who can forget a word like 'goblet'—four times. 'Pass me the goblin, sire.'"

"I was in danger of wetting myself," Bannister said.

"At your age, there's always that danger. How do you think she'll look on film? She seems so pale. Like a ghost."

"But there's not much call for *colour* on film, is there?"

"She'll be like an alabaster statue," Artie said.

"Pale and stiff?"

"And silent."

"She was a bit quiet, wasn't she? Not trained for the theatre like us. It's all in the diction, you know. You've got to be able to pronunciate."

"To what?"

"Pronunciate."

"It gets harder after a few drinks," Artie said.

"I wish it would."

"Naughty. I'm practically her understudy," Artie said. "If Eleanor isn't up to it, I shall be queen in her stead. It's a lovely frock—they've had it made so I can do the riding."

"You as the rider?" Bannister said. "There's always a first time for everything."

"Don't you start. At least I can still get my leg over a stallion. When was the last time you were in the saddle?"

"I can still manage it, I'll have you know. Though these days it's more of a canter than a gallop. I spent Saturday night with a peer."

"A *pair,* you trollop."

"Not a pair, a *peer,* rhymes with queer."

"Full of airs and graces, I suppose: they all expect you to kneel before them."

"I don't mind kneeling, as long as he takes his turn."

"I bet when you suggested that he nearly choked."

They spent a good few minutes giggling like school children.

"We ought to go back inside," Artie said.

"Why, have we run out of champagne?"

"No, but I told them I'd give them a song."

"Why, what harm have they ever done you?" Bannister said.

"I sang to a group of stevedores the other night, and let me tell you, there were tears on their cheeks when I'd done."

"I know, they really shouldn't mock the afflicted."

"They didn't *laugh*—"

"I keep telling you, you need fresh material."

"I wasn't *trying* to be funny," Artie insisted.

"That's easy to say now—they weren't to know."

"I'll give you a slap in a minute. If I had a voice like yours I'd be on a clifftop warning sailors about fog."

"You'd be on the clifftop luring them in."

"Like a *siren.*" Artie tossed imaginary hair.

"Like a factory whistle."

"Where were we?"

"About halfway down the third bottle."

"Third? Fifth more like," Artie said.

"Ah, then that explains the swollen bladder. Excuse me while I go and 'make water.'"

"There's a bucket under that tree you can use," Artie said.

"Are you taking the piss?"

"No, there's a maid fetches that!" They said in unison.

"Better?" Artie asked, as Bannister adjusted his robe and sat back down on the bench under the apple tree.

"Greatly relieved," Bannister said.

"Sounded like it. What were we talking about?" Artie said.

"I was about to say, what's the story with you and Teddy Kimball?"

"No story. Not even an anecdote," Artie said. He folded his arms.

"Fibber."

"He came to me for some advice, that's all I'm prepared to say."

"Advice on what, underarm shaving?"

"You may mock."

"Thank you, I was."

"There's a reason why you're old and alone, you know."

"I've just never found anyone I wanted to spend the rest of my life with," Bannister insisted.

"You want to hurry up, or you'll only have time left for a brief fling."

"Is that what you and Teddy had, then? A brief fling, and

then he flung you aside?"

"It doesn't *have* to be about sex, you know. Two men can just be friends," Artie said.

"He said 'no' then?"

"No, he didn't. Well, actually, yes he did. Several times. But you can't blame a girl for trying," Artie said.

"And then he came to you for advice?"

"He was looking for a clinic. Though why he thought I would know..."

"It's the way you scratch yourself down there, I've told you it's not ladylike."

"Not that kind of clinic. He wanted some help with his drinking."

"Could he not manage it by himself?" Bannister asked.

"You know very well what I mean. Some of these younger ones have quite a fondness for the strong stuff."

"You're not exactly a toe-teetaller yourself, love." One of Bannister's eyelids seemed to stop working then, and he had to wink a few times before he could get them both blinking in unison again.

"But they're not *like* us."

"No, we're lucky if we get tipsy, they can afford enough to do themselves real damage."

"Now, remember, I'm telling you this in confidence."

"Mum's the word, old friend, mum's the word. If I remember this tomorrow, I shan't—shan't *breathe* a word of it."

"Well, before he booked himself into the clinic, dear old Teddy decided he wanted to go out on one final spree..."

* * *

"Promise that you won't tell him you saw me, please," Veronica Fulbright said.

"I'm sure it won't matter to—" Eleanor said.

"*Please,* I need you to promise."

"All right, I promise." Eleanor was bemused by Veronica's apparent concern.

"It's always best to do what he says," Veronica said, "he can make life very difficult if you try and oppose him."

"What do you mean?"

"My brother prefers that everything be done his way, according to his timetable. You must have realised that?"

"He can be rather—"

"Controlling," Veronica said. "Some people like that. Not everyone wants to make their own decisions."

"I can assure you that I shall not be marching to your brother's drum," Eleanor said.

Veronica gave her a look that was somewhere between disbelief and pity.

"Just because someone knows his own mind, that doesn't automatically make him a tyrant," Eleanor said.

"When you have opposed him, have you found him ready to give ground—to compromise even?" Veronica asked.

"I haven't—"

"To begin with you won't be aware that he is controlling you. You do things to avoid upsetting him, and you think these are your own choices. Anything to avoid the raised voice or even the disappointed look. Tell me that isn't how it is with you," Veronica said.

Eleanor found that she could not.

"You are already under his spell," Veronica said, "watching him all the time, for any hint of displeasure. Hoping for some sign of approval; to hear that you've done the 'right thing.' Always trying to guess what he will want, before he has to say it. Always wanting to be the 'good girl.' He doesn't have to stand over you with a horse-whip. A real tyrant never needs to raise his hand or his voice."

"Leo is not like that," Eleanor said. "You're exaggerating."

"Am I? You've seen how he is with me; with his own daughter, even. Why do you think she had to sneak around behind his back? Leo has forbidden her to see Ollie Garvin, and so the two of them had to enter into an engagement without him knowing."

"But he is her father—"

"He isn't yours. And yet he has put an end to your relationship with Ted Kimball."

"That was my decision," Eleanor said.

"Was it? Really? You weren't persuaded by Leo's views in the matter?"

"I listened to his opinion."

"And when that wasn't enough, you believed the evidence he put in front of you."

"Leo didn't—"

"Didn't what? Didn't tell you that Ted Kimball was a violent alcoholic, and then present you with proof of the fact? Didn't tell you that Kimball was jealous of your relationship with him, and then provoke Kimball into demonstrating it? Didn't make you think that a relationship with Ted Kimball would jeopardise your future happiness and your career as an actress? My brother made you choose between him and Ted Kimball. Don't pretend to yourself that he didn't."

"You make it sound pre-meditated," Eleanor said.

"Because it is."

"Leo isn't that cold-blooded."

"Isn't he? Ask him why he had a photographer following Ted Kimball. Ask him why he can't bear to have the people under his 'care' find happiness in a relationship with someone else. Ask him."

"You are trying to turn me against him."

"What would I gain from that?" Eleanor asked.

"I don't know. Perhaps you don't want to have to share your brother with anyone else."

"Take him! With my blessing."

"You just want to blame your own unhappiness on him, rather than take responsibility yourself," Eleanor said, backing away.

"If you want to think I'm insane, go ahead, that's what Leo wants you to think. If you do not recognise a hint of truth in anything I have said to you, then you can safely turn your back and walk away. Trust that Leo has your best interests at heart. That is what he will tell you. It may be painful, but he is doing it for your own good."

"I don't know what to believe," Eleanor said.

"Believe what your instincts tell you to be true."

"I don't *know!*"

"Don't trust what I tell you. Or Leo. Find out for yourself. While you still can. Eventually Leo will have you doubting even yourself. And then he has won and you are his."

"You're frightening me."

"Good. That means there's still time—for you to see him as he really is."

"I will speak to him. I will make it clear to him that I intend to make my own choices."

"*Escape* from him. It is too dangerous to *defy* him."

"I will listen to what he has to say, but the final decision will be mine. He will see that I shall not be his puppet."

"You are already lost."

"She's *not*—" Fulbright said.

"Not what? She looks like she's wandered onto the wrong stage with the wrong script," Margot said.

"When you see what we've shot so far you'll see that she's..."

"I wasn't talking about the *movie*, you ox. Hadn't you better go and rescue her? She looks like the ghost of the blind flower girl."

"We'll talk later," Fulbright said. "When you're in a better mood."

"Don't hold your breath," Margot said, and lifted another two glasses of champagne from the tray of a passing waiter.

"More pain-killer?" Vickery asked, nodding towards the two glasses of champagne Margot McCrae carried: she seemed to have abandoned her cane. He accepted one of the glasses from her.

"You are smiling," Margot admonished, "don't let the others see. They will think I've amused you."

"You have, Margot dear. I'd quite forgotten what it was like to be among 'theatricals.'"

"You being not in the least bit theatrical yourself?" She sipped her champagne. "Damn it, you're smiling again."

"I will try not to."

"I have seen you flitting amongst our guests tonight, quite the investigative butterfly. What have you discovered?"

"That not everyone is telling the truth, and those that are, are not telling me all of it."

"*Really?* How terribly theatrical of them. Give me a 'frinstance."

"For instance, there is the matter of Linette's engagement ring. Apparently it used to belong to her maternal grandmother."

Margot was completely unabashed. "Did I not tell you that? How awfully remiss of me."

"Are there other things you aren't telling me?"

"Heaps of things," Margot said. "What sort of game would it be if everyone came right out and told you everything all at once?"

"Is murder a game, do you think?" Vickery asked.

"We haven't got to the murder. Yet."

"Do you think we will?"

"We have the setting and all of the necessary characters in place: it would be a frightful waste if we didn't have a murder now, don't you think?"

"I would prefer it if no one died," Vickery said.

"That's because you're the outsider. You are not mixed up in all the intrigue. It is your role to remain objective, so that you can discover which among us is Leo's murderer."

"Have we established that Leo is to be our victim?"

"He must be. Everyone here despises the man."

"But does anyone dislike him enough to take that irrevocable step, and bring his life to an end?" Vickery asked.

"We shall have to wait and see what transpires in Act II, shan't we?"

"Indeed."

"I saw you speaking with Leo's latest conquest earlier: what did you make of her?" Margot asked.

"Have you ever spoken to her?"

"Yes, I have—must have exchanged, oh, almost a dozen words between us. What did she say to you?"

"She seems under no illusion about where Leo's heart truly lies," Vickery said. "And she asked me if I thought it was wrong of her to use Leo's interest to further her own career."

Margot laughed hollowly. "Did she really? She's a *shameless* gold-digger, then?"

"I think she's rather under the impression that hanging on to Leo's arm will punish Teddy Kimball for being 'an absolute fool.'"

"That used to be me."

"It did?"

"Having Leo and Teddy falling over themselves to gain my attention."

"Perhaps it still is. I'm sure Leo has never forgiven Teddy for stealing you away from him, however briefly."

"The old horned hat? They're just like schoolboys, they never grow out of it," Margot said.

"Do you think Miss Trenton and Mr. Kimball would be good for each other?" Vickery asked. "Should we intervene and save their relationship?"

"I am not certain that Teddy would be good for anyone in his present condition. Or in any condition, if I am being honest. Perhaps I'm being unkind: my own expectations may have been too high."

"Do you still have feelings for him?"

"Who, Teddy? Heavens no. I never really did. And it was all so long ago. Before the accident. Eleanor Trenton is welcome to him."

Vicary was silent then, watching her closely.

"Don't try that with me, Benjamin. You and I have known each other far too long for that to work."

"Someday I may catch you unawares, and you will reveal your true feelings to me," Vickery said.

"Come visit me on my deathbed, perhaps then I shall have nothing I care to hide."

"You will outlive me, and everyone else here, I suspect."

"God, I hope not. 'Well preserved' is fine for a pickle, but not for a woman."

"Perhaps if you employed a little less vinegar, then?"

"It's not vinegar, it's vitriol, you should know that: it's far more effective."

"It would seem that tonight's curtain is descending. People are starting to wander off to their beds," Vickery observed.

"Are they? Don't they know it's only two o'clock?"

"Some folks are traditionalists: they prefer to retire *before* the cock crows."

"Lightweights, all of them. Will you escort me up? We're in the same cell block of this dank dungeon."

"You are not sharing your husband's chamber?" Vickery asked mischievously.

Margot gave him a look that would have turned a lesser man to stone, and offered him her arm.

"Will you be staying alert all night to observe who enters who's room?" Margot asked as they ascended the main staircase.

"I don't consider that necessary," Vickery said. "All that is required is to prevent any armed person from entering your husband's room."

"Then *you* will be sharing Leo's room tonight?" A smile twitched at her lips.

"I believe the driver, Malloy, has already been dragooned into serving at that post."

"The poor man, you really should rescue him," Margot said.

"I am sure our Mr. Malloy can look out for himself."

"And you don't consider him a suspect?"

"Why would I?"

"You haven't spoken to him, have you? Leo treats him abominably."

"Doesn't Leo treat *everyone* abominably?" Vickery asked.

"Everyone. Except you." They were standing outside Margot's door now.

"There is time for that yet, I fear. Goodnight, Margot."

"Do you think I should lock my door tonight?"

"That all depends, doesn't it?"

"Yes, I suppose it does. Goodnight Benjamin."

Chapter 5

A heavy morning mist obscured the landscape behind the keep, ghostly trees rising out of the whiteness. Vickery's attention was caught by the sound of a shotgun firing, and then a pigeon fell close to his feet. He picked it up: it was still warm, and missing its head. He carried it as he walked in the direction of the shooting.

"Morning, Mr. Vickery," Veronica Fulbright said. She was again dressed in men's tweeds, and held a shotgun pointed at the ground. "Thought I'd get in a little practice before breakfast." Vickery handed her the pigeon, which she placed with several others on the ground. "Thank you," she said. "I'm not allowed a retriever: Leo isn't a dog person."

"But you *are* allowed a gun?" Vickery asked.

"Ah—technically, no. I borrowed it from Sir Whatsit's cabinet. You won't tell, will you?"

"I saw and heard nothing," Vickery said. "If you break it open, I shall walk back with it for you."

Veronica broke open the shotgun and handed it to him.

"Six shots," Vickery said.

"What?"

"I heard six shots. And there are five pigeons."

"Missed one of the blighters," Veronica said. "I'm out of

practice with the gun."

"Will the cook roast the birds?"

Veronica picked them up. "They will have pigeon pie 'below stairs,'" she said. "Do people still say that?"

"Some people do," Vickery said.

"Cook will save me a piece of pie for supper."

"Because your brother doesn't like pigeon pie," Vickery said.

"That's right, how did you know? Magic again?"

"A lucky guess. Again."

"I don't believe you ever guess, Mr. Vickery."

"Please, call me Benjamin."

"Perhaps I will. And you will call me 'Miss Fulbright,' won't you?" She winked at him and hurried off in the direction of the kitchen, clutching her pigeons.

"Shooting, Mr. Vickery?" Linette asked as Vickery approached the rear of the keep. She held an unlighted cigarette between her fingers.

"I am merely the retriever," Vickery said.

"She didn't shoot at the bloody peacocks, did she?" Linette asked.

"Only pigeons."

"My father will explode if he finds out she got her hands on a shotgun."

"He takes a great interest in her behaviour."

"Of course he does. So would you, given that—"

"—he had her locked away, yes, she told me."

"Then you will understand why my father must remain vigilant," Linette said.

"I didn't tell him *why* I was locked up," Veronica said, appearing beside them, still clutching the pigeons.

"Aunt Veronica!" Linette was startled, and evidently embarrassed at having been caught gossiping.

"Forgot the shells," Veronica said, handing over a box of shotgun cartridges to Vickery. "Wouldn't want to be caught with those in my possession." Then she looked at Linette, expectantly. "Well?"

"Well what?" Again embarrassed.

"Aren't you going to finish your story?"

"I wasn't telling. I thought Mr. Vickery already knew."

"I do not wish to intrude on anyone's privacy," Vickery said.

"It's not a secret," Veronica said. "And it is what you might call *germane to your present hinvestigation.*" The last she said in her best imitation of a stage police constable.

"It is?" Linette seemed confused.

"Oh, yes. The reason my dear brother had me confined to a loony bin—sorry, private sanatorium—was because..." She paused for effect. *"I tried to kill him!"*

"With a shotgun?" Vickery asked, affecting not to be startled by her revelation.

"Bow and arrow," Veronica said. "I was distracted, missed his left eye by an inch. No chance to draw again. Now, tell me *that* doesn't make me a suspect!" She grinned her broad grin, daring him to contradict her.

"Your brother doesn't think so. He thinks you won't 'cook his goose' because you need his golden eggs."

"What comes out of my dear brother is not golden eggs, I assure you," Veronica said, her face reddening. "It is daddy's money he's throwing into that ridiculous moving picture of his. And I'd be willing to bet that even if he could shit gold, it wouldn't be enough to get the Ice Queen to prise open her legs."

"Aunt Veronica!"

The anger left Veronica Fulbright's face as quickly as it had arrived. "I'll ask cook to send up some pie for your supper," she said to Vickery. "She'll be careful to pick out every last piece of lead shot."

"I shall look forward to it, thank you."

Veronica turned and disappeared into the keep.

"I'm sorry, Mr. Vickery," Linette said.

"Don't be, it was most enlightening. Shall we go in to breakfast?" Vickery indicated that Linette should lead the way.

"I'm afraid that you're going to find *everyone* has a reason for wanting daddy out of the way," Linette said, as they headed down a gloomy hallway.

"He does rather inspire strong feelings in people," Vickery said.

"Do you have any idea who has threatened to kill him?"

"Your mother believes he may have sent the threats himself, in order to gain publicity for *Arthur and Guinevere.*"

"That's possible, I suppose," Linette admitted. "But then it is equally possible, I would say, that *she* sent them."

"Your mother? Why would she do that?"

In reply, Linette just smiled and shook her head. "I have given away enough family secrets for one morning, I am afraid." She skipped on ahead, then looked back over her shoulder. "If you haven't found out by then, ask me again after lunch. In the meantime, I think you should speak to Malloy."

"Everyone thinks I should speak to Malloy," Vicary mused, as Linette disappeared into the dining room. "Everyone except Mr. Malloy, who disappears whenever he sees me."

Chapter 6

The breakfast table was all but deserted. Linette and Oliver sat on one side of the table, sharing a private joke. Veronica sat opposite them, trying to give the impression of not listening to them. Margot McCrae, apparently, was breakfasting in her room. Dickie Bannister was still sleeping. No one had heard anything from Eleanor Trenton or Artie Delancey, though the latter was believed to be suffering from a hangover.

"Daddy's up," Linette said, "I heard him stomping about earlier.

"Almost forgot," Veronica said, "Saw Malloy in the kitchen and he said to advise you to hide, Mr. Vickery."

"Hide from what?" Vickery asked.

"I think you're about to find out," Garvin said.

A thundering sound came from the direction of the main staircase, followed by a bellow from Leo Fulbright.

"*Vickery!*" Moments later he appeared in the doorway. "There you are. A word in private, if you don't mind. *Now.*"

Vickery looked down at his untouched breakfast. Reluctantly he rose, bowing slightly to the ladies as he excused himself. He followed Fulbright into the library and closed the door behind him.

Fulbright's face was brick-red and he was breathing heavily.

He slammed a piece of paper on the desk in front of Vickery.

"*Well?*" Fulbright demanded.

"Another letter?" Vickery said.

"I know it's another bloody letter. It was pinned to my bedroom door this morning. What I want to know is how it got there."

"I would say that our letter-writer is here in the keep," Vickery said.

"You would, would you, Mr. Sherlock bloody Holmes? What else have you managed to deduce so far, do enlighten me."

"Well, as of last night, I have a list of suspects."

"Yes? And who is on this list?"

"I would prefer not to—"

"*Who?*" Fulbright demanded.

"Practically everyone."

"Are you taking the piss?"

"No, there's a maid who fetches that," Vickery said quietly.

"What?"

"Something I heard last night. I thought it was funny at the time. I need to speak to Mr. Malloy."

"Mister who?"

"Malloy."

"He's my *driver*. What's he got to do with anything?"

"Mr. Malloy was keeping watch last night. I want to know if he saw or heard anything."

"He said nothing to me," Fulbright said.

"Did you ask him?"

"Why would I ask him, he's—"

"Only the driver, yes, you said."

"If anything significant had happened, he would have told me."

"I'm sure he would. But I also wish to learn whether he saw or heard anything *insignificant* which might have a bearing on my investigation."

"I'm beginning to wonder if I wouldn't have been better to hire an ex-policeman instead of an ex-conjuror."

"In my experience, people of all stations experience some reluctance in confiding in a policeman," Vickery said, "even a retired one."

"Whereas they are comfortable telling *you* everything, are they?"

"Apparently so, yes. I think you would be surprised, and disappointed, to learn what I have heard during the last twenty-four hours."

"I am already disappointed, I am looking forward to being surprised in the very near future," Fulbright said. "Now understand this, Vickery, if I received any more of these," he prodded the letter, *"you* will be receiving a couple of letters from *me:* an 'F' and an 'O.' Do I make myself plain?"

"Exceedingly so, Mr. Fulbright."

"I want to know who is behind these letters, and I want to know by the end of *today.* Now get out of my sight."

Vickery turned to leave, then turned back, as if a question had occurred to him.

"This letter today, was there a second page to it?"

Fulbright looked up from the desk, expression slack for a moment. "One page," he said, "as you scc it."

"I see. Thank you."

Certain that Fulbright had just lied to him about the letter, Vickery exited the library. He stood in the hall a moment, regaining his composure, and considering whether he should add his own name to the list of people who might wish Leo Fulbright dead.

Vickery re-entered the breakfast room. The table had been cleared, and the room was empty except for Ted Kimball: he stood at the sideboard, pouring whisky into a glass. A plate of toast and marmalade sat next to the glass.

"Aren't you going to tell me it is a little early in the day?" Kimball asked.

"For breakfast? I should say it is a little late. I appear to have missed mine," Vickery said.

"I told them it was all right to clear, sorry," Kimball said. "I can ring and have them bring up a tray for you?"

"That isn't necessary. I have rather lost my appetite."

"I heard Fulbright shouting."

"Another letter appeared last night," Vickery said. "Mr. Fulbright finds them a trifle disconcerting."

"I wish whoever was behind them would stop messing around and just get on with it. If they did him in, there wouldn't be many to mourn the loss," Kimball said.

"You two must have been friends once?"

"I would still attend his funeral."

"If you will excuse me, I think I shall pop down to the kitchen and rustle up a late breakfast. And see if I can find that elusive driver."

"Golf?"

"Motor car."

* * *

"Dammit, Margot, you're my *wife!*"

"And what do you think that entitles you to, Leo? Everything that I am and everything that I own? Please be serious."

"We are supposed to be *partners*—in this *together.*"

"But I am not *in* this, am I, Leo dearest? You found someone else."

"Is that what this is about? A walk-on part in a moving picture? I offered you Morgana."

"I will not be your *witch!* Not while you appear on screen

with a new wife on your arm."

"She's *not* my wife. Margot, I'm not fucking her."

"I *am* your wife, and you're not fucking me either. Who are you fucking, Leo?"

"This is not about who I am sleeping with."

"It's about whatever I damn well say it is! You drag me out here to this god-forsaken folly and then parade your new mistress under my nose, in front of our friends."

"She's *not*—"

"—and then you have the absolute bloody gall to ask me if I wouldn't mind coughing up some cash to finance your little vanity project."

"This is not a vanity project. It's our *future*. If we miss this chance, it's over for people like you and me."

"But it's already over for me, Leo. I've been replaced."

"Would you listen to yourself? You can't expect me to believe that this is all about you missing out on the role that has all of a dozen lines in the script."

"No, it's not about that. It's about me being at the *end* of my career, and needing to hang on to my money for my retirement. I'm not handing it over to you to piss away on some speculative fantasy."

"It is not a fantasy. The studio is going to happen. I have the investment lined up. This is going to be better than what Korda is doing at Denham. Our own *motion picture studio,* Margot. We'll be in at the flowering of the British film industry."

"If it's going to be so blooming wonderful here, why is Hitchcock talking about moving to Hollywood?"

"Because he's a director for hire, not an entrepreneur."

"I'd love to see you say that in front of Alma."

"She's a better businessman that he'll ever be."

"And that's what you think you are, is it? You can't even keep your bank account in the black."

"This is on a *slightly* different scale than my personal finances."

"That's my point, you ass. You're only a week into shooting this thing, and you've already run out of money to keep the cameras turning. That's not *business* Leo. It's not even youth theatre. Your first movie is circling the drain, and you're talking about setting up a studio."

"I told you, I have an investor—"

"Oh, and who is this mysterious 'benefactor,' Leo? Anyone I know."

"As a matter of fact—"

"*No!* Please tell me you're joking? Not *him?*"

"I approached him about putting money into the film, we got to talking, and I mentioned our idea of a studio—"

"*Our* idea?"

"He was dead keen, Margot. He loves moving pictures, and the thought of being involved in the industry..."

"—and he also happened to have a niece who is a struggling actress. I *thought* I recognised that insipid little bitch. She's the spitting image of her mother. I can't believe you managed to keep *that* secret from me."

"It wasn't a secret: Eleanor uses a stage name, it's not that unusual."

"Where is she now, your little mouse-queen?" Margot asked Fulbright. He looked away, and she took this as her cue to continue. "You and Geoffrey have come up with a cosy little deal, and as part of it, his niece gets her name up on the silver screen. That's all fine and dandy, isn't it? But do you know the bit I can't work out? Why are you sniffing around me with your cap in your hand? If you've got Geoffrey's money, why do you need mine?"

"Sir Geoffrey's not investing in the film. He wants to see how it pans out before he will commit to the studio project. Once we have the film completed and a distributor in place, he'll sign the letter of intent."

"Geoffrey's not prepared to risk his cash on your *Arthur and Guinevere?* Perhaps he's brighter than I thought."

"When the film is completed, you and I will have our first major asset. That's why I want it to be *our* money—yours and mine—going into it. That way we will *own Arthur and Guinevere*. We can put that up as our stake, and be equal partners with Sir Geoffrey."

"You have really thought this out, haven't you?"

"I've been working on it for months."

"And you and I will be in it together?"

"That's the plan."

"Explain one thing to me."

"What's that?"

"All those months of planning, but not one word to me in that time. Why do I find out about it so late in the day?"

"I didn't want to bother you with the details," Fulbright said.

"You must think I was born yesterday."

"What do you—"

"You wanted to do this without me," Margot said, realisation dawning.

"That's not—"

"You were hoping you wouldn't need me. You weren't going to mention it until it was all signed and sealed. You thought Geoffrey would put up the money for *Arthur and Guinevere*. But when he declined, you had to come crawling to me."

"Margot, that's not how it—"

"You gave Guinevere to your talentless little ingénue because you thought she would bring the money with her, and when she didn't, you needed me to bail you out. How that must have stuck in your craw, Leo darling, to think you were free of me, and then to have to come back on bended knee."

"Do you *want* me to beg? I will if that what it takes."

Margot let him get down on his knees before she answered. "No, Leo, that's not what I want."

"Then what?"

"I want Guinevere."

"But it's just a *bit part*. Twelve lines at most."

"But I'm your wife, dammit," she mimicked him, "it should be me there at your side in *our* first film."

"Margot, you know I would, but Sir Geoffrey—"

"He's a *businessman*, Leo. He will understand: sacrifices have to be made. It's nothing *personal.*"

"Margot, I *can't*—I've agreed with him—the studio..."

"But nothing's *signed* yet, Leo. Everything is up for negotiation—between all *three* partners. We will all have an equal say."

"Please, Margot, don't do this."

"You don't have to give me an answer now, Leo," she said, ever-so reasonably. "Take some time to think about it. Sleep on it, if you like. Go and talk to Geoffrey."

"He's coming here," Fulbright said.

"What?"

"He'll be here after lunch. We're going to look over some plans. Possible studio sites."

"Well, won't this be a jolly little reunion."

"Promise me you won't make a scene."

"Leo, darling, as if I would!"

* * *

"Mr. Vickery." Fulbright's driver nodded his head in greeting. He had his jacket off and shirt sleeves rolled up. His shirt was open at the neck and without a collar.

"And what shall I call you, Mister—?"

"Malloy will do fine."

"Mr. Malloy it is then."

"Just Malloy." He wiped his hands on what had once been a white handkerchief. Malloy was trying to keep his injured jaw turned away from Vickery.

They were standing in a paddock out of sight of the keep, where the cars had been parked so as not to spoil Fulbright's image of a medieval idyll. Malloy had the bonnet open on a car with gleaming navy and black paintwork and shining chrome.

"This your car?" He asked.

"Do you approve of my choice?" Vickery was watching his face closely.

"Alvis Speed 20. They say it's a 'dignified' fast car. Up to seventy-five miles an hour, it probably is. At ninety, possibly less so." Malloy smiled.

"I had the feeling that you were trying to avoid me this weekend," Vickery said.

"I was."

"I would not have given away your secret."

"I know that."

"The bruise is colouring up nicely," Vickery said.

"Bit of an accident. Clumsy of me."

"To run into Fulbright's fist? Or rather, a backhanded slap."

Malloy looked at him directly for the first time.

"Leo Fulbright wears a signet ring," Vickery said. "Margot has a scar on her jaw in exactly the same place."

"I ought to know not to try and deceive you," Malloy said.

"I should hope that you wouldn't feel the need."

"You saved me from the hangman's rope: I'm still not sure why."

"Because it was the right thing to do."

"But what I did..."

"Was done for the right reason. I was sure then: I still am."

"You are a remarkable man, Mr. Vickery."

"As are you, Mr. Malloy."

"It's just Malloy."

"So you would have people believe."

"Aren't you going to ask me what I was doing to your car?" Malloy asked.

"You came out here so as to avoid the company of Mr. Fulbright. And you were also checking to see if any of the cars had been used last night. You discovered that none of them had been moved, and that none of them *could* have been, because a vital component has been taken from the engine of each."

"*You* took the—"

"Not I," Vickery said. "I would not know which parts to take. But *had* I taken them, I would have hidden them, perhaps wrapped in oilskin, submerged close to the edge of the pond at the front of the house."

"Not at the edge of the lake to the rear?"

"A possibility, but a greater danger of footprints giving away the hiding place."

"Should I retrieve them?"

"You are free to act as you see fit," Vickery said. "Myself, I would determine the exact hiding place, and then leave them there until they were needed."

"Why remove them in the first place?"

"To prevent any of our little assemblage making an early departure. It would seem that we are all expected to stay and see how this little drama plays out."

"Do you have any idea who is behind it?"

"Too many ideas, unfortunately. I shall need more information if I am to exclude those who are innocent, and uncover the identity of the guilty."

"Am I a suspect?" Malloy asked.

"I shall be keeping an eye on you," Vickery said, smiling. "This morning, when the latest poison pen letter was discovered, were you present?"

"No, I was in the next room. I heard Fulbright shout."

"Did you see him open the envelope?"

Malloy shook his head. "He was holding it when I went in, he'd already opened it."

"Do you recall of how many pages the letter consisted?"

Malloy paused, recalling the image to his mind's eye. "There were two sheets. I'm fairly sure."

"I think you are correct. Fulbright hides the second, and only shows us the first."

"Then he has something to hide," Malloy said. "The second sheet holds some clue as to why Fulbright is being targeted. He is guilty of something."

Vickery nodded. "That is a reasonable supposition. I would very much like to see the second sheet, but I fear that Fulbright will have destroyed it."

"I should have been there when it was delivered," Malloy said.

"Had you been at Fulbright's door, the letter would not have been delivered. At least, not then. Whoever it was would have waited until a time and place where there was no danger of their being observed. You could not have done more than you did."

"I'm sure Fulbright doesn't think so."

"I do not think we need be too concerned about what he thinks. As long as we stay out of arm's reach."

Malloy rubbed his swollen jaw and smiled. Vickery turned to leave.

"Should you ever decide to be undignified," Malloy said, "I hope you will consider making me your accomplice."

Vickery turned back, frowning. Then he smiled. "The Alvis Speed 20. I would definitely want you at the wheel, Mr. Malloy."

* * *

"Hello, Auntie Margot!"

Margot spun round, her face struggling to express neither surprise nor revulsion.

"Timothy!" She said, her smile a rictus.

The boy was about five or six, dressed in flannel shorts, shirt and grey sweater, and socks that seemed to have lost their elastic. He ran to Margot and wrapped his arms around her. She patted him on the head and then pushed him away, just as Vickery entered.

"Ah, Benjamin, may I introduce you to Timothy, Geoffrey's nephew. Timothy, this is Mr. Vickery: he's a *magician!*"

If Margot had been hoping that Timothy would show a typical youthful interest in magic, allowing her to slip away unnoticed, she was disappointed.

"There is no such thing as magic," Timothy asserted. "It's all nonsense designed to fool gullible people. I had a magic set for Christmas, it was rubbish."

"Have you come down with your uncle?" Margot asked quickly.

"No I drove myself down. Of course I'm here with Uncle Geoffrey. He's in the library talking to the butler, Creepy."

"Crawley," Margot corrected.

"Have you ever made an elephant disappear?" Timothy asked Vickery.

"No, I've never managed to eat a whole one," Vickery said.

The boy rolled his eyes. "I hope you're not the only entertainment we have this weekend!"

"Why don't you go upstairs. I'm sure I heard your sister calling you," Margot said.

"I doubt that. Eleanor thinks I'm an annoying brat. She said I should go out and climb one of the apple trees, as high as I can. Then jump."

"That sounds great fun. What are you waiting for?" Vickery asked.

"If I wanted to break my neck," Timothy said, "I'd ask to be in one of your magic tricks." He turned and trotted away, leaving Vickery standing white-faced and mute.

"Benjamin, I'm so sorry," Margot said, touching his arm. "He's just a child, he didn't know..."

Vickery recovered slightly and looked at her. "It's fine, Margot, really. I have heard much worse said."

"I will speak to Geoffrey. That sort of behaviour should not go unpunished."

Vickery held up his hand to stop her. "I would much rather you didn't," he said. "It is nothing. He rather caught me by surprise is all. I forget sometimes that parts of my story are known to all."

"You are somewhat infamous," Margot said. "I know people who would kill for that kind of notoriety."

"I did," Vickery said.

Margot stood aghast, mortified by her own insensitivity—until he winked at her.

Chapter 7

"Mr. Vickery, may I introduce my uncle, Sir Geoffrey Atterbury," Eleanor Trenton said, showing Vickery into the library.

Sir Geoffrey's handshake was firm and dry. His hair and moustache had once been red, but were now only slightly foxed. His eyes were a watery blue, and his lips dark, the colour of uncooked liver.

"Sir Geoffrey, thank you for sharing your keep with us this weekend, it's a remarkable place," Vickery said.

"It is, rather, isn't it? My late wife hated the place, but I couldn't bear to let it go. An Englishman's castle and all that."

"If you don't mind, I'm going to rest a while before dinner," Eleanor said.

"Of course, my dear, you run along. Mr. Vickery and I will have a nice chat over a cigar."

"Your brother's daughter?" Vickery asked, after Eleanor had closed the door behind her.

"My elder sister's, god rest her."

"Her mother died—"

"—in an accident, yes. Swimming. A villa on the coast—Rhodes I think it was. She'd taken a drink, perhaps more than one, and then gone for an evening swim. Her sot of a husband wasn't there to save her, of course. Must have been awful for the poor girl."

"Eleanor found her own mother?"

"Floating face down in the water, she said, a cloud—a cloud of blood blossoming around her head. It was a most awful thing. My sister was a wonderful woman. Eleanor has grown to be so much like her—sometimes I find it difficult looking at her. There's a portrait of my sister here somewhere, in one of the upstairs bedrooms, you should take a look at it. Remarkable likeness, you'll see."

"And her father?"

"Oh, she looks nothing like him, thank goodness."

"I meant, what became of him?"

"Nothing ever became of him, Vickery. Hopeless sort. He's around somewhere, I'm sure. But he and Eleanor are estranged. I've been more of a father to them than he was, to Eleanor and her brother."

"Timothy?"

"You've met him? He's a card isn't he?"

"Indeed, though I'm not sure if he was dealt from the top of the deck or the bottom."

"Eh?"

"Was Eleanor's mother an actress?" Vickery asked.

"Heavens, no! In school perhaps, we all do that. My sister was a wife and a mother, that was all she ever needed, I think. That's enough isn't it?"

"That is something every woman must decide for herself, I would say," Vickery said.

"I suppose so, yes."

"And Eleanor has decided that she wishes to act, in front of the camera."

"Apparently so, yes. It will be strange that there will be images of her that never age. We've always had portraits, and photographs now, of course, but these pictures will move. It will be like a ghost."

"I hadn't considered that," Vickery said.

Sir Geoffrey looked at him. "Hadn't you?"

"And you will be investing in this motion picture, for the sake of your niece?"

"Yes. Well, not in the film itself. I was too late for that, Fulbright already had all the funding in place. But he plans to have his own studio, based here at the keep, at least initially, we think. I shall be a silent partner, but it looks good to have someone with a title on the letterhead. Or so Fulbright believes: I'm never sure."

"And your money will be of some assistance?"

"Oh, yes—at first, at any rate—until *Arthur and Guinevere* is released. Films are a medium-term investment, apparently: two or three years before you see any real return."

"You are much better informed than I," Vickery said.

"Not really. Only what Fulbright has told me. He seems to know what he's about. I'm happy to trust his judgment."

"With advice from your solicitor and accountant, of course."

"Well, naturally. Though this is more in the way of a gentleman's agreement."

"Which is perfectly fine; providing that both men are gentlemen."

"Well, yes. But times are changing, Vickery. The old money is disappearing: look what happened in the States when the markets—well, you know what happened—I don't pretend to understand it. And there's taxes, we all understand *them*! There'll be hardly anything left for Timothy to inherit. It won't do for us to be sniffy about new money. People like Fulbright might well be this country's future."

"If he lives long enough," Vickery muttered.

"What was that?"

"Does Timothy live with you now?" Vickery asked.

"Well, he's away at school mostly, but yes, he calls the old hall home now. He's a bright boy, that one."

"That's certainly one possible description. Does he excel academically?"

"Not really. But then, neither did I. Didn't need to. He seems to understand money well enough. Better than I do. But other than that—" Sir Geoffrey shrugged. "His will be the last generation that can get by, I suppose. That's why I want to invest in this thing with Fulbright, give Timothy something to fall back on, just in case."

"Do you really think there is money to be made in moving pictures?" Vickery asked.

"Why shouldn't we be able to emulate the success they have been having in—where is it, California? With British acting talent and engineering, I don't see how we can fail."

"Unless the British talent heads for America?"

"Like old Charles Laughton? He was always good value. Larger than life. Saw him as Prospero at the Old Vic. That's the sort of talent we produce. And Fulbright, of course. America will never produce their like. They haven't the theatrical heritage we have. Take Shakespeare—English! Wrote his plays before there was a United States, and we're still watching them. All it needs is the right sort of imagination. And investment."

"I'm sure you're right," Vickery said.

"That Hungarian fellow has just built a studio down near the aerodrome. If that's not looking to the future of British motion pictures, I don't know what is. Shall I ring for some tea? All of this talking must be making you terribly dry."

"Tea would be lovely," Vickery said.

Sir Geoffrey got up and rang the bell: his butler appeared almost instantly.

"I saw your niece talking with Edward Kimball earlier. Have

they known each other a long time?" Vickery asked.

"They are on speaking terms again, are they? I suppose that's a good thing. Not sure I like Eleanor keeping company with him though."

"Because he's an actor?"

"Because he's a drunkard. I don't mind that a man takes a drink, so long as he doesn't make a fool of himself. Brawling in the street—grown men. It's not done, Vickery."

"Who was he fighting with, do you know?"

"No idea. Wasn't there. But I heard all about it. I just hope he's cleaned up his act, like he promised."

"Was he ever violent towards your niece?"

"Heavens, no! I wouldn't have allowed that kind of behaviour. I'm very protective of her, you know. He'd have been out on his ear, with my boot behind him."

"Eleanor would have confided in you if there had been...?"

"He never touched her, Vickery. I'm not so out of touch that I wouldn't have known—or found out about it. I have my own methods for keeping an eye out for my niece's well-being."

"I didn't mean to suggest anything. I hope I have not caused any offence."

"I don't offend easily, Vickery. Thick skin, especially after what happened. You seem like a decent enough fellow. I like that. You remind me of my cousin Raymond—he was a poofter too—but a good man all the same."

Vicary laughed. "You really do have your spies out there, don't you?"

"As I said, I'm not out of touch. I know a thing or two about everyone who's here this weekend, and most of what I know need go no further. You can rely on my discretion, I assure you."

"Then like cousin Raymond, I am in your debt."

"Eh?"

"Ah, here's the tea."

* * *

"What were you *thinking?*" Eleanor demanded.

"I was thinking that I needed to look out for you, because you don't seem capable of doing it yourself," Fulbright said. He was clearly uncomfortable being confronted directly.

"I am quite capable of taking care of myself. I don't need some arrogant Victorian patriarch to control my life. I am not your mentally unstable sister!"

"If I hadn't had that photographer follow him, you would never have known what sort of a man he is," Fulbright said.

"I know *exactly* what sort of man he is: I've been around men like him all my life."

"Then you ought to know better than to shack up with another one."

"It is not for you to decide who I should or should not become involved with." Eleanor's lips were pale and her eyes were glaring. "I will make my own decisions."

"Eleanor, please, you must understand that I have only your best interests at heart—"

"Do you think I am so feeble-minded as to believe that, Leo? You are only ever concerned with one person's interests."

"You are becoming hysterical—"

"Don't you *dare!*"

"I don't understand why you are so concerned with what happens to Ted Kimball," Fulbright said, changing tack. "You said you didn't love him. Have you changed your mind? Again?"

"No—I—How I feel about Teddy has nothing to do with this. It is *your* behaviour that concerns me," she said. "You have no right to—"

"Eleanor, I am disappointed with your—"

"Don't try and make me feel guilty. I have every right to be angry with you. What you did was unforgivable."

"I'm not going to apologise for doing what I thought was the right thing," Fulbright said.

"Then don't. But do not fool yourself into thinking you did it because it was the right thing *for me*. It wasn't. You were acting purely out of self-interest.

"You ungrateful—!"

"What am I meant to express gratitude for, Leo? All the sacrifices you have made on my behalf? Is that why you're going to give my part to your witch-wife?"

"I haven't said—"

"Don't deny that you're considering it. You just haven't decided which option is in your best interests yet."

"What makes you think—?"

"You invited your darling Margot down here this weekend because you want to sweet-talk her into giving you the money to finish *Arthur and Guinevere*. You lied to my uncle about having raised the whole budget for it."

"I underestimated what it would cost, I admit that," Fulbright said.

"And do you admit that Margot said she'd only give you the money if she can be your co-star?"

Fulbright breathed out loudly before replying. "She has said that. But I will talk her round, you needn't worry about that. I have years of experience dealing with Margot. I will make her—"

"I very much doubt that."

"I can control Margot," Fulbright insisted, angry that she would interrupt him.

Eleanor laughed out loud at this. "You can't even control your teenage daughter," she said.

"What's *that* supposed to mean? Linette obeys my—"

"Your daughter runs around behind your back doing exactly as she pleases . She has no more respect for you than Margot does."

"That's not true!"

"Really? Then I suppose you gave permission for her to become engaged to Oliver Garvin?" Eleanor asked. She smiled when she saw his expression. "Don't tell me you didn't know about it?"

"I knew about their relationship. I forbade her—"

"In her own interests, of course. And yet, your attempt to control her has amounted to—what?"

"I shall speak to her about this," Fulbright said. "There has been some mistake."

"Yes, Leo, I think there has." Her smile was cold. "And until you have your own house in order, kindly keep your nose out of mine."

* * *

"And what did you learn from your little encounter with Geoffrey Atterbury?" Fulbright asked. His face was flushed and he was breathing heavily.

"That you should never underestimate a toff," Vickery said.

"You didn't know that already? Rich bastards get rich—and stay rich—by being bastards. That's what my father always used to say."

"I thought your father was a clergyman?"

"Lay preacher—though he never said that from the pulpit."

"I might have attended church just to see that," Vickery said.

"Yes, well, don't go thinking that gives you and my father a great deal in common. He was working class, and old-fashioned in his thinking on a lot of things, if you take my meaning."

"Your father wasn't fond of cousin Raymond?"

"Who?"

"Never mind."

"Are you any closer to unmasking our poison penman?" Fulbright asked.

"I shall have a much better idea, once I have discovered why certain people are not telling me the truth."

"Who do you think is lying to you?" Fulbright asked.

"Practically everyone."

Chapter 8

"I know what you said to Leo," Eleanor said, "about wanting to replace me as Guinevere."

"And are you willing to step aside in order to save Leo's motion picture?" Margot asked. "Will you make that sacrifice for him?"

She stared into Eleanor's eyes, but the younger actress refused to look away.

"No," Eleanor said finally, still meeting Margot's gaze. Defiant.

"You've got backbone after all."

"I *want* this," Eleanor said. "I know I'll never be able to build my reputation the way you have. The long way. I haven't earned my dues. But this may be the one chance I have. If I don't play Guinevere, chances are that no one will ever hear of Eleanor Trenton. Can't you let me have this?"

"Are you trying to appeal to my better nature?" Margot asked. "I told Leo that I wouldn't give him the money for *Arthur and Guinevere* because I wanted your role in it. But that isn't true. It's not your *part* I want. I want to *be* you. I want to be ten years younger. Men grow older, and they get to play King Lear. What do we get? I've just been offered Lady Bracknell: don't you *dare* laugh. If I take it, I may as well just tell them it is fine to offer all the leading roles to younger women. You may not believe me, but I need Guinevere. Almost as much as you do."

"I am not seeking to replace you," Eleanor said.

"As if *you* could," Margot sniffed. She paced across the room and looked out of the window. "Do you know, the only happy women I know are the ones that gave up their own ambitions and settled down to raise a family. Perhaps I should have done that."

"That is ridiculous, you couldn't have walked away from the theatre if you'd wanted to," Eleanor said.

"I know. But sometimes I wonder—about the other life I might have had."

"If things are so terrible for women, shouldn't we be helping each other, rather than squabbling over scraps?"

"How do you propose we might do that?" Margot asked.

"Perhaps it is time that *we* become the writers and directors," Eleanor said, "and create parts for women that are really worth fighting over?"

"That shift will not happen in my lifetime," Margot said.

"Is that a reason *not* to fight for change?"

"You're talking about fighting a war. You'll have to win this battle first. I won't let you take this, not without a fight," Margot said.

"What are you really afraid of? Not me. I'm not here to take away anything you've achieved. And I'm not trying to steal Leo away from you..."

"I can keep Leo, but you're not prepared to give up Guinevere, is that it?" Margot stared at Eleanor. "Are you really prepared to fight for it?"

"I will do whatever it takes."

Margot smiled coldly. "You haven't got what it takes."

"And what is that?"

"You have got to be *ruthless*. You have to go out there and make that role yours. You have got to channel every ounce of your energy and anger into that performance, until everyone is looking at *you* on that screen, not Leo Fulbright. You have got to turn things up so high that people hold their breath, and then pitch it so low they lean forward in their seats to catch every word you whisper. They have got to believe Lancelot will betray his King for you, and you have to make every man want to feel your lips on his. When you weep, you've got to make every woman feel that her own heart has been broken. *That* is what it will take. And it will need more than an albino mouse to do it."

"What happened to you? What made you into this heartless—?"

"I became an actress. It's the price you pay."

"Perhaps you will blackmail Leo into giving you my part, that's your choice," Eleanor said. "But you will always know that you had to cheat to get it. You weren't Leo's first choice: I was. And you can whine and complain and blame the fact that life is so unfair because women age. But the truth is, if you'd had what it takes to make this role yours, he'd have given it to you in the first place."

"You *dare*—"

"If you want this role, *you* are going to have to fight for it," Eleanor said.

"I am going to take it from you."

"Over my dead body!"

"If you insist."

"I am going to go out there, and I'm going to show Leo Fulbright that *I* am his queen," Eleanor said. "I'm going to play Guinevere and make him forget he ever heard of Margot McCrae. I'm going to make him believe that he was right not to cast his poor little invalid wife in his first motion picture. Your reign is over, old woman—mine begins now!"

Margot applauded silently, mocking.

"Bravo, little mouse queen, bravo. Such a shame that you couldn't bring *that* passion to the sound stage."

The door opened, and Leo Fulbright leaned in.

"Is everything all right, ladies?" he asked.

"Everything is wonderful, Leo dear, Miss Trenton was just leaving to practice her lines."

Eleanor glared at her, then swept out past Fulbright.

"I heard you arguing," Fulbright said.

"We were comparing notes on you, dear. We were each convinced that we despised you more."

"I told her you wanted Guinevere, or you wouldn't provide the funding," Fulbright said. "She said over her dead body. Or yours."

"A fight to the death?" Margot smiled.

"Margot, please—"

"You made a mistake, Leo, thinking she could ever be a match for me."

"I didn't send her to try and argue with you, that was her choice."

"Then she has bigger balls than you," Margot said. "Unfortunately, that isn't saying very much."

Chapter 9

"**D**addy, no, *please!*"

"Where is he?" Fulbright demanded. "Never mind, I'll find him myself." He stomped out into the entrance hall.

"Help! Somebody, please!" Linette cried.

"What's wrong?" Vickery asked, entering through the French doors.

"Daddy's gone after Ollie. He has a *rifle!*"

"Actually, it's a seventeenth-century smooth bore flintlock musket," Sir Geoffrey said, entering the dining room. "Just passed him in the hall."

"Does any of that really matter? He can still shoot someone with it," Linette said.

"It's all right, your father doesn't have the balls for it," Sir Geoffrey said.

"What?"

"The lead shot—for the musket," Sir Geoffrey explained. "Still in there." He nodded towards the library. "He'd have to load it with a measure of gunpowder and a lead ball before he could fire. Even if he'd taken one of the paper cartridges, a trained musketeer can only load four shots a minute, and the musket is only accurate up to about a hundred yards, so the odds are all in your young man's favour."

"Then he can't kill Ollie with it?"

"Well, if he swung the musket hard enough," Sir Geoffrey said.

"Come on," Linette insisted, "we've got to stop him!"

"Garvin!" Fulbright bellowed, somewhere on the first floor.

Oliver Garvin appeared in the entrance hall just as the others came out of the dining room.

"Ollie, you've got to hide. Quickly!" Linette said. "Daddy knows we're engaged."

"How did he find out?"

"Aunt Veronica told Eleanor, and Eleanor told daddy."

"How did Veronica find out?"

"I don't know! That's not the important thing right now—he's got a gun!"

"Blimey! I'm guessing now isn't the time for a little man-to-man-chat with him, then?" Garvin said.

"Not unless you brought bandages," Vickery said.

"Where can I hide?"

"Take the car, go down to the village, to the inn, stay there until I can get away and meet you," Linette said.

"Are you two going to elope?" Sir Geoffrey said. "How daring!"

"I just saw a man with an axe—he was looking for Garvin," Molloy said, coming in from the courtyard.

"That was my father," Linette said.

"And it was a musket, not an axe," Sir Geoffrey insisted.

"No, it was that other actor chappie, Kimball. And he definitely had an axe."

"He must have found out about the photographs," Garvin said.

"What photographs?" Sir Geoffrey asked. Everyone ignored him.

"How did he find out?" Linette asked.

"I *don't know*! Maybe Aunt Veronica told the dog, and the dog told Kimball. Does it matter? Two people are trying to kill me!"

"You should hide," Molloy suggested.

"I've been saying that for *half-an-hour!*" Linette said.

"Run. We'll stall Fulbright," Vickery said.

"But what about Kimball?" Garvin asked.

"I'd suggest giving him a wide berth," Malloy said, "and if he throws the axe—"

"Yes?"

"Duck!" Everyone seemed to shout at once, as a shadow loomed in the doorway behind Garvin.

The stock of the musket slammed into the side of Garvin's head. His eyes crossed and then rolled to show all white. His knees buckled, and he fell to the ground.

"Got the little blighter!" Fulbright was triumphant.

Linette screamed.

Sir Geoffrey grabbed the musket. "I say, there was no call for that. I hope you haven't done any serious damage, this is a seventeenth-century antique!"

"Someone call a doctor," Linette pleaded, kneeling beside Garvin and cradling his head.

"It's not a doctor he'll need, it's a bloody undertaker," Fulbright said. "Get him up so I can knock him down again."

"Daddy, stop it, please!"

"I say, steady on," Sir Geoffrey cautioned, taking a step back.

"What's that—what's that ringing noise?" Garvin's eyes flickered open, but he seemed to have trouble focussing. "Is it me, or is it foggy in here?"

"It's you, dear. Please lie still. Daddy hit you with a musket."

"I've been *shot?*"

"No, darling, he hit you round the head with it."

"Is that why my ear is ringing?"

"I should think so. How do you feel?"

"A bit queasy. It might be those kidneys I had for breakfast."

"He may have a concussion," Malloy said.

"Is that bad?" Linette asked.

"Probably best not to let him fall asleep," Vickery said.

"I couldn't sleep with all this damn ringing, anyway," Garvin said.

"Somebody get some ice, in a tea towel or something," Malloy said, "it'll help the swelling."

"It's swelling just fine without the ice," Garvin said. "Do you think I'll have a cauliflower ear?"

"Get him up. I want a word with him," Fulbright said.

"Not now, daddy, he's *hurt.*"

"Let's carry him through to the library, lie him on a sofa," Vickery said.

"Sir Geoffrey's gone for the ice," Malloy said.

"Do you think he even knows where the kitchen is?" Linette asked.

"No, but he knows where the bell-pull is to summon someone from the kitchen," Malloy said.

Malloy and Vickery carried Oliver Garvin into the library and laid him on one of the chesterfields, propping him up with cushions.

"Ice is on its way," Sir Geoffrey said, "and I've ordered tea. Bit early, I know, but hot sweet tea usually helps when you've had a bump on the head. That's what nanny always used to give us. Or was it a mustard poultice?"

"Haven't felt like this since I cracked heads with Spotty Cartwright in the fourth year," Garvin said.

"Is he delirious?" Linette asked.

"He's a gibbering idiot!" Fulbright said. "The sooner we toss him out, the better."

"He's my *fiancé,*" Linette said defensively.

"The only way you're marrying him, is over my dead body."

"I am sure *that* can be arranged," Linette said coldly.

"I should put you across my knee!" Fulbright threatened.

"And Ollie should have you arrested for criminal assault," Linette said.

"I only hit him *once.*"

"In front of *witnesses,*" Linette said.

Fulbright looked around, as if seeing the others for the first time. "These aren't witnesses, they're my—guests."

"Ah, here's the tea," Sir Geoffrey said, pleased by the distraction. "And the ice for Mr. Whatshisname. Just put it down, Crawley."

The butler set the tray down on the table, gave the slightest of bows, and exited.

"Fulbright, why don't you be mother?" Sir Geoffrey suggested. Fulbright glared at him. "No? I'll pour then, shall I?"

As the others were adding milk and sugar to their teacups, Fulbright cornered Linette and began a whispered conversation.

"What do you think your mother's going to say about this?" He demanded to know.

"I imagine she will say that you are a Neanderthal who can't control his ugly temper."

"Not *this*—you and him—*eloping!*"

"We haven't eloped, we're still here. For the moment. And as for the engagement, I can tell you exactly what she said about that—"

"I said, congratulations, my dear, I'm delighted for you. I should like you to have grand mama's ring."

Margot McCrae swept into the room. She looked down at Oliver Garvin, placed the back of her hand against his forehead, then examined his swollen ear.

"No fever, no blood: you'll live," she said. "But I wouldn't go heading any footballs for a while."

"No, mother," Garvin said.

"Keep him awake," Margot said.

"How?" Sir Geoffrey asked.

"Talk to him. But avoid theatrical anecdotes, they can tranquilise a hippo. Leo, you and I need to have words, outside."

"But I'm not done here."

"You most definitely are," Margot told him. She led the way out of the library.

"As soon as he is on his feet," Fulbright said quietly, "I want him *out* of my house!"

"Er, actually, it's *my* house," Sir Geoffrey said, "not meaning to be pernickety, but you know what they say about an Englishman's home... Home, castle, you see what I mean. Ha, ha."

Sir Geoffrey was rescued from the full force of Fulbright's glare.

"*Leo!*" Margot called from outside the door. "Don't make me count to three!"

Fulbright exited, tail between his legs.

"What now?" Malloy asked.

"More tea anyone?" Sir Geoffrey asked brightly.

As he spoke, Malloy saw Ted Kimball walk past the window, a large axe resting on his shoulder: he looked to be whistling. Malloy signalled to Vickery and the two of them stepped out into the hallway.

"I just saw Ted Kimball carrying the axe. What do you think he's up to?"

"That would depend on which direction he was headed," Vickery said.

"To the front of the keep, I think."

"Probably not going to chop firewood, then," Vickery said.

There was a muted crash from outside, and a tinkling of glass.

"Definitely not firewood," Malloy said.

"But not someone's skull either, to look on the positive side," Vickery said.

"Probably just venting his anger in a little physical exertion," Malloy said.

Another crash.

"I think perhaps we should intervene," Vickery said.

"Let me say again: he was carrying a large axe."

"Perhaps hold off on the intervention, then, eh?" Vickery said. "We'll just go out and keep an eye on him. And ensure no one else tries to intervene."

"Good plan," Malloy said.

They opened the front door and walked across the courtyard.

"I do hope he has targeted the correct vehicle," Vickery said.

They tiptoed under the gatehouse.

"Who do you think he is angry with?" Malloy asked.

They remained in the shadow of the archway and peered cautiously out. Kimball had taken the axe to the little blue two-seater.

"Oliver Garvin," they whispered together.

"Should I go and tell Garvin?" Malloy asked.

"I fear that Mr. Garvin might try and come between Mr. Kimball's axe and his sports car. I think our young friend has had quite enough excitement for one afternoon."

Garvin's car was already in quite a sorry state. Its headlamps were both smashed, and one had been detached completely and was lying in the gravel. The bonnet had received several heavy blows from the poll of the axe and was crumpled like paper. The windscreen was shattered, there were deep rents in the doors and gashes in the leather seats. Kimball finished by bursting each of the car's tyres. Once this was complete, he stood back to admire his handiwork. Apparently satisfied, he hurled the axe into the pond. It bounced off a bronze dolphin with a dull clang, and then plopped into the water and sank from view.

"Now I think we may safely alert Mr. Garvin as to the fate of his motor car," Vickery said.

Vickery and Malloy retreated across the courtyard and back into the keep, and almost immediately encountered Oliver Garvin. He was tip-toeing across the great hall, a manila envelope clutched to his chest. When he saw them, he put his finger to his lips and shushed loudly.

"Linnie thinks I'm resting," he said. "Have you seen Ted Kimball? I was told he came this way. I must speak with him urgently."

"You and he have had some sort of disagreement?" Vickery asked.

"We may be about to. I owe him an apology."

"I think you may discover that he owes you an equal debt," Vickery said.

"I'm sorry about your car," Malloy said. "Hopefully a lot of the damage is only superficial."

"Damage?" Garvin said.

"It could have been a great deal worse," Vickery said, "had he encountered you before reaching the sports car."

"What has happened to my car?" Garvin looked at them as if they were lunatics, and then hurried out into the courtyard.

"That way to tea and muffins." Vickery pointed.

"But *that* way to the encounter between Garvin and Kimball." Malloy pointed in the opposite direction.

After a split-second's consideration, they both scurried back out into the courtyard.

Oliver Garvin was staring at his car, unable to speak. Kimball leaned back against one of the other cars, quietly smoking a cigarette.

"It would make a terrific *photograph*, don't you think?" Kimball asked.

"Photograph." Garvin's voice was tiny. He looked over at Kimball, then back at the devastation in front of him.

"How did—?"

"Axe," Kimball said.

"Ah."

"How much would a car such as that cost to buy?" Vickery whispered.

"MG Midget? A hundred and eighty or two hundred pounds new, I suppose. That one's a couple of years old," Malloy said. "Repairs and new tyres will set him back a few quid. Why do you think Garvin did it?"

"Something to do with photographs. Oh, wait, of course— Fulbright's second photographer, that was Garvin."

"It was?" Malloy frowned.

"Let me see, what's the shortest version? Artie Delancey took Mr. Kimball for after hours drinks at the *Pink Gardenia*—"

"But Kimball's not—"

"Indeed not. They were photographed leaving—and Mr. Kimball assaulted the photographer, smashing his camera."

"But there was a second photographer," Malloy said, "who captured pictures of the attack?"

Vickery nodded. "Oliver Garvin. Who was present, I think, on the instruction of Leo Fulbright."

"Blackmail?"

"Leverage, certainly."

"Nasty piece of work, our Mr. Fulbright," Malloy said.

"He plays a dangerous game, that much is true."

Oliver Garvin was finally able to look away from the

wreckage that had been his car.

"I was about to leave," he said. "You've scuppered that."

"Things don't always go according to plan," Kimball said.

"I deserve this, I suppose," Garvin said, "and worse. I had wanted to apologise to you, before I left."

"Is that right?"

"If I'd known what Fulbright meant to do with the photographs—no, that's stupid, of course I knew what he wanted them for. It just seemed like a splendid adventure—a bit of cloak and dagger. And then on the night, it got even more exciting—and all I could think about was trying to frame the perfect photograph—getting your face clearly. I am sorry, Mr. Kimball."

"Those more prints?" Kimball pointed his cigarette at the envelope. "I've already got a set for my scrapbook."

Garvin held out the envelope towards him.

"Then you have the only set of prints," he said. "And these are the negatives. I wanted to give them to you myself."

Kimball stared at the envelope for a while—then reached for it. "This is a decent thing—" he said

"I wish I could say my motives are entirely altruistic—but I just wanted to make sure Fulbright didn't have them. Now that he has terminated my employment."

"Does he know you're giving them to me?" Kimball held up the envelope.

"Not yet. I thought you might like to tell him. See his face."

Kimball smiled. Then: "About the car—"

"As I said, a salutary lesson for me. We all have to learn to take responsibility for our actions—you have taught Mabel and I that lesson."

"Mabel?"

Garvin nodded towards the battered blue sports car.

Chapter 10

"They're all dressed normally tonight," Margot said. "I'm tempted to go upstairs and put on fancy dress."

"Who would you be tonight?" Vickery asked.

"Perhaps Leo's right and I should be Morgana, the evil witch," she said. She waited for a response, but was disappointed. "Only you, my dear, would resist commenting on that being perfect casting."

"I make a point of avoiding the statement of the obvious," Vickery said.

"Don't you ever feel like being someone else?" Margot asked.

"I'm always being someone else," Vickery said. "Sometimes I feel like being myself."

"What is the real Benjamin Vickery like?"

"You wouldn't like him, he's very dull."

"I somehow doubt that."

"Mr. Garvin is still here," Vickery said.

"Poor man hasn't had the best of days, has he? What with Teddy putting dents in his car, and Leo putting a dent in his head."

"Has Leo finally accepted the engagement?"

"Heavens no, this is merely a temporary lull in hostilities. Linette will have to do something dramatic to win her father round."

"Such as?" Vickery asked.

"Threatening to emigrate to get away from him, that might work. Or getting married and asking someone else to give her away. Something that will ensure that Leo sees he's losing something important to him. If it isn't directly about him, he tends not to see it."

"That is how your relationship functions?" Vickery asked.

"Absolutely. I convince Leo that it is all about him, and he does whatever I want. Sometimes that means saying the opposite of what I think, but once I've divined the appropriate strategy, he's a pushover."

"You won't intervene on Linette's behalf?"

"If she's going to be married, she needs to develop these skills for herself, and who better to practice them on than her father?"

"You make marriage sound like a military campaign."

"No, no. It's much more like poker," Margot said. "You have to do what you can with the hand you're dealt. Do you play?"

"People tend not to want to play card games with a magician," Vickery said.

"Do people really think that what you do is magic?"

"What makes you think it isn't?"

They moved towards the dining table, which was almost fully occupied.

"Teddy, be a darling and move over so Benjamin and I can sit together," Margot said.

"Eleanor and I are not speaking," Kimball said sulkily.

"Then move the other way, you prune," Margot said.

"I'll move," Eleanor said. She got up and moved to the other end of the table.

"Did I say something wrong?" Margot asked. "Perhaps she was afraid I'd be tempted to stab her with a fork."

"Margot..." Vickery said.

"What?" Her innocent look was not at all convincing. "Did you see what she is wearing? Blood red? Is she determined to *advertise* that she's for sale?"

"You are terribly old fashioned sometimes," Vickery said.

Watching Eleanor Trenton take her new seat, Artie Delancey said: "I was hoping she would wear the blue dress."

"You were?" Bannister asked. "Why?"

"What? Oh, no reason. It's just a lovely dress."

Margot and Vickery took their seats.

"The food is from Sir Geoffrey's kitchen tonight: it has to be an improvement on yesterday's 'banquet,'" Vickery said. "What were those pellets they served with the pork, they were like catapult ammunition."

"Sage and onion stuffing," Margot said. "Leo managed to cut one of them open."

"He had an axe at the table?"

"The wine will be from Geoffrey's cellar too, he always had a fabulous selection," Margot said. "Goes over to France and selects it himself. Keeps some of it for years."

"Some things do improve with age," Vickery said.

"Unfortunately husbands aren't one of them," Margot growled, as Fulbright took a seat next to Eleanor.

"Sorry I'm late, did I miss anything?" Fulbright asked.

"Being present when good manners were taught," Margot muttered.

"What's the soup taste like?" Fulbright asked loudly. "It looks like bilge water. And someone pass me a decent wine glass, this one's not even big enough for sherry."

"Pass me a bigger knife," Margot said, "this one's not big enough for boor."

"Think pleasant thoughts and smile, Margot dear," Vickery said.

"I was: I was picturing Leo bleeding to death."

"Oh, look Auntie Margot, it's Sir Geoffrey's nephew," Vickery said, as the boy was helped into a seat at the table.

"Dreadful child." Margot shuddered.

"All children are dreadful," Vickery said. "Fortunately they don't all make dreadful adults."

"Though some do," Margot said, glaring across at Fulbright. "Is he really wearing a yellow shirt with a red tie? He looks like a boil that needs lancing."

"Perhaps you'd like some more wine?"

"I'd like a gun with six bullets," Margot said.

"That is rather harsh."

"I could have asked for a Thompson submachine gun," Margot said, reasonably she thought.

"Why *did* you come this weekend?" Vickery asked.

"To keep an eye on him."

"Why? You know exactly what he's going to do."

"Yes, but the fun will be in discovering how *I* react."

"Why don't you challenge him at his own game, and flirt outrageously with one of the other guests?"

Margot looked glumly round the table. "I've been married to Geoffrey and fucked by Teddy, that leaves Bannister and the six-year-old nephew. Oh, and Linette's fiancé, though he looks like he hasn't planted his flag on anyone's summit yet. Then there's that driver, Malloy, but I think you'd have more luck with him than I would."

"Do you think so?" Vickery looked up.

"Keep your fly buttoned, he'll be downstairs dining with the real people."

"Actually he's having dinner down at the local inn this evening," Vickery said.

"He is? Why?"

"Because I asked him to," Vickery said.

"Really? Do you think Leo and you-know-who have done you-know-what?" Margot asked.

"Not yet," Vickery said.

"How do you *know?*"

"Something in the way she looks at him."

"I think you're right. If she'd done it with him, she'd look like she'd been under a steamroller. Do you think she and Teddy—?"

"They are not on speaking terms, remember?"

"You don't have to be speaking to do it. I forget you've never been married."

"We're not going to be subjected to a showing of *Arthur and Guinevere* tonight, are we?" Vickery asked, in an attempt to change the subject of conversation.

"Don't worry, that reel isn't going to be found any time soon," Margot said.

"Why, what have you done with it?"

"Nothing too drastic."

"What *do* we have to look forward to tonight?" Vickery askcd.

"Once the drink's taken, Artie will delight us with a selection of popular music hall songs," Margot said, sounding anything but delighted at the prospect, "and then I think Teddy has a little something up his sleeve."

"Magic?" Vickery asked.

"Monologue."

"Sounds dreadful."

"It won't be, it will be rather wicked. I've had a sneak preview."

"Is Ted Kimball any good?"

"At monologues or fucking?" Margot asked. "Don't roll your eyes, people will think I've said something inappropriate."

"You think I would enjoy his performance then?"

"He's fine once the initial fumbling is done and he gets into his stride."

The soup plates were cleared away and the main course was served.

"Do stop staring," Vickery said.

"I wasn't staring, I was glowering," Margot said. "She's just picking at her food like a sparrow. And she's hardly touched her lips to that wineglass. It's not stage food, love, you can tuck in!"

"Young people don't know how to enjoy food," Vickery said.

"She's probably afraid she'll balloon like a heifer if she takes a whole forkful," Margot said.

"My mother always said that it didn't matter how big a woman was, as long as she had slim ankles. Men don't like women with ankles like tree trunks, she reckoned," Vickery said.

"Is that really what men look for?"

"How on earth would I know? I'm more interested in the size of a potential partner's feet."

"You are, why?" And then it dawned on her, and Margot slapped his arm. "You're incorrigible."

"Better to be incorrigible than a codger, according to Betty."

"Have you not got rid of that terrible girl yet?"

"I like her."

"She shows absolutely no respect for anyone."

"That's why I like her. That and her steak and ale pie."

"Sometimes you're impossibly *common*, you know."

"I rather thought I was just unique."

"I've heard other words applied to you," Margot said.

They ate in silence for some time: as predicted, the food was a significantly better than had been served on the previous evening. The roast beef was succulent and the gravy was flavoured with just the right amount of red wine.

"Whose conversations have you been dipping into this

evening?" Margot asked, as the dinner plates were being cleared away.

"You don't need to lip read to know what Leo's been talking about," Vickery said.

"I imagine he's been talking Geoffrey's ear off about the dawning of the British motion picture industry," Margot said. "Shame movies aren't still silent. I'd love a silent movie of Leo. I hope he manages to get a signature on something before Geoffrey sees that reel of *Arthur and Guinevere.*"

"Is it as bad as people are saying?" Vickery asked.

"Did I say that I had *seen* it? I'm sure I didn't say that."

"You do know it's rude to smirk at the table before the dessert has been cleared?"

"I *never* smirk. I smile ironically. What is in that bowl?"

"Syllabub."

"Isn't that sour cream?"

"Yes, but it's soured by alcohol," Vickery said.

"I know the feeling. Is it *supposed* to look like curds and whey? Perhaps you would like mine?"

"Traditionally it is made by squirting milk straight from the cow's udder into a jar of cider," Vickery said, "or so they say."

"You can definitely have mine."

"This is made with cream and sweet sherry, you should try it." Digging through the froth, Vickery extracted his spoon and sipped the liquor.

"Is that a nettle leaf on top?"

"It's a sprig of fresh mint," Vickery said.

"Like they put on potatoes?"

"Now who's being common?"

* * *

"Why did you have to stick your nose in, you dreadful woman?" Linette demanded.

"What do you mean?" Eleanor asked, shocked at being confronted in this way. Linette had cornered her as she came out of the WC.

"My father attacked Ollie and tried to send him away. You've ruined everything! Are you happy now, you interfering cow? I hate you!"

"I'm sorry, I never meant to—"

"Isn't it bad enough that you've come between my mother and father? Did you have to spoil what I had too? What is wrong with you?"

"I—"

"You're just as bad as my father. You just want to ruin everything for other people. You can't bear to see us happy."

"That's not true. And your father isn't—"

"Isn't he? Then why did my father pay photographers to follow Ted Kimball?"

"Teddy?"

"He didn't tell you that, did he? He sent Ollie to follow Mr. Kimball, he wanted some pictures that would force Kimball to give up his interest in you. And that worked out better than anyone hoped, didn't it? Provoking Mr. Kimball into attacking someone, then taking pictures to show what a terrible drunk he was."

"No..."

"You think my father didn't know what it would take to make you cast Ted Kimball aside? Leo Fulbright takes what he knows about you, and he uses it to get what he wants. If you don't believe that, you are fooling yourself and you deserve everything that will happen to you."

"Linette, I—"

"Keep away from me, and Ollie, you've done enough damage already."

Eleanor watched Linette walk away, trying to discount

what she had said. And found herself short of a convincing argument against what she had heard about Leo Fulbright.

* * *

Vickery stood on the terrace and breathed deeply. If he was being honest, it wasn't fresh air he needed so much as a break from the people inside. He was feeling very much like an outsider intruding on a family occasion, which in a way he was. He was here to work, and that work required him to observe and question the other guests. Something he could not do unless he returned to their company. He was on the point of making his way inside when he became aware of someone else exiting onto the terrace via the French doors. He stepped back into the shadows and watched Veronica Fulbright come out into the moonlight and glance about nervously. Seeing no-one, she hurried across the paved area and onto the path that would take her to the right, towards the wood. Her behaviour aroused his curiosity, and Vickery might have followed her, but he already had a good idea where she was going.

Only a few moments later, Vickery spotted another figure emerge from the woods. The man sauntered towards the terrace with his hands in his pockets.

"How was dinner?" Vickery asked, stepping out of the shadows. Malloy didn't seem surprised by this.

"The fare was bland, the company—interesting," he said. "You owe me four shillings and thruppence."

"I asked you to buy George a drink, not the whole inn."

"Ah, well, I had my dinner and we had a couple of drinks, and we got to talking, and then we had a couple more."

"What did you make of him?" Vickery asked.

"Good-looking fellow, a little younger than yourself. Not a rich man, I would say, but no pauper. And he seemed entirely genuine."

"You told him about the situation here?"

"That I did. He wasn't entirely convinced at first, wanted to be up here himself. But another drink or two and I had him round to our way of thinking."

"Four shillings and thruppence well-spent, then. Did you see Miss Fulbright as you were returning?"

"I did indeed. And made sure she didn't see me," Malloy said.

"A fine evening's work," Vickery said.

"Did I miss anything here? Has anyone murdered Fulbright yet?" Malloy asked.

"No."

"Ah well, the night is still young. I'm off down to the kitchen to see what Mrs. B has set aside for supper."

"More food, so soon?" Vickery asked.

"I have been walking all evening, ten miles at least."

"Only if you were considerably lost: it is a mile and a half along the bridleway to the village."

"Is that all? It seemed a lot longer in the dark."

"Sounds like the punchline to a joke. Enjoy your supper, Mr. Malloy."

"Sure and you've a dirty mind, Mr. Vickery. I like that." Malloy grinned.

Chapter 11

The drawing room seemed a little dark, furnished in Victorian style, though less cluttered. It also served as the music room, being home to a glossy baby grand piano. There were several high-backed chairs, and three sofas upholstered with faded tapestry fabric. Wing-backed chairs sat either side of a large marble fireplace. Off to one side was a round table draped in a fringed cloth with four chairs around it: it looked ready to hold a séance. Low tables were scattered about, and several aspidistras tried to rise above the questionable taste of their gaudy pots. Windows at one end of the room opened onto the grass in front of the keep; those at the rear would, in daylight, afford a pleasant view past the orchard to the lake.

Fulbright entered carrying a glass of brandy and made immediately for the armchair on the left of the fire. This was obviously Sir Geoffrey's favourite chair, and he looked mildly annoyed at Fulbright's presumption, especially when Fulbright, unbidden, opened a glossy walnut cigar box on the low table beside the chair and helped himself to one of Sir Geoffrey's cigars. With a sigh of resignation, Sir Geoffrey took the chair on the right.

The other guests filtered in, taking places on the sofas or standing nearby.

"This is the *drawing room,* not the parlour," Bannister was saying as he came in with Artie. "Parlours is what middle class people have, this is *upper* class."

"Pardon my ignorance, I'm sure," Artie said, favouring Bannister with a mock curtsey. "And is that what we call a pee-anna, or do the toffs have a posh name for that an all?"

"You are so *common,*" Bannister sniffed. He took a seat at the piano and lifted the lid. He began to play *Greensleeves* softly, in the style of a tea-room pianist.

Vickery offered to sit on one of the sofas with Linette and Oliver Garvin and entertain them with a little table-top magic. Garvin looked pale and there were dark circles under his eyes.

"Sit on my right, if you would, Mr. Vickery: I still have a terrible ringing in my left ear."

Vickery asked them to carefully examine a small wooden box with a drawer in it, it was a little larger than a matchbox, and to satisfy themselves that it was completely empty. Linette took it from Garvin's fumbling fingers and poked and prodded it, took out the drawer completely and held up both parts of the box to the light.

"Empty," she said, her tone certain. She slotted the drawer back into the box and held it out to Vickery. He declined to take it.

"Place it on the table," he said. "Tap the top of it—gently—three times." Linette did so. "Now open the box."

Linette slid open the drawer carefully, and something golden leaped out of it, startling her into a laugh. A brass grasshopper sat on the table, clearly a mechanical device powered by a watch spring. Linette picked it up suspiciously, turning it over, looking for the trick of it. At Vickery's request, she placed it back into the little wooden drawer, which it filled completely. She slid the drawer back into the box. Again she tapped the top of the box three times, then opened the drawer. The mechanical grasshopper was gone.

"Where did it go?" Linette asked. She shook the little box, separated the two parts again, and searched them carefully with eyes and fingertips.

"It went wherever you sent it," Vickery said. "Clearly you have a talent for magic."

"Except that I have no idea how I did it!" Linette said.

"Where's the music?" Artie asked.

"Upstairs," Bannister said.

"Wouldn't it be better down here on the piano?"

"Be a dear and fetch it for me?"

"Send the butler up for it, isn't that what posh people do?"

"I'll fetch it myself." Bannister sighed.

What occurred next only became clear in retrospect. There was a loud sound, something between a *snap* and a *twang,* people said, at the front end of the room. A brief hissing, followed by a loud, hollow *thud* over by the fireplace. Eleanor screamed, shocked by the sudden impact. Fulbright was the first to become aware of what had happened, having heard and felt the passage of something close to his face. His eyes flicked to the left, to where a crossbow quarrel was embedded in the leather of the chair wing, only inches from his head. His face was pale with the shock of it, but his colour swiftly rose.

"I've been *shot* at!" He thundered, leaping to his feet.

"The window!" Eleanor pointed to where the curtain still shivered. Vickery and Fulbright both sprang towards it. The window was ajar. They pushed it open and peered out. But no one was to be seen in the darkness. After a few seconds of trying to discern movement in the shadows, they pulled their heads back inside.

Vickery glanced around the room, noting which of the guests were present, and which absent. Margot McCrae, Ted Kimball, Veronica Fulbright, and Dickie Bannister were not in the room at that moment.

Sir Geoffrey was bending over, peering at the quarrel embedded in the chair.

"I say, you don't think this was meant for me, do you?" He asked. "This is where *I* usually sit."

"They were aiming for *my* head!" Fulbright insisted.

"How on earth did they manage to miss that?" Garvin muttered. Linette shushed him.

"Do you think we should send someone for the police?" Sir Geoffrey asked. "No telephone out here, I'm afraid."

"Do you think this is related to those poison pen letters?" Linette asked. "Perhaps we should fetch the police now?"

Fulbright's face was scarlet, and it took him a few breaths to regain his voice.

"We don't need the police for this—*nonsense!*" He said. He pointed a finger at Vickery and jabbed the air. "I said I wanted this sorted. Get it done!"

Margot entered. "What have I missed?" She asked brightly.

Fulbright scowled at her. "Where have you been?"

"I went up to fetch my wrap," she said. Then aware of her bare shoulders, she added: "Couldn't find it. I know I had it earlier when I was walking in the garden."

"Someone tried to kill me," Fulbright said.

Margot became aware that everyone was looking at her. "If *I* had intended to kill him, he would be dead," she said.

Bannister came into the room carrying his eyeglasses and a battered manila folder into which sheet music had been carelessly stuffed.

"Who's for a bit of Nanki-Poo?" Artie said, snapping open a fan and swishing it in front of his face. He took his place beside the piano and Bannister's fingers found the first chord.

"Leo escaped being murdered. Alas, Gilbert and Sullivan shall not be so lucky," Margot muttered to Vickery. "What's wrong with her?"

Eleanor Trenton was still standing, ashen-faced, staring at the window through which the crossbow had been fired.

"I wonder if she saw who was at the window," Vickery said. He moved towards her and asked his question. Eleanor shook he head: she had seen nothing, but had been startled by the sound.

"Thank goodness they missed," she said.

"Perhaps that was the intention," Vickery said.

Artie was just finishing his song when Ted Kimball entered the drawing room.

Kimball glanced towards Margot, smiled and nodded. She nodded back. And then, when Margot had looked away from him, Kimball nodded towards Artie. Artie looked uncomfortable, and gave the merest jerk of his head in acknowledgement.

"Sing us another one, Artie," Bannister said.

"I—I don't want to. Not right now," Artie said.

"Oh, come on, don't play coy."

"I'm not, really," Artie insisted, still seeming distracted.

Eleanor Trenton placed a hand on Bannister's shoulder and bent to whisper in his ear. He looked up at her and laughed, and began to play. Eleanor clasped her fingers together in front of her chest, looking as though she was going to perform something terribly 'proper,' but the rumble of the piano suggested not. Her voice, when she sang, was surprisingly deep and rich, with just the hint of archness that *Anything Goes* required.

Margot adopted an expression of cold disdain, but when she saw that Eleanor had captivated the audience, she turned on her heel and walked out. As applause followed Eleanor's performance, Artie Delancey also seemed less than pleased, though he pretended otherwise.

"That was lovely, dear. Perhaps we could try a duet?" He said. "You could take the man's part."

Eleanor walked away without responding.

"That wasn't called for," Bannister said. "What's wrong with you tonight?"

"You've got to admit, it was a bit butch," Artie said.

"Compared to you, dear, even I'm butch."

"Shut up and play the piano, Dickie."

* * *

"What happened to the booming bittern?" Margot asked.

"She's gone to her room unwell, thinks it might be something she ate," Vickery said.

"And Teddy has gone to 'rub her tummy' has he?" Margot asked, glancing around the drawing room.

"I thought perhaps he had gone to prepare for his performance."

"That's supposed to be a secret. You mustn't let Leo know. I need to get him out of the way," Margot said. "Don't look at me like that: I'm not going to lure him to some secluded spot and bludgeon him to death with a blunt instrument. Not without an alibi."

"Going off on your own to look for a wrap and not finding it, that's not much of an alibi," Vickery said.

"Shooting at Leo's head and missing isn't much of a murder," Margot said. "Am I your only suspect?"

"Veronica Fulbright, Mr. Kimball, and Mr. Bannister were all absent at the moment the shot was fired in through the window," Vickery said.

"Have you checked the soft earth outside the window for

footprints?"

"Whatever for?" Vickery asked.

"Isn't that what proper detectives do? To help narrow the list of suspects. For a start you could see if they were male or female."

"Miss Fulbright wears men's shoes."

"She does?"

"Brogues," Vickery said. "I thought women noted such things."

"Only in other women they regard as a friend or a threat," Margot said.

"And what sort of shoes was Eleanor Trenton wearing this evening?"

"An open-toe high-heel sandal, patent leather, darker shade of red than her dress, why?"

"Just testing your theory. Does Mr. Kimball play darts, do you know?"

"Haven't a clue, why?"

"I was thinking of challenging him."

"To a game of fifty-one?" Margot asked.

"That as well. Do you think he could hit the bull's-eye?"

"Sober, probably. Do you think he shot the crossbow at Leo?"

"I would certainly like to know where he was when it was fired."

"Teddy wasn't with me," Margot said. Was there a challenge in that remark, or a defensiveness? "Where are those two off to?" She nodded towards Linette, who had taken Oliver Garvin's hand and was leading him out.

"A romantic moonlight stroll?" Vickery suggested.

"Do people really do that?" Margot asked. "It seems such a cliché."

"It is just an excuse to be away from the presence of others," Vickery said.

"Do you think they are up to no good?"

"I did not see Mr. Garvin carrying a flag, if that's what you are asking," Vickery said.

"I wasn't thinking any such thing! What a filthy mind you have."

"I think I should question Mr. Bannister regarding his recent whereabouts," Vickery said.

"You don't suspect *him* of trying to kill Leo? We've known Dickie for years."

"And do people grow fonder of Leo, the longer they are acquainted with him?"

"We grow more tolerant. We have to."

"Sometimes we find our tolerance put to the test," Vickery said. "Mr. Bannister is, I think, much more attached to you than he is to Leo."

"Lesser of two evils," Margot said, "we are both acquired tastes."

"I know in whose company I should prefer to pass my time," Vickery said.

"Yes, but that's because we are both vitriolic misanthropes, no one else would put up with us."

"Perhaps. But Mr. Bannister and I are also kinsmen, after a fashion."

"You are both sexagenarians?"

"I am sure Mr. Bannister would feel complimented to be described so, whereas *I* am deeply offended."

"Touchy about our age, are we Benjamin?"

"Only when people add ten years to it."

"Ten?"

"Yes. Well, the best part of ten years."

"Perhaps you *are* human, after all," Margot said, smiling. "Your secret is safe with me."

* * *

"Mr. Vickery, I can't tempt you into giving us a song? Artie seems to have lost his voice. The poor boy looks quite ill," Bannister said.

"Something he ate?" Vickery asked.

"More likely to be something he drank, the way he's knocking it back. He's not usually like this."

"You are feeling well yourself?"

"Perfectly fine, why do you ask?"

"You were absent for a while earlier."

"I was?" Bannister thought about this. "Popped upstairs to get my music and my specs," he said. "Missed all the fun with Leo being shot at."

"Did you see anyone else while you were upstairs?" Vickery asked.

"Saw that awful boy being dragged off to bed by his nurse. Looked like she'd tried to drown him in the tub, or vice versa, they were both soaked. Passed Margot on the stairs."

"Going up or coming down?"

"She was coming down as I went up."

"Did you see Teddy Kimball?"

"No, sorry. I thought he'd stayed in the dining room, lingering over the cigars and brandy, if you get my drift? You're sure I can't tempt you?" Bannister nodded towards the piano.

"I never sang. And it is some time since I played accompaniment."

"That's a shame. Does you good to keep your hand in. What time is it?"

Vickery consulted his pocket watch. "Twenty-five minutes after eleven."

"Time for one more song," Bannister said. He placed his fingers on the keys. "Any request?

"A little Coward?" Vickery said, with a wink.

Bannister laughed a throaty laugh and began to play, singing "I met him at a party..."

Bannister was only part-way through the last chorus of *Mad About the Boy* when Fulbright's voice reverberated through the open doorway: he was evidently standing in the entrance hall given the way the sound echoed.

"Never mind that mawkish mooning, come out here if you want to be properly entertained!"

There was some grumbling and people began to shuffle out, more from a sense of duty than a desire to be 'entertained' by Leo Fulbright. But once out in the entrance hall, they looked about in confusion: there was no sign of their host.

"That's right, gather round, gather round!" The voice boomed again. They all looked up, to where Ted Kimball stood on the first landing of the great staircase, owning it as his stage. He had a glass in one hand and a bottle of whisky in the other, and his voice was a perfect imitation of Fulbright's.

Chapter 12

"Now is the winter of our discontent," Kimball boomed, "made glorious summer by this quart of scotch."

"How *much* has he had?" Bannister asked, clearly impressed.

Kimball turned and looked up the stairs to where a figure stood half in shadows, the red of her dress more subdued there.

"Eleanor, come down and watch, please?"

She shook her head and stepped back, singing softly the verse of *Anything Goes*.

"Was she crying?" Bannister asked, looking up at the retreating figure.

"She's fine," Kimball said, "just tired. Now then, we present this evening's entertainment," he said, slipping back into Fulbright's voice. "*The Tragedy of Hamlet, Prince of Limerick.* Our scene, a castle on Eire's shore..."

And then, using Fulbright's voice to perform in best mock Shakespearean tones, he began a recital of the tragedy, rewritten in the poetic meter of the limerick.

> *A ghost called me here from my bed,*
> *I'm your father Hamlet, so he said,*
> *I was killed by your uncle,*
> *That ugly carbuncle,*
> *Used poison to kill me stone-dead.*

My father had come from the grave
His poor soul he asked me to save
His method was simple
I should lance that fat pimple
My uncle, the murderous knave.

But things are not simple, I said,
My mother is now in his bed,
That cold-hearted bitch,
That selfish old witch,
Is fucking your brother instead.

Margot had been watching this with a bemused smile, but at some point it must have occurred to her that watching her ex-lover imitating the husband she had betrayed with him was perhaps just a little too much to endure. Shaking her head, she turned and went back into the drawing room. She opened the French doors and stepped out.

"Not staying to watch the show?" Vickery asked. He was standing on the terrace, looking out towards the lake.

"I sent Leo down to the summer house to get my wrap," she said. She drew the wrap more tightly around her shoulders. "I should go and tell him I found it."

Vickery stepped back into the shadows as Margot hurried away, so that she might not see him when she glanced back, as he knew she would. She went for some way along the path towards the summer house and the lake, then—believing she was unobserved—she cut across the lawn back towards the orchard. From there, Vickery had no doubt that she would make her way back round to the front of the keep.

* * *

Back inside the keep, Kimball was nearing the end of his recital.

> *The last act of a play, so they say,*
> *Needs rhyming couplets and swordplay,*
> *This is Shakespeare, my dear*
> *So we have nothing to fear,*
> *There'll be blood and his cast he will slay.*
>
> *The stage will be running with blood,*
> *The red stuff will flow like a flood,*
> *The weak-hearted will faint*
> *Seeing all this wet paint,*
> *But will know it is for their own good.*
>
> *And there we must leave our sad tale,*
> *The plan of poor Hamlet did fail.*
> *Revenge he did seek,*
> *But his delivery was weak,*
> *And his blood ended up in a pail.*

Applause accompanied Kimball's bow, which he silenced with open palms. His eyes flicked towards the dial of his wristwatch.

"'Lo, what sound is that?" Kimball-Fulbright asked aloud.

Behind him, the mechanism of the grandfather clock clicked loudly, and it began to sound the hour.

"Upstaged by a bloody clock!" Kimball counted the strokes silently, pantomiming impatience. Then his voice boomed out in Fulbright's best Falstaffian tones. "We have heard the chimes at midnight!" He paused to draw breath, and seemed about to speak again, but was prevented from doing so.

A scream, loud and penetrating, filled with anguish and fear, that was enough to still the heart and chill the blood. And then the sound of something substantial cast bodily into water.

"Eleanor?" Kimball said, shocked back into his sober self.

He glanced towards the back of the house.

"The lake?" Bannister asked, looking around as if to determine the source of the terrible sound.

"No, it came from the front," Linette said.

"The pond then," Bannister said.

Everyone crowded out into the courtyard. The darkness was impenetrable.

"Someone fetch a lantern!" Sir Geoffrey called.

Malloy appeared, carrying two lit oil lamps. He passed one to Garvin. They led the way across the courtyard and under the gatehouse.

"Eleanor?" Kimball shouted. They all held their breath to listen, but there was no sound but for a gentle breeze.

"Eleanor!" Kimball called again, louder. But to the same effect.

Malloy and Garvin approached the edge of the pond, lamps held out before them. Vickery appeared at Malloy's side.

"You heard the scream?" Malloy asked.

"I came at once. Cast the light to your left."

There was something pale and round beneath the surface of the water. The light passed across it, then returned and remained steady. The pale shape revealed itself to be a human face.

This should have been a pre-Raphaelite *Ophelia*, but there were no vivid sunny colours here, but rather the sense of something discarded in a dark muddy puddle. Around her, the slimy black leaves of decaying water lilies waved on their stems like malignant serpents ready to envelop her and drag her body into the depths. Her face was luminously pale in the thick greenish water, pale blue eyes open and staring, but unseeing. Everyone gazed down at her, their own eyes burning as they longed for her to blink. Her hair drifted around her head like weeds, swayed gently by the movement of the water.

And amidst the pale fronds played a pinkish mist of her life's blood.

"What's going on here?" Fulbright asked, coming up behind the group and unable to see what they were staring down at. He forced his way through, and finally comprehending what he was seeing, he fell to his knees in the mud.

"Eleanor?" His voice was a whisper.

Passing his lamp to Vickery, Malloy pulled off his shoes and waded into the water. He bent and lifted the water-logged corpse. For a moment he stood in the lamplight, holding the dripping victim like something from a Victorian melodrama. Then he dragged his legs through the murk, bringing her ashore, and at the same time raising a terrible stench of rotting vegetation. Without looking at anyone, Malloy carried her back towards the keep like a tragic hero returning with his drowned lover.

The others followed Malloy, but Fulbright remained on his knees staring into the inky water of the pond. Vickery stood with the lamp, waiting for him to stir, not wanting to disturb him. He was about to go inside and leave Fulbright to his thoughts, when he saw the other man lean forward and pick something out of the dirt.

"Leo?" Vickery said softly.

Fulbright, startled, thrust his hand guiltily into his pocket and struggled to his feet.

"She's really dead?" Fulbright asked.

Vickery nodded.

"But why?" Fulbright asked quietly.

Vickery regarded him a moment in silence, then said: "Let's go inside out of the cold."

Chapter 13

"We can't just leave her on the floor. Can't we take her upstairs and put her into bed?" Bannister asked.

"She's soaking wet," Margot said.

"It doesn't matter where she is. She's not going to know the difference," Fulbright said, coming in behind them.

Margot cast a silencing glance in his direction, and for once he had the sense to take heed.

"We should cover her with a sheet, at least," Margot said.

Sir Geoffrey rang for the butler, and a sheet was sent for.

"Malloy, a word if you wouldn't mind," Vickery said.

"Mr. Vickery?"

Vickery led Malloy off to one side.

"I want you to go out and make sure all of the cars are still inoperative: we don't want anyone trying to make an escape. Move the missing engine parts to a new hiding place, just in case. And you'll need to put my car back in running order if you are to—"

"Someone has to go and fetch the police," Fulbright said, looming over them. "There's no telephone here to call them."

"Mr. Malloy is going to take my car and return with the local doctor, and the police," Vickery said.

"Then he can take the Rolls," Fulbright said.

"Mr. Vickery's car is faster," Malloy said, with just a hint of pleasure.

"You trust him?" Fulbright asked, ignoring Malloy.

"With my car? Of course."

"I meant, are you sure *he's* not the murderer?" Fulbright said. "He could flee in your car."

Vickery favoured Fulbright with a withering look. "Malloy is only the *driver,* what possible motive could he have for murdering Miss Trenton?"

"I will be back as swift as I can, sir," Malloy said, taking the keys from Vickery and ignoring Fulbright.

"I don't like that boy's attitude," Fulbright said as Malloy left.

"Is that why you hit him?" Vickery asked. He turned without waiting for a response. He addressed the rest of the assemblage: "Why don't we all go into the drawing room? We can have some coffee sent up. I think it may be some time before any of us get any sleep."

"Who put you in charge, Vickery?" Fulbright demanded to know.

"You are right, of course. Excuse my presumption," Vickery said. He turned his back on Fulbright and approached Sir Geoffrey. "We are guests in your house, Sir Geoffrey. Until the police arrive, it is only right that you should take charge."

"Er, yes, thank you Vickery." Sir Geoffrey's face was white and his eyes large and staring. "Ah, here's Crawley with the sheet. That's better. Much more respectful. Let's all go into the drawing room and wait, shall we? Crawley, bring some coffee up, would you?"

They all trooped through into the drawing room, Fulbright muttering under his breath. They sat or found places to stand around the room, unconsciously arranging themselves into a circle facing Sir Geoffrey. He dropped into his armchair. Vickery stood protectively behind and to one side of Sir

Geoffrey's chair. He had positioned himself so that he could see through the open door into the entrance hall.

"Where's Artie?" Bannister asked.

"Haven't seen him since dinner," Kimball said.

"Has he gone to bed?" Bannister asked.

"We will ask Crawley to go up and check," Vickery said.

"Artie doesn't know about—" Linette glanced towards the open door leading into the entrance hall. "We should make sure that he doesn't just stumble across the body. That would be an awful way to find out."

"I will keep an eye out for him coming in," Vickery said. He glanced through the door into the entrance hall.

"What about Timothy?" Sir Geoffrey asked, standing up suddenly.

"Nanny is with him, sir," Crawley said, entering with a tray of coffee. "She will break the news to him gently when he wakes."

"I should probably do that," Sir Geoffrey said. He didn't sound convinced. "She was his sister..."

"Children are usually better handled with a woman's understanding," Crawley said, "if you don't mind my saying so."

"No, you're probably right, Crawley." Sir Geoffrey sat down, relieved.

"Crawley, would you go up and look into Mr. Delancey's room, please?" Vickery asked. "No one has seen him for some time."

Crawley looked towards Sir Geoffrey, who nodded his assent. Crawley gave a tiny bow and exited.

"What do we do now?" Linette asked.

"We wait," Margot said. "Malloy will return with the police soon."

An awkward silence followed. The guests glanced at each other, but looked away without making eye contact. The coffee went mostly untouched. Seconds ticked by, ponderously marked by the mantel clock. There was a brief stir as Crawley returned and bent to whisper something to Sir Geoffrey: he nodded and waved the butler over to Vickery, where the same pantomime was repeated.

"Thank you, Crawley," Vickery said.

The butler gave a grudging bow and exited.

"Artie Delancey is not in his room, his bed has not been slept in," Vickery said. "None of the staff have seen him since the dining table was cleared."

"You don't think he's lying dead somewhere too, do you?" Bannister asked.

"No, I'm sure he just stepped out for some air and will return shortly," Vickery said. "When the police arrive, we can have a proper search for him."

"What's keeping them?" Kimball asked.

"There's only a bobby in the village," Sir Geoffrey said. "Can't have a murder investigated by a bobby. They will have to telephone the station over in Crowmans Heath to get an Inspector, and he'll be at least an hour getting here. Assuming he's not been called off somewhere else."

"And in the meantime we have to sit here with a murderer in our midst!" Linette said.

"*Linette!*" Margot admonished.

"The girl's right," Fulbright said. "Unless that fool Malloy is the killer, in which case we'll be waiting more than a couple of hours for the police to arrive."

"Perhaps Artie is the murderer," Linette suggested.

"Don't be *ridiculous!*" Bannister said. "Artie would never hurt anyone one. Would he?"

"In which case, it *must* be one of us in this room," Linette said.

"Why are we all assuming that the murder has to be one of

us?" Fulbright asked. "We're not on a desert island: someone else could have come here and killed her. Perhaps it was some passing vagrant."

"I'm sure we would all like that to be true," Margot said, "but it seems unlikely doesn't it? Especially since she was stabbed with that bloody sword."

"We don't know that for a fact," Fulbright said. "We should wait until the doctor has—"

"You saw her," Margot insisted, "she was stabbed by something that went in the front and out her back. It was a sword. You don't need to wait for the doctor to tell us. Go and look at your blasted stone: I bet the sword isn't in it."

Linette and Garvin exchanged looks, then got up and hurried out together, hand in hand. They returned after only a few moments.

"Mummy's right: Excalibur is missing," Linette said.

"That doesn't prove it was used to kill Eleanor," Fulbright said stubbornly.

"Oh, come on Leo, how many other swords do we have here?" Margot said.

"Several, actually, Margot," Sir Geoffrey said, "scattered about the place. As well as several pikes and axes, and a Japanese katana, and a number of antique firearms."

"Murderer's paradise," Fulbright muttered.

Another period of silence followed, and again people cast suspicious sideways glances at one another.

"If Artie had been here, he could have given us a song," Bannister said. "P'raps not appropriate under the circumstances, though."

"Should we have asked Malloy to bring the vicar as well?" Linette asked.

"What for?" Fulbright asked. "All they are ever interested in is money for the church roof. Those places must all be Gerrybuilt."

"Not much of a church-goer, Fulbright?" Sir Geoffrey asked. "Why doesn't that surprise me?"

"The churches are already full of hypocrites," Kimball said, "they don't need another one."

"Gentlemen, a little respect please; for yourselves if not for anything else," Vickery said.

"I think I heard a car," Linette said.

Silence followed as they all strained to listen. Then came the unmistakable thud of a car door. Then another.

"About bloody time!" Fulbright said.

"Only one car," Kimball said, "that can't be right." But no one was listening. They all leaned expectantly towards the open door into the entrance hall.

"Sir Geoffrey?" Vickery indicated that he should go through into the entrance hall. "If everyone else would please wait here," he said. He followed Sir Geoffrey out and closed the door.

The door into the courtyard was open. Malloy stood in the entrance hall next to a short, stout man who was wearing a brown derby, tweed jacket, and round tortoiseshell glasses. His trousers would have benefited from the application of a flat iron and his bowtie seemed to have been fastened in haste.

"This is Doctor Cole," Malloy said.

"Doctor, thank you for coming. Sir Geoffrey Atterbury I believe you know. I am Benjamin Vickery."

The doctor shook hands with them both. He seemed pale and a little breathless.

"And the police?" Vickery asked Malloy.

"They should be along shortly," Malloy said, with just a hint of a smile. "They were right behind us."

"Malloy made very good time from Crowman's Heath," the doctor said, his colour gradually returning.

There was a crunching of gravel outside, and then a dark blue Wolsley with POLICE above the windscreen drove in under the gatehouse. It shuddered to a stop in the courtyard.

Two large uniformed constables squeezed out of the rear seat of the car. They had been obliged through lack of headroom to sit with their domed helmets in their laps. They hastily donned these and adjusted the chin straps as their superior climbed out of the front passenger seat. The Inspector was an altogether less beefy fellow, and his porkpie hat had remained on his head, though it appeared to have been knocked out of position. He adjusted it as he approached the front door, casting an annoyed glance at his driver, though whether this was because of the jolting he had received, or the fact that they had failed to keep pace with Malloy, wasn't clear.

The Inspector was a grey man, wearing a grey raincoat and a large ill-advised moustache: because his hair was dark and his sideburns and whiskers almost red, the moustache looked fake.

"I am Inspector Debney: I shall be leading the investigation into the death of Helena Trenton."

"Eleanor," Malloy corrected him.

Inspector Debney looked down at the shrouded form on the floor. "The body should not have been moved without proper authority," he said.

"We lifted my niece out of the pond to see whether she might be revived," Sir Geoffrey said, "surely you cannot object to that, Inspector?"

"People should not have trampled over the ground by the pond: a herd of elephants couldn't have done a better job of spoiling the murderer's footprints," the Inspector said.

"People walked there before they were aware that a murder had taken place," Vickery said.

"Valuable evidence gone. It makes my task all the more

difficult," Debney said. "Doctor, I should like you to make a preliminary examination of the body. Bring me your findings as soon as you can."

"We should move the body out of the entrance hall," the doctor said.

"A cool room with a large table?" Vickery suggested.

"That would be ideal," said the doctor. "I shall also need hot water and a towel."

"There are empty store rooms downstairs near the kitchen," Sir Geoffrey said. "I'll have Crawley prepare one." He rang for the butler.

"Where are the other guests?" Inspector Debney asked.

"I'm surprised they're not all out here already," Sir Geoffrey said.

Vickery held up the key to the drawing room door.

"We can't keep them locked up," Sir Geoffrey said, "much as we might like to."

Inspector Debney took the key from Vickery and passed it to one of the constables.

"Go in and keep an eye on them, Crabtree."

"Sir." He touched the peak of his helmet and went to unlock the drawing room door. There was a babble of voices, which was cut off when he closed the door behind him.

"I shall want to speak to each of them in turn," Debney said.

Crawley appeared and under instruction from Sir Geoffrey listened to the doctor's requirements. He hurried back down the servants' stairs to make arrangements. He reappeared a few moments later.

"Brierly, fetch Halstead in to help you," the Inspector said. "Then I want you to take statements from the domestic staff."

"Yessir." Constable Brierly hurried out and returned with the driver. Halstead smelled strongly of cigarettes. The two constables wrapped the sheet more tightly around Eleanor

Trenton's body and lifted it from the stone floor. Manoeuvring carefully, they carried it down the narrow stairs, Crawley leading them and the doctor following behind.

"Sir Geoffrey, I should like to speak with you first," the Inspector said.

"Of course. Let's go into the library." Sir Geoffrey led the way.

"Wait here to be called," the Inspector told Vickery. "I'll deal with you next."

Vickery bit his tongue and nodded politely.

"Typical of the species." Vickery sighed.

"What do we do now?" Malloy asked.

"We submit to their questioning. I suggest you go downstairs: that constable will speak to you along with the other staff. No reason why you should have to put up with any more of the Inspector's rudeness."

"I might even get breakfast while I'm down there," Malloy said. "Shall I ask them to send something up for you?"

Vickery looked at his pocket watch: it was a little after three in the morning. "No, thank you, I shall wait until I have spoken to the Inpsector."

Vickery paced the entrance hall. It was after a quarter-to when Sir Geoffrey came out of the library and closed the door behind him. He looked mildly annoyed.

"That young man has the manners of an ox," Sir Geoffrey said. "Sat himself behind my desk without so much as a by-your-leave; fired questions at me, cutting off my answers as if he couldn't be bothered to listen, and then ushered me out of my own library when he'd had his fill of me. Quite intolerable. I shall speak to the Chief Constable."

"We must make allowances, Sir Geoffrey," Vickery said. "He has the task of investigating a murder, an unpleasant undertaking in itself. And his first priority must be to bring the killer to justice. I'm sure he wished to complete your interview as quickly as possible, so as not to intrude on your grief any more than he had to."

"'Spose you're right, Vickery. But a little courtesy wouldn't go amiss. I'll get Crawley to bring tea and breakfast things up to the drawing room. No one's going to want to stand on ceremony this morning. Then I'm going to check on Timothy. If anyone wants me, send Crawley up, I'll be resting in my room."

Sir Geoffrey went to summon the butler.

Doctor Cole came up the stairs in his shirt sleeves, a sheet of paper in his hand with a few notes written on it.

"Debney?" The doctor asked.

Vickery nodded towards the library door.

The doctor knocked and went inside. He re-emerged after ten minutes. "He wants you in there now," the doctor said. He sounded as though Debney had rather offended him.

Vickery tapped on the library door and entered. He sat down opposite the Inspector and waited for him to speak. Debney was reviewing the notes he'd taken while speaking to Sir Geoffrey.

"I know about you, Mr. Vickery," the Inspector said, without looking up. He didn't sound impressed.

Vickery chose not to respond. He'd sat opposite policemen before, and was accustomed to their tactics. Debney looked at him, brow furrowed. "I'm aware of the Alhambra incident. And that you have subsequently assisted the police in a minor way in several investigations."

"I am always happy to help, Inspector," Vickery said.

"I want to make it very clear that I will *not* be requiring your assistance here. There is no place for an amateur sleuth in a murder investigation. Leave it to the professionals, Mr. Vickery."

"I would not dream of intruding," Vickery said.

"Sir Geoffrey has indicated that only four of the guests were not within his sight at the time of the murder," Debney said.

"Leo Fulbright, his wife Margot McCrae, Artie Delancey, and myself," Vickery said.

"Where were you at midnight, Mr. Vickery?"

"I was taking the air, out on the terrace. I am not aware that anyone saw me there, so doubt if anyone can corroborate my alibi."

"Why did you not watch the performance inside with the others?"

"I have spent too much of my time around theatres and theatrical types. Since my retirement, I try to limit myself to only a couple of hours a day in their company."

"Do you recognise this, Mr. Vickery?" The Inspector held up a piece of gold chain, about four inches in length.

"May I?" Vickery took the chain and examined it closely. "A piece cut from a watch chain."

"Do you own more than one watch chain, Mr. Vickery?"

"I *own* several, but I only ever wear this one." He indicated the chain he currently wore. "For reasons of sentiment."

"A family piece?"

"From someone close to me, yes."

"You said the piece was cut, not torn?" Debney asked.

"Gold is malleable, if you pull it, it stretches—like toffee. None of the links appear deformed, so it is more likely to have been cut from the whole, rather than torn from it."

"Can you be certain?"

"Not unless you have the fragments of the broken links of the chain," Vickery said.

"We do not," Debney said.

"The chain was found where?" Vickery asked, handing it back.

Inspector Debney looked as though he was considering withholding this information. Then said:

"It was found clutched in the hand of the victim."

"A very convenient clue," Vickery said.

"The killer was careless."

"Or perhaps the opposite," Vickery suggested.

"Meaning?"

"I don't want to suggest theories when I have nothing with which to back them up," Vickery said. "As to the owner of the watch chain, I would suggest asking Leo Fulbright: he wears a watch chain of this type."

"How well did you know Eleanor Trenton?" Inspector Debney asked.

"Not at all. I met her for the first time this weekend."

"Any other connections to her?"

"She is, as I am sure you know, Sir Geoffrey's niece. I knew of him, but had not met him until yesterday. She worked for Leo Fulbright, and there was a rumour that they had begun a relationship, though I very much doubt it. I have known Leo and Margot for twenty years."

"Tell me about these poison pen letters Leo Fulbright has been receiving."

"Mr. Fulbright asked me to come down and look into it," Vickery said.

"Have you discovered who is sending them?"

"Not yet. A curious thing is that Leo Fulbright refuses to share the full contents of the letters with anyone. I suspect that the writer of the letters believes that Fulbright is guilty of something."

"He's being blackmailed?" Debney asked.

"Possibly. Or someone is seeking revenge. Perhaps he will be less reticent in revealing the contents of the letters to a *professional* detective."

Debney wrote *Fulbright – Letters?* in his notebook.

"Do you believe the letters are connected to the murder?" The Inspector asked.

"Lacking knowledge of the content, I have not formed a definite opinion."

"Thank you Mr. Vickery. I may have more questions for you. Please do not attempt to leave without seeking my approval." Debney looked down at his notebook, effectively dismissing Vickery.

"Perhaps I might propose a couple of lines of enquiry that you may wish to pursue," Vickery said. "Not that I wish to tell you your business, but I have observed a great deal this weekend."

"Oh, yes?"

"I would suggest sending one of your constables to the inn in the village: at least one of the guests has had meetings with someone there. Talking to the landlord may help to identify an additional suspect, or perhaps prove an alibi. Or disprove one."

"You are not going to tell me who I should look for there?"

"I think it will become clear to you when you interview the other guests."

Vickery rose and moved towards the library door. He turned as he was leaving. "Have you located the murder weapon yet?"

"My men are searching. It is only a matter of time before it is recovered."

"I would advise searching the pond. Someone, probably the murderer, has already used it as a hiding place—for components taken from the guests' vehicles to render them unusable."

He gave the smallest of bows and exited.

Vickery located Doctor Cole in his make-shift examining room, a low-ceilinged space with a stone floor off a corridor near the kitchen. It was empty except for a large wooden table, on which the shrouded corpse now lay.

"We're not used to this sort of thing here, you know." He nodded towards the body under the sheet. "Murder is most uncommon, despite what you might read in those mystery novels."

"You are not an aficionado, doctor?"

"They often contain interesting details about poisons, but what they suggest about the evidence revealed by a brief examination of a body, well..." He shook his head. "I'm sure you are expecting me to be able to tell you that this poor woman died between, say, 11pm and 11.10, so that you will then be able to test everyone's alibi for that precise window of time, and so identify the murderer as being the butler. But it is not possible for me to provide such a neat approximation. The temperature of the body gives us an idea, but this poor girl was submerged in cold water, which affects the accuracy of the calculation."

"She died a minute or two after midnight," Vickery said. "A scream was heard. And the sound of her apparently falling into the pond."

"Midnight is consistent with my initial examination," the doctor said. "But I cannot give you an absolute confirmation: she might have been killed an hour before that, perhaps more. As I told the Inspector, that is our margin of error, I'm afraid."

"Thank you, doctor, I understand. Are you able to tell if water was taken into her lungs?" Vickery asked.

"You are asking if she was dead before the body entered the water? I may be able to confirm if water is present in the lungs, but couldn't be sure of its absence without a more intrusive examination."

"I should also like to know if this button came from her dress. It was found close by, but I do not believe it came from her." He held up the red cloth-covered button.

"It did not. Her dress was fastened by a zipper and a hook-and-eye," the doctor said, without needing to check under the sheet.

"What can you tell me about the injuries to the body?" Vickery asked.

"A single stab wound," the doctor said. "The entry point is here, just below the rib-cage." He indicated on his own chest. "And the exit wound was just below the scapula—the shoulder-blade. The blade ruptured the heart, and death would have been almost immediate."

"Then the weapon used was—"

"At least twenty inches long, probably longer, with a double-edged blade, approximately an inch-and-a-half wide at the broadest point, tapering to a point."

"A sword, then. A two-handed longsword?"

"Something of that nature," the doctor said.

"And she was stabbed once, from a low angle and upwards?"

"Yes."

"Thank you again, doctor. I think we may be able to identify the murder weapon shortly. Do you know where Malloy went?"

"Right here," Malloy said from behind them. He was holding a thick bacon sandwich.

"You heard what the doctor said?"

"Did he just describe Excalibur?" Malloy asked.

"Excalibur?" The doctor frowned.

"A replica," Vickery said, "a prop for a motion picture."

"Is it missing from the stone?" Malloy asked, pushing the remainder of the sandwich into his mouth.

Vickery nodded.

"The stone? From which the sword was drawn?" The doctor asked.

"We even have a Merlin upstairs," Malloy said, mouth full. "And another magician right here."

"Don't mind Mr. Malloy," Vickery said, "he suffered a blow to the head in the recent past."

"I noticed the bruise."

"There's another young man upstairs you ought to take a look at," Vickery said. "Mr. Garvin has also suffered a blow to the head, though rather more recently."

"What sort of place is this?" The doctor asked.

"Technically, it is a Victorian folly," Vickery said, then added in a conspiratorial tone: "And most of the folk upstairs—are *actors!*"

"How are the staff taking it?" Vickery asked, after they had left the doctor.

"They're upset that a young woman has been murdered," Malloy said, "but they didn't know her, so I think they're more upset about their daily routines being interrupted. And they don't much like the idea that there is a killer in the house. Mrs. B had to speak sharply to one of the maids who was threatening to leave."

"The police constable questioned you all?"

"Yes. The butler, Crawley, seemed most put out at being questioned by a uniformed officer: he felt he should have been spoken to by the Inspector himself. How was your interview with the Great Detective?"

"He was rude and arrogant, as expected," Vickery said. "I rather feel that he will be no match for the subtlety of our murderer."

"You offered him the benefit of your insights?" Mallory asked. "You've spent a whole weekend with these people."

"I made some suggestions. They were not well-received."

"Eleanor Trenton deserves better than his bumbling efforts,"

Malloy said.

"I have been instructed not to interfere," Vickery said.

"Then you cannot investigate *the murder*," Malloy said. "But you were asked here to investigate the poison pen letters: did Inspector Debney say you could not pursue that enquiry?"

"He did not," Vickery said. He smiled.

"In the case of the poison pen letters, what would be your next move?" Malloy asked. "Is there anything I can do to help?"

Chapter 14

Malloy stood on the threshold, feeling uncomfortable about entering. Vickery had already stepped into Eleanor Trenton's room.

"Is something wrong?" Vickery asked.

"It feels like an intrusion," Malloy said.

"Does it?" Vickery asked. "You are wondering how Miss Trenton might feel about us going through her private things. But Miss Trenton no longer has feelings, Mr. Malloy, someone has seen fit to put an end to them."

"I understand that. But it still feels—strange."

"When conducting an investigation, we must put aside our own emotions, and we cannot be diverted from our purpose by a wish to avoid hurting the feelings of others. To be a detective is to be beyond the confines of common decency."

"And beyond the law?" Malloy asked.

"Sometimes *justice* must be sought outside that which is, in the strictest sense of the word, legal. You have some experience of this, you know how I work. We may need to act in accordance with what is *morally* right, rather than what is strictly prescribed in law."

"Do you really think Eleanor Trenton could have sent the poison pen letters?" Malloy asked.

"It is a possibility that we must consider," Vickery said. "Particularly if we need an excuse to search her room."

"We *are* doing it for her," Malloy said, to convince himself. He crossed into the room, and his shoulders relaxed. "Can't remember the last time I was in a lady's bedroom," he said, his smile nervous.

"I do not think we shall need to be here long," Vickery said. "I fear that someone has been in before us."

"The police?"

"They have not yet begun their searches."

"Perhaps the maid?"

Vickery shook his head. "The Inspector asked that she leave the room undisturbed until the police have seen it. No, someone has been here, and almost certainly taken away anything that might have proved useful to us."

"What had you hoped to find?"

"Clues, Mr. Malloy! Something that will tell us why someone might wish Eleanor Trenton dead."

"Photographs or letters?" Malloy suggested, glancing around the room without touching anything.

"Perfect," Vickery agreed. "Or a diary or some other revealing document."

As he was speaking, he opened drawers and peered into them, shifting garments with quick movements of his hand. He pushed one drawer shut and opened another. Both men were wearing their leather driving gloves.

"Can I help?" Malloy asked.

"Try the wardrobe."

It was a big old bow-fronted wardrobe, veneered with highly polished walnut, the inside smelling faintly of mothballs.

"Three dresses," Malloy said, "and matching shoes for two of them—the black and the peacock blue. No red shoes."

"She was wearing the red shoes," Vickery said, without

looking up. "High-heel open-toe sandals in patent leather."

"You are also an expert in women's fashion?"

"Margot described them to me."

"She must have liked this dark red colour," Malloy said, feeling the soft fabric of the dress.

"Indeed. She has matching lipstick and nail polish here on the dressing table," Vickery said. "Help me pull the bed away from the wall."

They shifted the heavy bed and examined the gap between the bed and the wall. Then they dropped to their knees and peered under the bed. All they recovered for their efforts was a stray hair grip.

"We are wasting our time," Vickery said. "If there was anything here, it is gone."

"Handbag?" Malloy said, passing the heavy leather object to Vickery.

Vickery emptied it on the counterpane and ran his hands over the contents. After a quick glance, he scooped everything back into the bag.

"Nothing?" Malloy asked.

"Miss Trenton had a fondness for liquorice pastilles. She occasionally suffered from acid indigestion, and she recently took a pair of shoes to the cobblers to have them re-heeled. She has a ten shilling note and a handful of change in her purse. Beyond that, all her handbag tells me is that she had a recurrent problem with her teeth, there are two receipts from a dentist, and that she was taking dancing lessons with a gentleman called Ramone, with whom she may recently have had a disagreement."

"How could you know that?"

"An appointment card. The last entry, dated three days from now, has been scored out heavily, and the card has been torn in two."

"Perhaps she discovered that dancing just wasn't for her."

"I think we can safely assume that Miss Trenton was able to dance quite as well as she could sing. No, I rather think that 'Ramone' may have attempted to lead where she had no intention of following."

"Does that make him a suspect?" Malloy asked.

"No. I am sure that Ramone is quite used to having his advances rebuffed by attractive female students. I think we're done here, don't you?"

"Do you think we should search the other rooms?" Malloy asked, as they closed the door behind them.

"That would not make you feel uncomfortable?"

"We need to find the murder weapon, don't we?" Malloy said.

"I think it unlikely the murderer would have hidden it in their own room. They would know that the police would instigate a search as soon as they arrived."

"In which case, they might have hidden it in *someone else's* room, in order to throw suspicion on them?" Malloy suggested.

"That is a possibility we should consider," Vickery agreed. "You should search the other rooms while I go downstairs. Start with Fulbright's—and see if you can find any of the missing pages of the poison pen letters while you are there."

"And what will you be doing while I do that?" Malloy asked.

"I shall be distracting Fulbright so he doesn't come up and find you rifling through his things. Don't want him hitting you again, just as the bruise is beginning to fade." He touched his fingers to Malloy's discoloured jaw. "And I will keep an eye on our friends from the constabulary."

"Is this how it is going to be?" Malloy asked.

"How what is going to be?"

"Working together. I get the dangerous jobs, while you keep lookout?"

"Mr. Malloy, you are entirely free to choose what you will and will not do. I hold no power over you, and would not wish to."

"You will give me a signal if Fulbright or one of the policemen come this way?"

"I promise that I will." Vickery turned to go. Malloy grabbed his arm.

"Wait! What will it be? The signal? I wouldn't want to mistake it or ignore it."

Vickery thought for a moment. "I shall shout 'Someone's coming!' at the top of my lungs."

"I was expecting something a little more subtle." Malloy sounded disappointed.

"You were? Why?"

"Won't that rather alert them to the fact that I'm here up to no good?"

"Hadn't thought of that."

Vickery reached forward, and Malloy felt the fingers brush his neck just behind his ear.

"I shall blow this station master's whistle instead," Vickery said. He seemed to have retrieved said whistle from behind Malloy's ear.

"Where did you get that?" Malloy asked.

"A station master's jacket pocket," Vickery said. "I used to pick pockets as part of my stage act. Meet me downstairs in half-an-hour."

Malloy looked at his wristwatch, only to discover that his wrist was bare. He looked up to find Vickery with the wristwatch in his hand, comparing the time on it against his own pocket watch.

"A couple of minutes slow." Vickery adjusted Malloy's watch.

"When did you take that? I didn't feel—"

"I distracted you, when I touched the side of your face." He handed the wristwatch back. "Nice watch."

"A present from an admirer," Malloy said.

"'Bertie' has very good taste," Vickery said.

"How—no, wait, it's engraved on the back." He grinned triumphantly.

Vickery smiled. "Downstairs in half-an-hour. I'll have the cook prepare coffee and cake. She admires you as well, I think."

He left Malloy blushing in the upstairs corridor.

* * *

Vickery found Fulbright sitting alone on the terrace, staring morosely at his hands folded in his lap. Whether he was upset for Eleanor Trenton or for himself, it was impossible to tell. He looked up and scowled, then seemed to think better of saying what he had intended to say. He looked back down at his hands.

"I was just thinking about her," Fulbright said. "Eleanor. She wasn't a great actress. She could never have dominated the stage like Margot. But motion pictures are different, the camera can be closer than a theatre audience. Expression can be more subtle. She could have been great on the screen..."

"But we will never know," Vickery said. "People have said that the early footage was a little disappointing."

"That was my fault. I terrified the poor girl, so that she didn't know—"

"—a goblet from a goblin?" Vickery said.

"You heard about that? Of course you did, actors are such dreadful gossips."

"And now the film is lost?" Vickery said.

"Lost?" Fulbright seemed confused. "You mean the print we brought to show here this weekend? Yes, that's missing. But the negative is still at the studio. We can have another print off that easily enough. If we decide to."

"The future of the film is in doubt?" Vickery asked.

"It always has been. Eleanor's death just makes it—" He shrugged.

"Could Eleanor have been murdered in order to put an end to *Arthur and Guinevere?*" Vickery asked.

"There are much less drastic ways of sabotaging a production," Fulbright said. "And more effective ones."

"But still, removing the leading lady—?"

"Everyone seems to think that Guinevere was a much bigger role than it is. There are only a dozen lines spoken—"

"Forty-seven," Vickery said.

"Eh?"

"Forty-seven lines. In the photoplay. Excluding one-word responses. I checked," Vickery said.

"It's still only a few minutes of screen time. Most of the existing footage is salvageable, and the rest of what she'd done we could reshoot in an afternoon. We would have to have redone most of it anyway. To suggest that she was murdered to sabotage the film is ridiculous. And besides, who would benefit from it?"

"Two names suggest themselves," Vickery said.

"Do they?" Fulbright asked.

"Your sister for one," Vickery said.

"*Veronica?* What would she get out of it?"

"You are spending her inheritance on your motion picture."

"It is not being *spent*, it is being *invested*. We shall get our money back and a good deal more besides."

"She gave her consent for it to be invested?" Vickery asked.

"I don't *need* her consent."

"No, you control everything. But perhaps as a courtesy...?" Vickery said.

"Veronica doesn't care about the money, as long as there's enough for her to live in comfort and security," Fulbright said.

"She did care about George," Vickery said.

"What's he got to do with anything?" Fulbright asked.

"Revenge? As a motive for murder," Vickery suggested.

"Revenge?" Fulbright said.

"Veronica believes that you took away her only opportunity for a life of happiness with the man she loved," Vickery said.

"Pshaw!" Fulbright said.

"Perhaps she decided to punish you by taking away someone you loved?"

"Eleanor? I did not love her."

"But you allowed people to *believe* that you were lovers," Vickery said.

"Veronica didn't kill Eleanor, out of revenge or any other motive. George left her a long time ago, she's over that now. And my sister trusts me to do what's best for her. Ask her. Yes, she attacked me once, but she is better now. And I'd prefer it if you didn't go around suggesting otherwise to the police. And please do not go putting ideas into her head and upsetting her. She is not the murderer."

"If what you say is correct, we must look for another culprit," Vickery said.

"Me?" Fulbright said.

"I was about to suggest another name," Vickery said. "But since you put your own name forward, we should consider if you might be responsible for Miss Trenton's death."

"I'm not," Fulbright said flatly.

"Inspector Debney knows you weren't with everyone else after dinner," Vickery said.

"I went up to my room after dinner. I worked for a while, preparing my notes on the script pages for the next day of shooting on *Arthur and Guinevere*. Then I turned out the light and went to sleep," Fulbright said.

"You were alone throughout this time?" Vickery asked.

"Margot and I have separate rooms here, as you know," Fulbright said.

"An attempt was made on *your* life the previous evening," Vickery said

"Someone shot a crossbow at my head," Fulbright said. "Whether they intended to kill me or just scare me, it is hard to say."

"And prior to that you had received a number of threatening letters," Vickery said. "It might help to identify the murderer if you could share with me the content of those letters."

Fulbright shot an angry glance at Vickery.

"I shall be quite happy to provide full details of these poison pen letters—*to the Inspector.*" Fulbright's glare dared Vickery to push the matter further.

"You asked me to find out who sent the letters, but you will not give me information that could help me to do so. Even now, when it might help name a killer."

"You said you had another name," Fulbright said. "Who else do you suspect?"

"Why, Margot, of course," Vickery said.

"Margot!"

Vickery made his exit before Fulbright was recovered enough to give vent to his thoughts regarding this suggestion.

* * *

"Inspector," Vickery said. He stood in the open doorway of the library.

Inspector Debney was sitting behind Sir Geoffrey's desk, seemingly lost in thought. If at all possible, he looked less happy than he had previously.

"Mr. Vickery?"

"When we spoke previously, I neglected to pass on to you an item that was picked up near the pond when Miss Trenton's body was found."

Vickery approached the desk and placed the small red button in front of the Inspector.

"From Miss Trenton's dress?" Inspector Debney said.

"Miss Trenton's red dress had no buttons," Vickery said.

Inspector Debney looked at it, but didn't pick it up.

"Perhaps a coincidence?" He said. "Dropped at some other time."

"Perhaps," Vickery said. "But it was retrieved from the wet mud, and it is unstained: it cannot have lain there long."

"Did anyone else wear red this weekend?"

"Not that I am aware of," Vickery said.

"And you picked this up beside the pond just after midnight?"

"I did not pick it up, Leo Fulbright did."

Inspector Debney frowned. "Everything seems to lead back to him," he said. "There is the absence of an alibi, his violent and overbearing nature, the watch chain. And now this."

"I agree, Inspector. Circumstances are such that it appears Leo Fulbright is guilty of the murder of Eleanor Trenton. And that is what the killer wishes us to believe. He wishes us to accept at face-value that which *appears* to be true. Fortunately, Inspector, you and I are able to see beneath this too-convenient façade, and can already see glimpses of what *really* happened. Is that not so?"

"Er—of course," the Inspector said. "The murderer must believe we are amateurs if he thinks we would fall for his ruse..."

"The button is an important clue, I think," Vickery said.

"Yes, well, now I have this," Inspector Debney still didn't touch the little red button. "I can see things beginning to fall into place—"

"Excellent! Then I should not disturb you any longer, Inspector. It is customary, I believe, to bring all of the suspects together in the drawing room when you name the murderer.

Let me know when you're ready to do that, and I will assemble the guests," Vickery said.

"I—er—I will, thank you."

Chapter 15

"No sign of the sword," Malloy said. "The police haven't come up with anything, and I checked all of the rooms, including the empty ones. But this place is such a warren, there could be hundreds of places we haven't checked."

They were standing on the path by the kitchen garden between the keep and the little orchard.

"There is also rumoured to be a secret passageway," Vickery said, "though I think even Sir Geoffrey doesn't know where it is. And Victorian folly builders were fond of adding fake priest holes. So as you say, there could be many places where Excalibur could be hidden. There is one more obvious one that I think you should check, but we can talk about that later. Am I right in thinking that you did not discover any of the missing pages of Fulbright's poison pen letters?"

"There were some flakes of burnt paper in the grate in his room. I think we can assume that he destroyed them," Malloy said.

"That is as I feared," Vickery said. "Fulbright remains tight-lipped about the full contents of the letters. It is really most inconvenient. I feel sure that the threats in the letters have a bearing on what happened last night, or if they don't, they can explain some of the unusual behaviour we have witnessed."

"Guilty secrets make people behave guiltily?" Malloy said.

"Yes. And most of these secrets are completely irrelevant to the situation at hand. They only serve to cloud things."

"Was the attack on Fulbright's life connected to the letters, do you think?"

"Possibly," Vickery said. "Our letter-writer may have decided to take more direct action since the letters did not seem to be having the desired effect."

"Are the murder and the attempted murder the work of the same person? It would be a bit of a coincidence to have two different murderers, wouldn't it?"

"Perhaps that is what the murderer wishes us to think," Vickery said. "But what if the attempt on Leo Fulbright's life was not a genuine one? It may have been arranged in order to make us think of *him* as a victim."

"But why do that?"

"Because if we regard Mr. Fulbright as a *victim*, we are less likely to regard him as a possible murderer."

"But he didn't fire the crossbow at himself," Malloy said.

"No indeed, he would have needed an accomplice."

"Someone who was a very good shot, and who he trusted."

"That is a very good point, Mr. Malloy. It does seem somewhat unlikely. But until we have all of the facts, we should not discount it as a possibility."

"Whether the attempt on Fulbright's life was genuine or not, it does not rule him out as a suspect in the murder of Eleanor Trenton," Malloy said.

"We should proceed on that basis," Vickery said.

"You were in the drawing room when the crossbow was fired at Fulbright," Malloy said. "Who was in the room at the time?"

"Eleanor Trenton, Sir Geoffrey, Artie Delancey, Linette and her fiancé, Mr. Garvin, all were present when the crossbow was fired through the drawing room window."

"None of them could have fired it. Who does that leave?"

"Margot McCrae, Ted Kimball, Veronica Fulbright, and Dickie Bannister were all absent from the room," Vickery said. "They must be regarded as our suspects for the attempted murder of Leo Fulbright."

"Have the police determined who was missing last night at the time of the murder?"

"They have information from several people, and the list seems to be consistent: Artie Delancey was absent, as were Margot McCrae, Veronica Fulbright, and Leo Fulbright."

"Then they are our suspects for the murder of Eleanor Trenton," Malloy said. "Two names appear on both lists."

"Margot McCrae and Veronica Fulbright."

"Didn't the Fulbright woman try and kill her brother once before?"

"With a bow and arrow," Vickery said. "Not so very different from a crossbow."

"Though we ought to consider the fact that someone may have used the crossbow in order to direct attention away from themselves and towards Veronica Fulbright," Malloy said.

"Quite right. While I am certain that she has a motive for wanting her brother dead, I am not aware of any such bad blood between Veronica Fulbright and Miss Trenton."

"What would she gain from killing Eleanor Trenton?" Malloy mused. "I can't imagine that they were rivals in love, can you? That excludes any revenge motive."

"True," Vickery said. "Unless she wished to have her revenge on her brother. She holds Leo responsible for separating her from the man she loved."

"But why kill Eleanor Trenton? Perhaps Leo Fulbright cared for her, and he needed her for his motion picture, but it seems too far removed somehow," Malloy said. "Why not hurt Fulbright more directly? I'm sure that would have been George

Starling's preference."

"Indeed, we must consider him as a possible accomplice. If the motive wasn't revenge, it might have been money."

"How could Veronica Fulbright gain financially from Eleanor Trenton's death?" Malloy asked.

"It is not that she would gain money, rather that she might lose less. Leo Fulbright is providing the funding for his own motion picture, using money he and his sister inherited from their father."

"If Veronica thought her brother was 'wasting' their money, she might wish to try and put an end to the shooting of the motion picture. Eleanor's death might lead to the movie being abandoned..." Malloy said.

"I think I shall have a chat with Miss Fulbright and try and ascertain her whereabouts last night. She led us to believe that she was visiting George at the inn in the village. But that might have been a ruse. George might have made his way here, either alone or having met up with Miss Fulbright."

"There was time for them to get back to the keep before midnight, even if they stayed at the inn for last orders," Malloy said.

"The people at the inn might tell us if Veronica Fulbright arrived last night, or whether George left."

"And on the night of the attempt on her brother's life," Malloy said.

"I shall challenge her immediately. Unless she happens to be holding a loaded shotgun."

"Why should she be holding a shotgun?" Malloy asked.

"Pigeons," Vickery said. He turned to go.

"*Psst!*"

Vickery turned back. "What?"

"It wasn't me," Malloy said. He looked around, but could see no one else. He shrugged.

"*Psst!*" The sound came again, from the bushes nearby. A slight figure crawled out from under them. "It is I, Artie Delancey."

Artie Delancey's hair was sticking out in all directions and his cheeks were smeared with dirt. The knees of his trousers were dirty and the toes of his shoes scuffed. He approached them cautiously in a half-bent scuttle. His eyes were wide and he appeared to have passed beyond fear into a state of constant nervous vigilance, his head jerking this way and that like a bird fearing the approach of a cat.

"The police are here?" He asked in a breathless whisper, never quite making eye contact.

"Yes," Vickery said.

"Then it is nearly over." Artie nodded rapidly, but it wasn't clear whether he was relieved or upset by the presence of the police. "And she is really dead?" There was a flash of pathetic hope in his eyes.

"I'm afraid she is," Vickery said.

Artie nodded his head sadly. He had known what the answer would be, even while hoping that the reality might be different.

"Why don't you come inside and warm yourself by the fire, Artie?" Malloy said.

Artie looked at him with a combination of relief and gratitude, but it quickly vanished and he looked away. "I can't!" Eyes wide. "It's not safe!"

"Why isn't it safe, Artie?" Vickery asked. "Who are you afraid of?"

"Can't say." Artie licked his lips nervously. "I've done a bad thing. I should be punished. But I don't want to *die!*" He let out an anguished wail, and then darted off, running doubled-over and flat-footed.

Malloy made to go after him, but Vickery restrained him with a hand on his arm, for at that moment Inspector Debney appeared through the door from the kitchen.

"Highly suspicious," the Inspector said.

For a moment they weren't sure if he was referring to Artie or to them.

"Inspector?" Vickery said.

"Arthur Delancey, our missing suspect," Inspector Debney said. *"I've done a bad thing*—that sounded very much like a confession."

"But would he have asked if Eleanor Trenton was dead if he had killed her?" Malloy asked.

"Yes, if she was still breathing when he pulled the sword out of her," the Inspector said.

"We should be careful not to read too much into what Mr. Delancey said," Vickery cautioned. "He has been greatly disturbed by what has happened."

"He sounded insane," Inspector Debney said.

"I do not believe we just heard a confession of murder, Inspector, but rather the admission of someone who did nothing to *prevent* the killing," Vickery said.

"I would expect you to take the side of one of your own kind," the Inspector said.

"And what *kind* might that be, Inspector Debney?" Vickery asked.

Patches of pink coloured Debney's pale cheeks.

"Theatrical types," he muttered. "You can hardly claim to be impartial."

"But I am, Inspector, and I shall seek to protect anyone that I believe to be innocent. Theatrical type or otherwise. In seeking the guilty, we must always take care not to run rough-shod over the innocent."

"Say what you like, that young man is harbouring a guilty secret," Debney said.

"There I can agree with you," Vickery said. "He knows

something about the murder, and Mr. Delancey believes that possession of this knowledge places him in mortal danger."

"He knows something about the murder because he was responsible for it," the Inspector said. "I regard him as my prime suspect at this point."

"On that I must disagree," Vickery said.

"That is your prerogative, Mr. Vickery. But I am expected to solve this crime and bring the guilty to face justice, however you may feel about them. I shall have my men search for Delancey, and seize him."

"Then I would ask you to remind your constables that *Mr.* Delancey should be treated as an innocent man, until you have proof of his guilt."

"Not that you wish to tell me how to do my job, eh?" Inspector Debney asked.

"I shall make close observation of how *all* of the guests here are treated during the course of your investigation," Vickery said.

"We shall behave properly and without prejudice," the Inspector said. He seemed offended that Vickery was suggesting they would do otherwise.

"I ask nothing more," Vickery said.

Inspector Debney gave a curt nod and went back inside, in search of his constables.

Malloy made to speak out, but Vickery silenced him with a gesture, until he was sure Debney was out of earshot.

"At least we know Artie Delancey is not dead," Vickery said.

"We have to help him," Malloy said.

"For the moment, he may be safer wherever he is hiding. He has avoided discovery thus far."

"We should find him, calm him down. Warn him about the police search."

"He has come to us once, that means he trusts us. It would

be a mistake to pursue him. We must hope that he comes to us again. And we must be ready to protect him when he does."

"What do we do in the meantime?" Malloy asked.

"I keep asking questions, and you keep searching for Excalibur," Vickery said.

"Where do I look next?"

Malloy didn't like the look of the smile that flickered across Vickery's lips.

* * *

"They *can't* think Artie did it, surely?" Bannister said.

Sir Geoffrey's butler had brought up another selection of breakfast foods and set them out in the dining room. Having now been interviewed by Inspector Debney, the guests had gathered round the dining table to drink tea and fill plates with food that they only nibbled at. Leo Fulbright, and Sir Geoffrey and his nephew, were the only ones absent. It had seemed like a long day already, and yet it was still only ten-thirty.

"I heard he confessed," Kimball said.

"He did not," Vickery said. "He was in a very agitated state, and admitted that he had done something he knew was wrong."

"But he didn't say what?" Kimball asked.

"No, he didn't," Vickery said.

"I can't really imagine Artie as a murderer," Linette said. "Can you?" She looked at Garvin, who shook his head.

"Artie Delancey isn't the murderer," Margot said. "It's ridiculous to suggest he could be: he's an understudy at best, not a lead player."

"But the police are out searching for him," Bannister said.

"Perhaps they know something we don't," Veronica Fulbright said.

"Nonsense!" Margot said. "Inspector Debney knows only what we have told him."

"Artie didn't do himself any favours by disappearing like that," Bannister said.

"Perhaps he knows who the murderer is," Linette said. "If he does, he'd be afraid of being killed himself."

"That's a bit melodramatic," Margot said.

"It would explain why he ran and hid himself away," Bannister said.

"It is one possible explanation," Vickery said.

"Do you think the police will arrest him?" Linette asked.

"If they find him," Kimball said.

"What can we do?" Bannister asked. "If they're going to arrest him whether he's guilty or not—"

"The only thing that will help Artie Delancey is the real murderer being unmasked," Margot said. She looked towards Vickery, and gradually every eye turned the same way.

"You're a detective, Mr. Vickery, you could investigate the murder," Veronica Fulbright said.

"I am not really a detective as such, Miss Fulbright."

"But you have solved mysteries before. What about Hattie Graham and her so-called 'cat-burglar'?" Margot said.

"Inspector Debney has made it crystal clear that he does not want my assistance."

"Then don't assist him," Veronica Fulbright said, "conduct your own investigation."

"I shouldn't—" Vickery said.

"Don't pretend you haven't been snooping around already," Margot said.

"I was investigating the poison pen letters sent to Mr. Fulbright," Vickery said.

"Then investigate the murder for *us*," Margot said. "We are all being treated as suspects until the murderer is found. Help us."

Margot could see that he needed only a little more

convincing. She glanced towards Dickie Bannister, who was already rallying to the cause.

"Do it for Artie, Mr. Vickery," he said. "None of us want to see the poor boy in a jail cell again."

"I second that," Kimball said.

"I could only conduct an investigation with your help," Vickery said to them all. "I would need you to submit to my questioning."

Having spent the early hours of the morning being interrogated by Inspector Debney, not everyone seemed keen to endure another similar ordeal.

"Talking to Mr. Vickery won't be as bad as being grilled by that sour-faced Inspector," Garvin said.

"Leo will never agree to it," Vickery said to Margot.

"Then we won't tell him," Margot said. "When you talk to him, don't let on that it is an interview."

"You all agree to be part of this?" Vickery asked. He looked around the room, and they all nodded, some more enthusiastically than others. "Very well: I accept your invitation," he said.

* * *

"Miss Fulbright, a word if I may?" Vickery said.

Veronica Fulbright was unarmed, and the smile of her greeting was perhaps more cheerful than the circumstances might dictate.

"Mr. Vickery, good day to you." Then, noting his sombre expression, she added: "Terrible thing that happened last night."

"It is a terrible thing to see a young life cut short," Vickery said, watching her face carefully.

"Makes one realise that we should seize every moment and make the most of it," she said.

"I have some questions, if you wouldn't mind?"

"Anything to help. But can't say that I saw anything that might be of any use."

"We don't always recognise the importance of the little things, until someone comes to put all of the pieces together," Vickery said.

"Then ask away, Mr. Vickery."

"Did you see Mr. Kimball play *Hamlet* last night?" Vickery asked.

"No. I watched for a couple of minutes, but it made me uncomfortable, hearing someone else speaking like Leo. I'm sure it was a wonderful performance, but..." She shrugged. "I couldn't watch."

"You went out?"

"I didn't feel like being around everyone. Sometimes these moods overcome me, and then all I can do is take myself off somewhere until it passes."

"And last night, where did you take yourself off to?" Vickery asked.

"Do you think I could have murdered Eleanor Trenton? Is that the reason for these questions, Mr. Vickery?" Her tone had become challenging.

"I am trying to establish whether you *could* have murdered her, and to do that, I need to know where you went after dinner yesterday evening. Until we know who *didn't* commit the crime, everyone must be viewed as a *potential* murderer."

"That's not a very nice thing, is it, to be suspicious of everyone?"

"No, Miss Fulbright, it is not. Which is why I intend to remove the shadow of suspicion away from the innocent as soon as I am able. But I will need their help to do that. Hence my questions."

"I understand." Veronica Fulbright nodded firmly.

"Last night...?" Vickery prompted.

"I went outside to get some air, then I went up to bed." She nodded again, as if that was the end of it.

"You went out onto the terrace immediately after dinner?"

"I did." Again the firm nod.

"How long did you remain on the terrace?" Vickery asked.

"I don't know, I never looked at my watch. Half an hour perhaps. Just wanted to let my dinner settle before I went off— off to bed."

"Quite so, I did the same thing myself," Vickery said. "But before you went up to bed, you took a stroll? Through the woods?"

"I—I did, yes. Only for a few minutes. It was a nice night."

"And then you were seen to pass through the wicket gate in the hedge onto the bridleway."

"*Seen?* Who says I did that? They're..."

"I myself saw you, Miss Fulbright, from the terrace," Vickery said.

"Well, yes, then I must have passed through the gate. I had quite forgotten. I walked along the path a little way —"

"When you passed through the gate, did you turn left and walk towards the village, or did you turn right and follow the path around the front of the house towards the main road?"

"I—I walked towards the village," she said.

"Did you meet with anyone, Miss Fulbright," Vickery asked.

"Of course not! Who would I be meeting in the village?" She made the idea sound preposterous.

"I meant only, did you encounter anyone who would be able to confirm to the police that they had seen you walking in that direction. It would help in establishing your whereabouts at the time of the murder."

"Oh. No, I passed no one on the path, I'm afraid."

"And no one saw you return to the keep?"

"I saw no one, but whether they saw me, well, you'd have to ask them, wouldn't you?" She stared at Vickery, determined not to be caught out again.

"Quite so. I myself did not see you return this morning," he said.

"*Last night,* you mean," Veronica Fulbright corrected him.

"Yes, I must do, mustn't I? Thank you for your assistance, Miss Fulbright. I am sure that there is nothing to be concerned about, if you tell the Inspector the truth, as you have told it to me."

"Thank you, Mr. Vickery."

"You should have Sir Geoffrey's man have a go at those," Vickery said, pointing to the dried mud on her brogues.

"Yes, I will. I forgot to put them out for him last night."

"Easily missed," Vickery said. "One last question, if you would indulge me further? On the night the crossbow was fired at your brother, were you taking a stroll into the village then too?"

"I—er—think I probably was, yes. I don't really know my way about the countryside here, so I have taken the same path for my strolls."

"Thank you, Miss Fulbright," Vickery said.

Chapter 16

Dickie Bannister was sitting on the bench under the apple tree, clouds of smoke swirling around his head. He was wearing a green tweed jacket, plus-fours and a red wool waistcoat.

"Go on, say it," Bannister said, as Vickery approached.

"Say what?"

"I look like a bloody gnome sitting here smoking this thing." He waved his pipe.

"I was thinking Father Christmas," Vickery said. "May I?" He took a seat next to Bannister.

"I almost cut off the beard, blasted thing only collects bits of food. But Margot is convinced the picture will go ahead without Eleanor Trenton."

"It was going to go ahead without her anyway. Leo finally took your advice and gave Guinevere to his wife. It was decided before—before last night."

Bannister nodded. "It's the right choice. What on earth was he thinking, casting that girl?"

"They say there's no fool like an old fool." Vickery wafted smoke away from his face.

"Is the pipe bothering you?"

"It smells like burning hair."

"Does it? No, that's the blasted beard!" Bannister batted his chest, smothering the glowing strands of hair. He knocked out his pipe on the heel of his shoe and scuffed the ash into the dirt. "I feel a bit guilty if I'm honest."

"Why?" Vickery asked.

"Well, I never had a good thing to say about the poor girl. About the way she looked. How she moved. Her voice. It wasn't her fault she wasn't Margot McCrae."

"She was no match for her, that's true. But you have to admire the way she stood up to Margot. How many times have you seen that?"

"I've seen grown men wilt under Margot's glare," Bannister said. "If she'd had a few more years—chance to toughen up a bit, so she could take the knocks—who knows? She just wasn't ready yet. She didn't belong here."

"Do you think that's why she was killed?" Vickery asked.

"Because she was in the wrong place? Or because she wasn't ready yet? It amounts to the same thing in the end, I suppose. She was in someone's way, they decided to get rid of her. That makes for a short list of suspects, doesn't it?"

"Well, I wouldn't—"

"You *know* who was missing last night when the clock struck midnight: Leo Fulbright and Margot McCrae."

"And Artie Delancey," Vickery said.

"*Artie*? What would he gain by killing her?"

"Didn't he believe he was Eleanor Trenton's understudy?"

Bannister laughed at this, and the laugh turned into a coughing fit. His cheeks were purplish and his eyes were streaming by the time he managed to catch his breath again. He kept shaking his head.

"It's not that Artie wouldn't pass, god bless him," Bannister wheezed. "But I don't think the world of motion pictures is yet ready for a male leading lady, do you?"

"What I believe is less important than what Artie himself believes," Vickery said.

"Artie's not naïve, he wouldn't have survived in this game if he was. He's a dreamer, but he doesn't have any illusions. If he gets to ride a horse in that Guinevere frock, even if no one sees his face, that's the best he can hope for, and he knows that. He'll tell you that himself."

"I wish he would. But I can't seem to get near him: every time he sees me, he disappears. I can't help but wonder if he has something to hide."

"He's just looking out for himself. He has to," Bannister said.

"Do you know where he went last night?"

"He's a grown man, I'm not his mother. I think he was still upset because he'd had a falling out with Teddy. He probably just needed some time on his own. He wasn't to know he was going to need an alibi, was he?"

"If you speak to him, will you tell him that I'd like—"

"He'll come and find you when he's ready, I'm sure of it. Artie's a good lad, he didn't murder Eleanor Trenton."

"You don't think so?"

"No," Bannister said. "I know who my money's on."

* * *

"How's the sleuthing going?" Margot asked.

"Badly," said Vickery. "Too few suspects."

"Why is that bad? I thought the idea was to narrow down the field until you identify your man. Or woman."

"The field has been narrowed down to you, Leo, and Artie Delancey," Vickery said.

Margot seemed unfazed by this. "I don't really see Artie as a murderer, do you?" She asked.

"I don't see Artie at all, he's avoiding me. It's all most suspicious."

"Aren't suspects *supposed* to act suspiciously?"

"This isn't a game, Margot, there's a young woman lying dead under a sheet down there."

"Artie didn't kill her," Margot said. "If he's acting suspiciously, it's because he knows something about what happened last night. He's probably struggling to decide whether he should tell you or not, but he'll get there, and then he'll come and tell you."

"If Artie is innocent, then the murderer is—"

"Either Leo or me, you said. If Eleanor was killed in the heat of the moment after a violent argument, then Leo is your man. If her murder was the result of a coldly calculated plot, then I'm your woman. Otherwise there's something wrong with your selection criteria, and you need to re-audition your cast of suspects, cast your net wider."

"How am I to do that?" Vickery asked.

"I have no idea. I saw one of that Rinehart woman's plays once, couldn't make head nor tail of it. If I remember correctly, the butler did it."

"You are the second person to mention the butler."

"There you are then, he must be guilty. Or innocent. Sometimes the trick is to make the obvious suspect guilty. Or is it the other way round?"

"Now you are just trying to confuse me."

"Isn't that what I would do if I was guilty?"

"Unless you were trying to protect someone else," Vickery said.

"Do you really think I would risk my own neck to save Leo's?"

"I think you might."

"So does Leo. You men are terrible romantics." Margot got up to go. "Oh, and if you want Artie to answer your questions, send your man Malloy after him."

"He's not mine."

"So you would have everyone believe, Benjamin." She exited.

"Infuriating woman!"

"I heard that!" Came floating back through the open door.

* * *

"I warned her not to defy my brother," Veronica Fulbright said. "I told her to escape while she still could. She didn't listen to me."

"Is that what you were talking about last night?" Vickery asked. "It seemed like a very heated conversation."

"She said she was going to confront Leo, tell him to stop trying to control her life. She should have listened to me."

"Then you didn't *threaten* her?"

"*No!* She threatened me," Veronica said, in her own defence, then realised she had said more than she intended. Vickery raised an eyebrow, and she felt that she had to continue. "Well, it wasn't a threat, exactly. She just warned me not to interfere in her life. Or she might feel compelled to interfere in mine."

"Did she say how she might do that?" Vickery asked.

"She saw me with—a friend. Leo doesn't like me to have friends, he doesn't approve. Eleanor saw me on the train with someone, just talking."

"A gentleman friend?"

Veronica blushed. "Please don't tell my brother."

"I won't. And you must not blame yourself, you were not responsible in any way for Eleanor Trenton's death."

"But if my brother killed her—"

"*If*," Vickery emphasised. "There is some indication that he may have done, but I am far from being able to say that I know the identity of the murderer. There are still many questions I must ask. Do you understand that?"

Veronica nodded, but looked far from convinced.

* * *

"I am sorry to intrude on your grief, Sir Geoffrey," Vickery said.

Sir Geoffrey was sitting alone in his library, the desk in front of him completely bare. Now that the Inspector had finished with the room, he was trying to make it his own again. He waved Vickery into a chair opposite him.

"Please, don't feel you must apologise, Vickery. I appreciate the work that you're doing here. I shall be most relieved if you can bring this matter to a discrete conclusion."

"How is Eleanor's brother taking the death of his sister?" Vickery asked.

"Poor Timothy is inconsolable," Sir Geoffrey said.

Vickery knew this to be far from the truth: The boy had already made a couple of attempts to get into the room to see his sister's body, and had tried to press the doctor to provide him with all of the grim details of her murder.

"He's just a child, it won't have sunk in yet," Sir Geoffrey said, as if reading Vickery's thoughts. This acted as a timely reminder not to underestimate him. "It will hit him hard when it does."

"There are questions that I must ask everyone," Vickery said.

Sir Geoffrey nodded and indicated that he should proceed. "You want to know where I was at midnight last night. I've already told the Inspector: I was watching that Kimball fellow taking the mickey out of Fulbright, he'd got him down to a tee. You know, of course, that there's no love lost between Fulbright and myself. Kimball was very cruel. But it was massive fun." He chuckled, but then must have realised that while he had been laughing, his niece was being murdered outside. "I wish I had been more aware," he said. "That Eleanor wasn't there. I might have gone to seek her out. I am normally much more attentive, but I thought she was safe here. In my house. With her friends."

"Do you remember when you saw her last?" Vickery asked.

"I remember us all being at the dinner table. There were no empty chairs."

"Timothy was there also?"

"Oh, yes, he was there up until dessert. Then Crawley took him off to bed, before the grown-ups got out the brandy and cigars. That must have been after nine. I'm sure you remember better than I."

"We moved from the dining room into the drawing room around nine-thirty," Vickery affirmed. "I went out onto the terrace for some air. I don't smoke these days. Don't like to be around the smell of the smoke."

"Bad lungs?" Sir Geoffrey asked.

"Bad memories," Vickery said. "Do you remember who was speaking to whom in the drawing room?"

"Let's see—there were a few people I don't really know. I sat down with that character actor fellow for a while."

"Dickie Bannister."

"That's the chap. What a card! Terrible old gossip, swears like a sailor, absolute hoot! Tears in my eyes, never laughed so much. And if even *half* of what he said is true—scandalous! You theatricals are a rum lot, Vickery."

"I'm an ex-theatrical," Vickery reminded him.

"And yet, here you are," Sir Geoffrey said.

"As are you."

"I'm not going to pretend I wasn't enjoying myself: Fulbright hooked me and reeled me in with all his talk of a British motion picture industry, and spending time with actors has been the tops!"

"You may find it palls with time."

"I dare say. I'm only doing it for Eleanor, of course." He looked away, caught out again by his recent change of circumstances. "Well, I suppose that's all over now, isn't it?"

"Do you recall when Eleanor left the drawing room last night? Whether she left with anyone?" Vickery asked.

"I'm sorry, no. People were in and out, it was a pleasant evening, and a few people stepped out for a while, like you. I think Linnie Fulbright and her young man slipped off for a moonlight stroll, down by the lake. I do remember Eleanor having quite a heated discussion with Fulbright's sister. But I don't think it amounted to much. Veronica seemed a bit upset by it, she slipped out and headed down the servants' stairs to the kitchen, probably in search of left-over dessert. Did you try the syllabub? Splendid stuff."

"Just before midnight, when Kimball was standing on the stairs performing, do you recall who was watching?"

"I know Fulbright wasn't. I don't think Kimball would have been so bold if he had actually been there. Linette and her young man were there, I remember him laughing out loud, and her trying not to laugh. Your man Malloy was there."

"He is not mine."

"My mistake. Veronica Fulbright was there for the start of it: she looked shocked rather than amused. I think she was afraid her brother would come back in and catch us all laughing at him."

"Back *in?*"

"Eh?"

"You said she was afraid Fulbright might come *back in*, not *back down*. Had he gone out? I thought he had gone upstairs."

"Oh, he might have done. I could have sworn he went out into the courtyard, but I might be mistaken? Is it important?"

"I don't know yet. I'm just trying to get an idea of who was where during the course of the evening."

"Ah, yes, checking alibis and such. I read one of those

mysteries, *The House at Red Corner* or whatever it was. Not really my cup of tea. Much preferred his Christopher Robin."

"You were telling me who was in the hallway at midnight," Vickery said.

"Was I? Oh, watching young Kimball, splendid fellow. Yes, well, I know Timothy saw it: he was hiding at the top of the stairs, thought we couldn't see him, the little scamp!"

"Was he fully dressed?"

"Pyjamas and dressing gown, why?"

"Merely curious, since he was supposed to have gone to bed some time previously."

"You know how boys are. Doesn't hurt to indulge them once in a while."

"What about Artie Delancey?"

"Now *that* I don't think should be indulged. Don't really want Timothy mixing with that sort. No offence intended."

"I meant, was *Mr.* Delancey present in the hallway watching Mr. Kimball's little show?"

"Oh, sorry. Not sure. Didn't see him there."

"And Margot Fulbright?"

"She was there. For a little while, at any rate. She went back into the drawing room with an odd sort of smile on her lips. Not sure what that was about."

"Thank you, Sir Geoffrey, you've been most helpful."

"I hope you catch him, Vickery. Whoever did this terrible thing to my niece."

"It will be for the police to arrest the murderer," Vickery said. "I am merely gathering information while people's memories are fresh."

"And let me say, you are doing a splendid job, very thorough. Look, why don't I shove off, and you can use the library, question people here in peace?"

"That's very kind, but—"

"Don't usually let people loose in here, you know what people are like with books, using them to prop up wonky bed legs or belting spiders with them..."

"I thought people usually stole them to read," Vickery said.

"Read?" Sir Geoffrey said. "Well, if they want to do that, they can take what they like. My father bought most of these as a job lot in a house sale. I'll let you get on."

Chapter 17

"Mr. Garvin, may I have a word?" Vickery asked. Garvin moved towards the open library door, Linette close behind.

"Alone, if you wouldn't mind," Vickery said.

"Oh, right, sorry, Linnie. He has to do us one at a time—"

"So he can compare our stories for discrepancies," Linette said.

"She's a smart one," Garvin said, closing the library door behind him. "You will be questioning her too?"

"I think she will *insist* upon it, don't you?" Vickery asked.

Garvin grinned. "You need to be careful, she might have this thing solved before you or the police do. She's already been asking questions. She thinks there is someone you should talk to at the inn in the village: Inspector Debney has gone off to find him."

"Her aunt's mysterious gentleman friend."

"You knew already?"

"It's my job to know," Vickery said. He picked up a large magnifying glass from the desk.

"Do detectives really use those things? It's a bit Sherlock Holmes isn't it?"

"It's for you," Vickery said, handing him the magnifying

glass.

"Er, thanks..."

"On the desk are two typewritten documents. One of them is the most recent poison pen letter sent to Linette's father. The other is a document belonging to another of the guests," Vickery said.

Garvin looked down at the two sheets. "Different paper," he said.

"One is a standard bond, smooth, typically used for typed documents. The other is smaller, heavier and with a textured surface, better suited to the nib of a pen," Vickery said.

Garvin laughed. "This one's from Ted Kimball's skit from last night: I remember this bit about Claudius being a thief and a cad and a shit!"

"Were they typed on the same typewriter, do you think?"

"It's the same typeface, and they were both typed with a red and black ribbon, you can see a smidgeon of red on the descenders, the 'g' here and the two 'y's' on this line. And the same here on the other sheet."

"The same *kind* of typewriter then, but from the exact same machine?"

"Hard to say. They *look* the same—" Garvin applied the magnifying glass, looking closely at one sheet, then the other. And then he held the sheets out at arm's length and squinted at them. "It's like you said before, some of the letters are very slightly out of line. The 'p' is rotated very slightly to the right, it is more obvious on the upper case."

"And the 't'?" Vickery asked.

"That seems to be consistently higher than the other characters. As does the 'u', while the 'r' is lower. The letter is quite short, it would be helpful to have the others so we could make further comparisons. But I'd say there are enough similarities between the two pages to say that they were typed by the same machine."

"I agree," Vickery said.

Garvin seemed pleased with this, then his brow creased as he began to think through the implications of what they had discovered.

"Does this mean that Ted Kimball is the writer of the poison pen letters?" He asked.

"I would say that he has access to the same typewriter as the sender of the letters," Vickery said.

"Or the same typist?"

"That also is possible, but I do not believe that someone would contract a typist to make good copies of a poison pen letter."

Garvin nodded. "Do we ask Mr. Kimball where his skit was typed?"

"That might show our hand a little too soon," Vickery cautioned, "and alert him to our suspicions. I should like to have more proof before we confront our letter writer."

Garvin laid the magnifying glass on the desk and stared down at the two sheets of paper. "I don't know why, but I assumed the letters would be connected in some way to the murderer," he said, disappointed.

"Perhaps they are," Vickery said.

"But we know Kimball isn't the killer, he was standing in front of us all when the murder took place."

"That certainly appears to be the case," Vickery said. "Perhaps the letters were not sent *by* the murderer, but rather *to* the murderer."

"But they were sent to Linnie's father."

"Who was not standing in front of us all when the murder took place," Vickery said.

Garvin paced over to the window and looked out. Vickery watched him as he gently put his fingers to the bruised ear where Fulbright had hit him the previous day.

"The fact that Leo Fulbright has a violent temper, does not mean we should assume he is capable of murder," Vickery said. "We shall require more damning proof before we even mention this theory outside this room."

Garvin turned and leaned back on the windowsill. "You're not going to mention this to Linnie?" He asked.

"I do not intend to mention it to anyone. However, I fear that the accusation will be made by someone else before very much longer."

"How will you prove who really killed Eleanor Trenton?"

"By asking questions," Vickery said.

"Is there anything more I can tell you?"

"Do you remember who was watching Ted Kimball on the stairs at midnight?" Vickery asked. "I have already been given a list, but it would be helpful to have the names confirmed."

"Because anyone who *wasn't* there is potentially our murderer," Garvin said. "All right, let me see if I can remember. I was standing next to Linnie, I was leaning against the wall because I was still feeling a little unsteady. Linnie's mother was watching from the doorway into the drawing room. The old man, Merlin, was hanging onto the newel post on the right as you look up the stairs. Linnie's Aunt Veronica was sitting on the bottom step to the left. Who does that leave? That driver chap, Malloy, he was standing near the top of the narrow staircase that leads down to the kitchen. The library door was shut, and Sir Geoffrey was leaning against that with a snifter in one hand and a cigar in the other, he was looking quite the country squire. But then, so was Aunt Veronica!"

"Is that everyone?"

"I think so. Linnie's father wasn't there, he'd been sent off on an errand somewhere so that Kimball could do his little performance."

"Do you recall where Leo Fulbright had been sent?" Vickery asked.

"Sorry, no."

"Upstairs or outside?"

"Could have been either. He was looking for something. Linnie might know."

"We know that Eleanor Trenton herself was absent. Do you remember when she left the company? And whether she was with anyone?" Vickery asked.

"I saw Eleanor talking to Aunt Veronica, both of them seemed to get into a bit of a tizzy about something. And then Eleanor asked us if we knew where Linnie's father was. She looked rather stern when she went out to look for him."

"Out?"

"Out of the drawing room. She went upstairs, I think."

"Do you know what time this was?"

"Haven't the foggiest, sorry. No reason to look at the time. But it must have been well before midnight, because Linnie and I went out for a stroll round the lake after that, and we got back just before Ted Kimball took to the stage."

"You and Linnie went out through the drawing room doors onto the terrace?"

"That's right."

"Did you see anyone else outside while you were walking?"

Garvin shook his head. "There was no one on the terrace when we went out, and there wasn't a soul down by the lake, which was rather the point."

"Thank you, Mr. Garvin. I should probably leave you in peace now, so that you can write up your notes." Vickery, picking up the two sheets of paper from the desk, noted Garvin's quizzical look. "For the newspaper account you are going to write. Best to get things down while they are still fresh.

"Yes, yes I will. Thank you. Are you going to speak to Linnie now? Probably best to speak to her straightaway, before she and I have had chance to compare stories and iron out our inconsistencies. And she'll be sitting out there waiting for you anyway."

Vickery moved towards the door. "I shall ensure that Miss Fulbright does not disturb you—for at least the next half-hour."

"Brilliant. Thanks ever so much."

As her fiancé had predicted, Linette was sitting on a chair in the hall. She stood as soon as Vickery opened the library door.

"Is everything all right?" She asked, trying to peer over Vickery's shoulder as he closed the door.

"Splendid," Vickery said. "Mr. Garvin has given me permission to escort you to morning tea. He will join us on the terrace shortly."

"It's not his head, is it? He said he woke up with the most terrific headache. I asked that doctor to take a look at him, and he said Ollie was fine, no signs of a concussion or anything. He just needs rest and a bit of peace and quiet—" She caught herself then, smiling in her mild embarrassment.

"You can talk to me while he rests," Vickery said.

"I should be with him. Sitting quietly."

"The whole point of my interviewing the two of you separately," Vickery said, "is that you are not together."

"Oh, you need to be able to compare and contrast our accounts, see if we tell you the same thing. I do hope Ollie got his facts straight, he's not always as precise as he might be. Just little details."

"Mr. Garvin has been most thorough, I assure you. Now, let's ring for some tea, shall we?"

*

"You don't take milk?" Linette asked.

"When I was abroad, we often had only condensed milk, so I gave it up completely."

"Condensed milk? The tea must have been—" She pulled a face.

"It was, *very*." Vickery pulled the same face.

Linette laughed. "Sometimes you seem terribly old-fashioned, and yet at other times... I'm sorry, Ollie must have told you what I'm like. He says I talk too much."

"He said nothing of the sort. I got the impression that he rather fancied you."

Linette laughed again. "I should bally well hope so! We're—"

"*Engaged*, yes I know." Vickery put his finger to his lips and winked.

"It's not a secret anymore." Linette held up her hand to show off the ring, an oval cut sapphire with a round brilliant cut diamond on either side. "Beautiful isn't it? We could never have afforded a ring like this."

"Your grandmother would have approved, I'm sure."

"Oh, yes. Ollie is wonderful, everyone loves him."

"With the obvious exception," Vickery said.

"Daddy hates everyone," Linette said. "I'm sorry, that's a terrible thing to say. And I'm sure he wouldn't have actually *killed* Ollie yesterday."

"But he does have quite a temper," Vickery said.

Linette looked down into her teacup. "Everyone's going to think he killed Eleanor, aren't they?"

"Some people will think that. Others may suspect someone else."

"That's the horrible thing, isn't it? We all end up looking at each other, wondering: Did *he* do it? Could it have been *her*?"

"The horrible thing is that a young woman is lying dead in a cold room," Vickery said.

"You are right, I'm sorry. We shouldn't be feeling sorry for *ourselves*, should we? It is just a temporary inconvenience to us, but for Eleanor it is—"

"Her life is over. And all we can do for her now is to try and ensure that her murderer is identified and punished."

"Do you think it is right, doing what we do to murderers? Taking another life seems so—"

"It is very Old Testament."

Linette nodded. "You don't think about these things until, well, until it could be someone you know."

"Does it make a difference whether the murderer is a friend or a stranger?"

"No. Murder is murder. Ask me questions. If I can help you, I will."

"At midnight last night you were watching Ted Kimball give a recital in the style of your father," Vickery said. "Can you remember who else was watching him?"

"I will tell you who wasn't there, that's what you really want to know, isn't it? If they weren't watching Teddy, they obviously had the opportunity to commit the murder."

"I thought it might be easier to recall who you *did* see."

"My father wasn't there, you already know that. Teddy wouldn't have dared do that if daddy had actually been there. Artie Delancey wasn't there. And my mother left after a few minutes, I suppose she thought watching it would be some sort of betrayal of my father. Those are your three suspects: my father, my mother, and Artie. Apart from that, there's only Sir Geoffrey's butler, Crawley, but the butler only ever does it in stage plays. Oh, and there's that ghastly boy, Timothy."

"He was watching from the top of the stairs, I am told."

"By whom?"

"Sir Geoffrey."

"He'd say whatever he had to, to protect the boy."

"There is also your aunt's mysterious gentleman friend," Vickery said.

"Is there? I suppose she has been acting rather oddly of late, but then, well, you've met her. Lovely woman, but a few penn'orth short of the full shilling, as my father says. I think she went out yesterday afternoon to meet someone at the inn in the village, but as to whether she has found herself another man, well, I very much doubt it, don't you?"

"Did anyone else leave before the end of Mr. Kimball's performance last night?" Vickery asked.

"No, just my mother."

"Do you know where she went?"

"Back into the drawing room, so she might have gone through the French doors out onto the terrace."

"And do you know where your father went?"

"No, sorry. If I knew, I'd tell you."

"When you were walking round the lake, did you see anyone else?" Vickery asked.

"Is that what Ollie said we did? Went for a romantic moonlit stroll, arm-in-arm around the lake? He's such a darling."

"I don't understand."

"We didn't get much further than the orchard. He became dizzy and we had to turn back. We sat on that bench under the tree, he had his head between his knees because he felt queasy again. *Très romantique*," she said, grinning.

"You sat there until going back in to watch Mr. Kimball perform?"

"Yes," Linette said. "When he was feeling a little restored, Ollie sat up and rested his head on my shoulder. It was rather nice. It doesn't always need to be 'hearts and flowers,' does it?"

"Most of the time, it isn't," Vickery said. "The quieter moments are the ones you miss most, looking back."

"Do you think my parents ever have quieter moments?"

Linette asked. She laughed at her own question. "They're always on stage when there's someone else around. I don't suppose it's any different when they only have each other for an audience."

"Your parents are both people with strong emotions," Vickery said. "That does not mean that the feelings they express are not genuine."

"But you can never know what another person is *really* thinking or feeling, can you?" Linette asked.

"You can only observe the outward signs, and put yourself in their position and imagine what you would think and feel in such a situation," Vickery said.

"And you can ask them questions," Linette said, "and see if what they say is in accord with what they do?"

"That is so. You, for example, wish to give the impression that you are very different from your father, and would never lose your temper, even if provoked. And yet—"

"And yet?" Linette was suspicious now.

"And yet, late yesterday afternoon, you quarrelled with Eleanor Trenton. Quite loudly, I understand."

"Who told you that?"

"Sound travels, Miss Fulbright. You were heard by more than one person to call her a 'dreadful woman' and an 'interfering cow.'"

Linette blushed. "I'm sorry about that now, of course, given the circumstances. But at the time—"

"It was she that revealed to your father the secret of your engagement?" Vickery asked.

"Yes," Linette said. "She had no right. What was it to do with her? She only said it to try and hurt my father."

"But your fiancé was the one who was hurt."

"Poor Ollie, he didn't deserve... Not that Eleanor deserved what happened to her. You have to believe me when I say that

I didn't want her to be harmed. You do, don't you?"

"You are more like your father than you might wish to believe," Vickery said. "And you have also inherited certain traits from your mother. That is a formidable combination, I would say."

"Is that a bad thing?" Linette asked: she felt that she was somehow being judged.

"The relationship between your parents has endured partly because they provide a balancing influence for one another. I would like to think that those characteristics you have gained from each will do the same."

"I'm not sure that was an entirely glowing endorsement."

"It was not intended to be so. Your tea is cold: shall I ring for more?"

"No. Thank you."

Chapter 18

Malloy was standing at the side of the pond leaning on a long-handled hoe he had taken from the gardener's shed. He had removed his shoes and socks and was staring at the water with the expression of a man contemplating having a tooth drilled.

"That's where they found her *body!*"

Malloy turned, startled by the voice. It was Sir Geoffrey's nephew, Timothy.

"Yes, it is," Malloy said.

"Are you really going to get in there and swim around in it?"

"I have to see if I can find the—find Excalibur."

"You mean the *murder weapon!*"

"You don't fancy a paddle, do you? Save me having to get wet?"

"I'm not getting in there, that water has got my sister's blood in it!"

Malloy looked back at the pond with even greater reluctance.

"What you need is a great big magnet on a piece of string," Timothy suggested.

"Do you have one?"

"No, mine's tiny. It came from a fishing game. You can pick up pins with it, but not swords. When are you going to start?"

"Soon," Malloy said.

"I bet it's *really* cold in there," Timothy said. "And dirty."

Malloy looked down at his white shirt, then back towards the inky water. He pulled the shirt off over his head.

"How did you get that bruise on your chin?" Timothy asked.

Malloy was tempted to say he got it while drowning a brat in a pond, but he thought better of it.

"Someone hit me," he said.

"Why?"

"Because I kept asking questions." Malloy was beginning to shiver.

Timothy laughed. "That's not true. Is it? You're covered in goose bumps, and you're not even in the water yet."

Malloy moved towards the water's edge. Mud squelched between his toes.

"Watch out for alligators," Timothy said. "And leeches, they stick to your skin and suck your blood out."

Malloy was knee deep in the water now.

"If you see anything swimming towards me, shout," he said.

"I will." Timothy sat on his haunches and began his vigil, scouring the surface of the pond for tell-tale ripples. "What about mosquitoes?"

"It's too cold for mosquitoes," Malloy said, trying not to let his teeth chatter.

"That's lucky."

"I'm the luckiest man alive." He planted the hoe on the bottom of the pond, gripped it tightly, and swept his leg left and right, exploring the bottom of the pond with his foot."

"Aren't you afraid you'll step on the sword and cut one of your toes off?"

"I wasn't afraid of that, no." Malloy hadn't given this any thought, until now. He began probing the bottom of the pond with the end of the hoe instead.

"Are there any fish in there?"

"Haven't seen any yet."

"If there are fish, do you think they might have nibbled my sister's body?"

"Fish don't have teeth."

"Sharks do," Timothy said, "they're fish. And piranhas. I read about them in a book about jungle explorers. They eat people."

"Explorers?"

"No, piranhas."

"You're right, there's no piranhas. But I think I just stepped on a dead frog."

"Can I *see*?"

"Shouldn't you be inside, getting spanked or something."

"Oh, I'm never spanked."

"You surprise me."

"No sword?" Timothy asked.

"No sword."

"You're going to have to go deeper, towards the fountain, and get your head under."

"What I need is a small boy on the end of a piece of string," Malloy muttered.

"What?"

"It's not 'what,' it's 'pardon me.'"

Timothy giggled. "You sound like nanny."

"Your nanny sounds like an Irish bloke?"

"No, she sounds like a Scottish bloke."

As he swept the hoe back and forth, it became snagged in something soft. Thinking it had become entangled in weeds, Malloy drew it out. Wrapped around the end of the hoe was a hessian sack. The words 'Jersey Potatoes' were clearly legible on the fabric: it had obviously not been in the water long. But it did not contain the sword. Malloy wadded it up and threw it towards the bank, as close the boy as he could without actually hitting him. He resumed wading through the soupy water.

"You made it to the middle!" Timothy said.

Malloy placed a hand on one of the hideous bronze dolphin-monsters, pleased to have made it without the need to submerge his head in the murky water. The cold greenish-black water lapped under his armpits, and he shivered. He decided he would circle the fountain, and then work his way back to shore in a widening spiral, probing the bottom of the pond with the staff as he went. But he had taken only a single step when his foot slipped across the surface of a slimy rock and unable to maintain his balance he fell face forwards with splash.

Malloy's head broke the surface. He spat out the pond water and gasped for air. As the water drained from his ears, he became aware of shrieks of laughter from the bank. Timothy was doubled-over, hands on his knees, red-faced and crying with laughter. His gasps for breath were louder than Malloy's.

Sir Geoffrey's sour-faced butler came striding out of the gatehouse and hurried towards the boy. He cast a glance towards Malloy, silently accusing him of being responsible for Timothy's undignified outburst. He took the boy by the arm and led him, protesting, inside.

"Don't worry about me, I'm alright," Malloy spluttered, "no help needed here!"

He spat loudly, and then set about completing his search of the pond as quickly as he could.

When the head of the hoe struck something metallic, Malloy felt a rush of anticipation, but it was not the missing sword: it was the axe Kimball had used on Oliver Garvin's sports car. Malloy hurled it towards the bank in frustration.

As he approached the edge of the pond, Malloy became aware that he was being watched from the bushes to the right of the gatehouse. At first he thought it was the boy, back to renew his enjoyment at Malloy's discomfort. But the outline of the concealed figure was an adult. Pretending he was unaware of his watcher, Malloy trudged up out of the water and towards his discarded shoes and shirt. His skin was covered with a greenish slime, and his trousers blotched with something darker. He looked down at his white shirt, and then at his stained hands.

"I should have given this more thought," he said to himself. "I'm going to need a towel."

"You're going to need hosing down and scrubbing with a yard brush," said a voice behind him. Malloy turned. Crawley held a greyish towel out towards him. "It's not one of the good ones," Crawley said.

Malloy took the towel and nodded his thanks.

"You are to go round to the rear and in through the kitchen, do *not* go through the house. They are filling a bath for you below stairs. I brought clean clothes down from your room. And, for future reference, the pond is *not* for swimming."

"I was *not* swimming," Malloy protested. "I was *drowning.*"

"Next time, do it in the lake." Crawley turned back towards the gatehouse, pausing only to shout into the bushes to his right. "And you, boy, get out of there, you're trampling the Narcissi."

A figure detached itself from the foliage, stared past the butler at Malloy, and then turned and ran.

"Who was that?" Crawley asked.

"Artie Delancey," Malloy said, scrubbing at his arms with the old towel.

Crawley looked with horror at the rapid discolouration of the towel. "He was watching you swim."

"I was not swim—"

"In round the back, *not* through the house," Crawley repeated. "It's bad enough those police constables blundering about the place, moving the furniture and scratching the floor. We don't need you ruining the rugs as well." With that, he disappeared back inside.

* * *

"I suppose they all think *I* did it?" Fulbright said.

"Did you?" Vickery asked.

"Don't be a bloody fool, if I was going to kill her, do you think I would have painted myself into this corner—made it look as if only I *could* have done it?"

"You are not the only one who lacks a satisfying alibi: there are two others," Vickery said. "But to answer your question, one way for a murderer to divert attention is to make himself seem *too* obvious a suspect, perhaps even to claim that someone has staged circumstances so as to incriminate him."

"That's too ridiculous even to work on stage, never mind in the real world. Do you really think I could have killed her?"

"In the heat of the moment, perhaps."

"Because of my temper," Fulbright said.

"You must admit, it does rather cast you in a poor light."

"I didn't kill her. And neither did Margot."

"Why would you think Margot was a suspect?" Vickery asked.

"Because she also lacks a satisfactory alibi, as you put it, or has she provided some proof that she was elsewhere at the time of Eleanor's death?"

"She was with you," Vickery said.

"She told you that? No, of course she didn't. You guessed."

"She asked you to go upstairs and fetch the wrap she had left there. I imagine she made sure that you would not be able to locate it. And a few minutes later, she followed you up."

"And why do you deduce that she would go to such lengths to ensure I was kept away from the assembled company?"

"Are you aware that Mr. Kimball is an accomplished mimic, and that his vocal imitation of you is really very good?"

"That's what they were up to down here, is it? All having a jolly old laugh at my expense?"

"Don't the common folk always mock their king in private?" Vickery asked.

"What did he say about me?"

"I believe he performed a routine using your voice, though the content did not relate to you directly."

"But he still made me look a damned fool!"

"One assumes that was his intention, yes. I did not see the performance, but I have had sight of the script. Considerable effort appears to have gone into it."

"There was a script? That wouldn't have been Kimball's work, he has trouble composing a telegram."

"You do not think he wrote the routine?"

"He would have had a co-writer at the very least," Fulbright said.

"Interesting," Vickery said. "Do you know if Mr. Kimball is in possession of a typewriter?"

"I doubt it, his messages are always handwritten. Penmanship like a doctor's."

"But there would be a typewriter at the film studio?"

"One in the office, another backstage, and probably one in the props cupboard. Plus whatever the current writer is using, though some of them would be more at home with a wax crayon."

"Do you have a typewriter, Mr. Fulbright?"

"A big old Underwood, sits on a table behind the desk at home. I've used it twice. Or attempted to. How anyone gets the letters onto the paper in the right order is beyond me. But that's what secretaries are for."

"Do you have a secretary?"

"Had several, none of them stayed above a month. All useless. If you want to know about typewriters, talk to Bannister, he operated one during the war. He can hit the keys better than any woman I've ever seen. When he's sober."

"Does he drink as a result of his experiences in the Great War?"

"He sat behind a desk in Whitehall. He drinks because it is the only thing that gives him the courage to walk out on stage every night. Is Bannister the third suspect?"

"I beg your pardon?"

"You said there was Margot, me, and one other."

"Artie Delancey."

"Artie?" Fulbright didn't sound as incredulous as Bannister had.

"Do you think he is capable of murder?" Vickery asked.

"Artie's tougher than he looks. You should have seen him after the beating he took last year. Three men. You couldn't recognise his face. Look at him now and you'd never know."

"He was on the receiving end of violence, but did he fight back?"

"If he had, he probably wouldn't have survived."

"Then you do not believe he is capable of violence?"

"Put him in the ring with the gloves on, no. But put him in the shadows with a dagger, perhaps."

"Or a sword?" Vickery asked.

"Have you found it yet?"

"Malloy is still looking."

"That why he looked like he had been swimming in a sewer?"

"My fault, alas. Why do you think Eleanor Trenton was murdered?"

"Because of me," Fulbright said, without hesitation. "Someone wanted to hurt me, by taking her from me. And they rubbed salt in the wound by making it look like I was the one who killed her."

"You do not think that she might have had enemies of her own?" Vickery asked.

"She was a girl, she wasn't old enough to have made enemies."

"Then we come full circle and must ask again who might have a motive for wishing you harm?"

"We are back where we started, with you having achieved nothing," Fulbright said. "If you had gotten to the bottom of this business with the letters, Eleanor would still be alive."

"You think the letters and the murder are connected?" Vickery asked.

"It stands to reason, doesn't it? When the letters did not produce the desired effect, they turned to more dramatic action."

"'Dramatic action,' an interesting choice of words. This whole thing does seem a little theatrical, doesn't it? A dead woman found floating in a pond like Ophelia. Murdered using a medieval broad sword. With the whole thing surrounded by the mystery of the poison pen letters."

"Well, I suppose so—"

"And all the time, you are refusing to share with me the content of those letters. What is the letter-writer trying to force you to do? And how did they think murdering Miss Trenton might be the final encouragement you needed?"

"The letters are the ramblings of an idiot—"

"They were written by someone who bears a grudge, for some wrong they believe you did to them, perhaps years ago. If I knew what the subject of the letters was, I might be able to identify the murderer. I want to see the rest of those letters, including the missing pages."

"I burned them." Fulbright was defiant.

"You will have to share the contents of the letters with the police."

"If I must share that information with a *professional* investigator, I will."

"Then you *do* have something to hide," Vickery said.

"And I also *do* have an alibi for the time of the murder," Fulbright said smugly. "I was with Margot."

"That is not enough, a husband and wife providing alibis for one another, with no corroboration from anyone else. Who is to say that you are both telling the truth? Or who is to say that you and Margot were not accomplices, committing the murder together, and then covering up by providing each other with a plausible alibi? The *professional* investigators will want to dig much more deeply into the relationships between you and Margot and Eleanor Trenton."

"Let them, I have no guilty secrets to hide."

"Those letters seem to indicate otherwise," Vickery said.

"They are gibberish, no one will take them seriously."

"You took them seriously enough to engage me to look into them. And now that you have connected them with a murder, the *professional* investigators will, I am sure, want to take them very seriously indeed. Even if you *are* innocent, your name will be connected with murder on the front pages of tomorrow's newspapers. Is that the publicity you wanted for your motion picture?"

"I have nothing more to say to you—get out!"

* * *

Malloy sat in the zinc hipbath set in front of the fire in a low-ceilinged room off the kitchen. The warmth had finally worked its way into his blood, and he was feeling content once more, especially so since the cook had slipped him a good measure of whisky to make sure he 'didn't come down with a chill.' Malloy closed his eyes and breathed deeply.

"No sign of the sword?"

Malloy's eyes snapped open. Vickery was leaning against the mantelpiece.

"No, and it wasn't in the pond either," Malloy said.

"Cook asked me to bring this in," Vickery said, pointing to a large folded white towel sitting on the hearth. "She said this wasn't one of the ones they used for the dog, if that means anything."

"Crawley," Malloy said, as if that explained everything. "How did your morning unfold?"

"I appear to have narrowed it down to three suspects," Vickery said.

"Quick work."

"Unfortunately, I don't think any of them actually did it."

"And none of them had the decency to confess?"

"I have spoken to two of them, but have been unable to corner Artie Delancey."

"You should have been outside chest-deep in pond water," Malloy said.

"I should?"

"Artie Delancey was hiding in the bushes, watching me."

"A secret admirer? That explains Margot's comment: she said you might have a better chance of questioning Artie than I did. Did you speak to him?"

"Crawley frightened him off."

"I know that feeling," Vickery said. "What happened to the Inspector and his handful of coppers?"

"Debney has gone off to the village to try and locate a mysterious 'someone' who might have 'hinformation germane to the hinvestigation.' He's taken one of the plods with him, and the other two have gone off wandering around the lake looking for footprints that might lead them to the murder weapon. They'll be back shortly for more tea, I expect."

"We need to locate Artie Delancey before they do. Will you

do something for me?"

"What, *now?*" Malloy glanced down at his naked self in the cooling bathwater.

If Vickery had been wearing glasses, he would have looked over the top of them, instead he raised an eyebrow and pursed his lips.

"Does it involve wading navel-deep in pond scum in my underwear?" Malloy asked.

"No."

"And it doesn't involve getting wet?"

"Not very. But it may involve undressing again, at least partially."

"Tell me more!" Malloy grinned.

"I want you to go and see if you can tempt Artie Delancey out of the bushes so that he'll speak to you."

"And how am I going to do that?"

"I was thinking perhaps you might go out and wash one of the cars. Preferably mine. If you're out there alone, he might be inclined to approach you."

"Do you really think that will work?"

"If you turn on the Irish charm. And if that fails, try taking your shirt off again."

"Do you know how *cold* it is out there?" Malloy protested. "It's only the beginning of May: I should still be wearing a vest!"

"If you catch cold, I'll rub goose grease on your chest," Vickery said.

"Is that what you had to do in the olden days?"

"That and drink raspberry vinegar."

"I'm surprised you lived past childhood, what with that and the Black Death."

Vickery gave Malloy his best schoolmasterly scowl. He took a hipflask out of his pocket.

"What's that?" Malloy asked.

"Brandy."

"What's it for?"

"I will give you a clue: it's not for washing the car."

"Do you want me to get Delancey drunk?"

"Is that what you usually have to do?"

"Usually I'm the one needs the brandy," Malloy said.

"Well, here you are then." Vickery passed him the silver flask and turned to go.

Malloy uncorked the flask and took a good belt from it.

"Watch out Artie Delancey, here comes the Irish Charmer," he muttered.

Chapter 19

Malloy walked round the keep across the grass by the pond, over to where Vickery's car had been parked on the circular part of the driveway. He whistled brightly to call attention to himself. A bucket of warm soapy water hung from one hand, and a larger bucket of cold water for rinsing from the other. He had a chamois leather and a linen cloth over his shoulder. He set the buckets down beside Vickery's car and stretched, trying not to make it obvious that he was looking around for Artie Delancey. Seeing no sign of the young man, and for want of anything better to do, he dipped the cloth into the soapy water, then slapped it onto the roof of the Alvis and began washing it. He quickly became absorbed in the task, forgetting that he was supposed to be seeking Artie.

"What are you washing Vickery's car for?" Fulbright asked.

Malloy turned, he hadn't heard his employer approach.

"For two bob," Malloy said.

"Idiot," Fulbright said, "can't you see it's going to rain?"

"There's a shame," Malloy said, "for I won't have chance to wash the Rolls as well."

"You and I are going to have serious words when we get back to town tomorrow," Fulbright said, trying to sound ominous. But Malloy was too distracted to be aware of the threat.

Malloy was more eager than ever to escape Fulbright's presence, knowing that Artie would never show his face while the big man was there. Malloy looked up at the clouds and made tutting noises.

"I think you're right about the rain," he said. "You should probably get yourself indoors before the heavens open."

Fulbright looked at him suspiciously. Malloy tried on an innocent smile.

"Why do I always get the feeling that you're up to something, Malloy?" Fulbright turned without waiting for an answer, stomping back towards the gatehouse, muttering.

Malloy watched him pass into the shadow of the archway, then glanced towards the pond, wondering if Fulbright might be the murderer of Eleanor Trenton. He thought he saw a brief movement in the bushes not far away. Not wanting to startle his quarry, he turned his attention back to the car, pretending he'd seen nothing. He glanced up at the clouds again and shivered. Ah well, he thought, it's in a good cause. He slipped his braces down off his shoulders and let them hang, then pulled his shirt off over his head. He opened the car door and dropped the shirt on the front seat. He stretched, and bent to retrieve the cloth from the bucket of soapy water. In an effort to stop his teeth chattering, he started to sing to himself. After a few minutes he glanced round again, as casually as he could. But he could make out nothing amidst the foliage. Perhaps he had been mistaken before.

"Pretend that you don't see me." An urgent voice. Startled, Malloy peered through the smeared wet glass into the car. Artie Delancey sat huddled on the floor behind the passenger seat. How long had been there? Malloy cracked open the door a half-inch and leaned close to the gap, wiping at the paintwork with his cloth as he did so.

"Are you all right?" He asked.

"Been better," Artie said.

Malloy looked at him more closely. Artie had his arms wrapped around himself; stubble stood out stark on his pale cheeks. He looked unwashed, his red-rimmed eyes staring.

"No one must know I'm here," Artie said, "I'm in danger."

"Why?"

"Because of Eleanor."

"Did you kill her?" Malloy felt he had to ask the question.

"*No!* But I saw her dead." Artie began to cry. The streaks down his face said this wasn't the first time.

"What have you got yourself mixed up in?" Malloy asked. "Whatever it is, we'll help you. Mr. Vickery will find you a way out of it."

Artie was shivering violently along with his sobs now. Malloy opened the boot of the car and took out a tartan travelling blanket. He passed it into the back of the car. Artie hid himself under it.

"Do you know who killed Eleanor, Artie?" Malloy asked.

"Who are you talking to?" A voice asked. Malloy turned, looked down. Timothy.

"I was just singing to myself," Malloy said. He leaned back on the car door so that it clicked shut.

Timothy seemed unconvinced by this answer. "What were you singing?"

"I don't know what it's called. It's something my mammy used to sing to me, when I was little."

Timothy considered this and seemed satisfied: Why would Malloy lie to him?

"My mother never sang to me," Timothy said. "Nanny does. Well, she tries to. But she's a terrible singer. I told Uncle Geoffrey that she sounds like someone strangling a cat." He snorted laughter at his own wit.

"Don't let your Nanny hear you say that now," Malloy

warned.

"I'm not afraid of her," Timothy said, drawing himself up to his full height.

"She's watching from the upstairs window," Malloy said.

"She is?" Timothy turned quickly. "I can't see her."

"She's pointing at you."

"Where? You don't think she heard, do you?"

"No, but I think she wants you to go inside."

"You won't tell her, will you? What I said about her singing."

"It'll be our little secret. You run along now."

And run the boy did.

Malloy opened the car door a little. "You still in there?" He asked.

"Still here," Artie said.

"What can I do to help you?" Malloy asked.

"I'm hungry. Was sick that night, haven't eaten since."

"I'll fetch you some food," Malloy said. "Wait here."

"Not here. It's not safe. Someone could see me."

"Then where?"

"The summer house near the lake. Come when the others are at lunch. Just you."

"Are you sure you'll be safe until then?" Malloy asked. "Artie?"

Malloy looked into the car. Artie and the blanket were gone.

"That proves he knows how to stay hidden, I suppose." Malloy reached for his shirt.

* * *

"We're to meet while the others are at lunch," Malloy said. "He was terrified. I don't think he's the killer."

"Nor do I," Vickery said. "But he knows something that will help us identify the murderer, of that I am quite sure. Why else would he be in fear of his life?"

"If the killer finds him before—"

"You said he was quite adept at hiding," Vickery said. "The murderer is unlikely to find him before lunch time, and so are we. We must decide how best we can help Mr. Delancey."

"If he will let me, I can protect him," Malloy said.

"His best protection will be to share with us what he knows," Vickery said. "While he is the only person who knows it, he is in grave danger. The murderer will try and silence him before he can speak. But once he has told us—"

"All three of us become potential victims," Malloy said.

"Perhaps, but the risk to Mr. Delancey becomes less once the burden is shared: his death no longer provides the killer with a neat solution."

"I've asked the cook to prepare some food. I've said that I want to have a picnic in the orchard. I think she believed me."

"How could she not?" Vickery smiled.

"What should I do when I get to the summer house?"

"Allow Mr. Delancey to eat, and make him feel safe, as far as you are able. I would suggest taking a walking stick with you, one with a heavy head. Then he will see that you can protect him with it, should you have to."

"And then?"

"When he feels ready, he will tell you what he knows. From what you have said, I think he will be distressed by what he tells you. You must be ready to provide comfort to him."

"How do I do that?" Malloy asked.

"Wrap those big arms of yours around him and make soothing noises," Vickery said.

"He's not a child."

"No. But we all feel like children when we are afraid."

Malloy looked equal parts unconvinced and uncomfortable. "Come with me," he said.

"Mr. Delancey will be watching. Should he see that you do

not arrive alone as promised, he may bolt. And we shall not have another opportunity to help him. Besides, I need to keep an eye on those policeman and make sure they don't head in your direction."

"I feel that I'm out of my depth," Malloy said.

"I can think of no one better-suited to the task," Vickery assured him.

* * *

On Vickery's advice, Malloy took a circuitous route toward the summer house, making several stops to determine that he was not being followed. Satisfied that he was not, he now approached his destination. He had a sack over one shoulder, containing sandwiches wrapped in waxed paper and a bottle of cook's homemade dandelion and burdock beer. He swung a walking stick as he strode along, his hand gripping the smooth knob that was almost the size of a cricket ball. He whistled, the same tune he had attempted earlier, to alert Artie to his approach.

Malloy came out of the trees and stopped a few yards short of the summer house. The air was still. Except for the humming of insects, there was silence. He moved on, stopping again when he reached the open doorway.

"Artie?" For some reason he felt the need to whisper. He received no response, and so tried again, louder. "Artie!"

Stepping inside, he spied the tartan blanket on the floor, the bundle too small for Artie to be hidden under it. Malloy glanced around and under the furniture, satisfying himself that the little shelter was empty. He stepped outside and walked all around the summer house, listening attentively.

"Artie?" He called. "Are you here?" This silenced the birds, and brought no response.

Malloy glanced towards the lake, where the sun glittered on the water. He wondered if Artie might have gone down to the water's edge. Would he have risked such exposure? He took a few steps in that direction, then stopped and drew a hand up to shield his eyes as the sun was reflected suddenly on something like a mirror. He blinked away the after-image, his brain already subliminally registering the shape that he had glimpsed in the reflection.

Malloy dropped the picnic sack and ran towards the lake.

"No, no, no," he repeated as he headed for the bright metal that had caught his attention. He stopped at the edge of the water and stared.

Excalibur. Standing up straight in the lake as it did in the legend.

"No!" Malloy said again, drawing out the vowel in his anguish. He waded into the chilly water, towards the sword.

Lying in the shallow water was the body of Artie Delancey. The sword had been driven through his chest, pinning him in place like a pale moth.

Malloy carried Artie Delancey's body back up to the keep. He took it in through the rear of the house and down the stairs, where he laid it on the wooden table next to Eleanor Trenton. He placed the sword Excalibur down between them.

* * *

"Artie was going to be the Lady in the Lake," Bannister said, when Vickery broke the news to him. "In the film. He was going to be under the water, thrusting his arm up into the air, holding Excalibur. Poor Artie."

"Malloy has gone to fetch the doctor again. Then he and I are going to find who killed the Lady in the Lake," Vickery said. "And we are going to make sure they pay for what they have done."

"I know you two will do right by Artie," Bannister said.

* * *

Artie Delancey's room was not quite how Malloy thought it would be. He had expected to find things scattered everywhere, but instead the room looked almost unoccupied. Clothes were neatly folded and put away, the ones in his suitcase wrapped carefully in tissue paper. His shaving kit was spotless, and everything on his dresser was lined up with regimental precision.

"We've only got a few minutes, while the police are preoccupied with Artie's body," Vickery said. "I want to look around before they come up here."

The room was almost identical to that occupied by Eleanor Trenton. They divided the labour as they had before, with Vickery searching the drawers, which were all but empty, and Malloy opening the wardrobe.

"Two dresses, white and blue," Malloy said. "They're not quite the same quality as those we found in Eleanor Trenton's room."

"Artie didn't have a wealthy uncle or well-to-do admirers," Vickery said, pushing the last drawer closed. "I hope Bannister knows where to contact his family."

"Three pairs of shoes," Malloy said, on his knees peering into the bottom of the wardrobe. "White and blue, as you'd expect, and also red ones."

Vickery turned round quickly. "*That* is the final clue!" He said.

"The shoes?"

"The missing red dress." Vickery said. "The small cloth-covered button I retrieved from Fulbright's pocket—was from Artie's missing red dress."

"Where do we look for it? We've already searched every room," Malloy said.

"We don't need to look for his dress, we've already found it. We just didn't know it was lost at the time," Vickery said.

"Artie's red dress is... in Eleanor Trenton's wardrobe!" Malloy said.

"An apple in an orchard," Vickery said. "The perfect hiding place."

Chapter 20

"Inspector Debney and I have completed our investigations, and reached our conclusions," Vickery said.

The guests were all gathered in the drawing room, their chairs arranged in a rough circle, with everyone looking expectantly toward Vickery. Inspector Debney stood beside him: he looked somewhat uncomfortable, but nodded agreement. Two of the constables held positions in front of the exits from the room. Malloy stood off to one side by the sideboard.

"Would you like to go first, Inspector?" Vickery asked.

The Inspector seemed startled by this, as though he had not expected to be asked.

"Er—you go ahead, Mr. Vickery. I will—I will add any details that I think you have missed."

"Thank you, Inspector." Vickery gave a little bow in his direction, a half-smile on his lips, then he turned back to the assembled guests. "In a case such as this, there are two versions of events. The first is what *seems* to have happened: this is what the murderer wishes us to believe. The second is what *really* happened, and this is what the murderer seeks to hide from us.

"I want to begin with the first version, that which we all initially believed to be true," Vickery said.

Inspector Dabney gave a slight cough and seemed to see

something interesting out of the window.

"At a minute or two after midnight we all heard a scream and the sound of something heavy falling into the pond in front of the keep. We hurried out, and discovered the body of Eleanor Trenton lying in the pond. She had been stabbed with a sword."

"Excalibur," Linette said.

"Excalibur," Vickery agreed. "The murder weapon is what our friends in the constabulary refer to as the *means*. To prove that someone is a murderer, we need to show that he or she had access to our 'sword in the stone.'"

"Everyone did," Garvin said, "it sat in the hall all weekend."

"Did you try and draw the sword from the stone?" Vickery asked him.

"Didn't everyone?" Garvin smiled sheepishly.

"And were you able to pull the sword free?"

"Well, no, but there's a trick to it, isn't there?" Garvin said.

"Only Fulbright knew how to pull the sword from the stone," Kimball said.

"Leo Fulbright wanted us all to believe that only he knew the secret for releasing the sword. But that wasn't really true, was it?" Vickery said.

"I swore them to secrecy," Fulbright said.

"As magicians, we rely on the discretion of our technicians not to reveal the workings of our apparatus, we call them professional secrets. But sometimes a technician can be persuaded to give up his secrets—given sufficient payment from a rival magician. Or simply out of spite, if they feel their master has treated them unjustly or disrespectfully."

Fulbright's colour rose, from anger or embarrassment, perhaps both.

"Sometimes it is only a desire to impress that causes a person to reveal the secret, to be seen as someone special," Vickery continued. "Artie Delancey knew how to draw Excalibur from the stone, he revealed the secret to me, believing that I may not have divined the trick. Artie learned it from someone on the film set. The secret was passed from one to another, until all knew it."

"You are saying that anyone here could have pulled that sword from the stone?" Garvin asked.

"There are few secrets kept among actors," Vickery said.

"Isn't that the truth," Kimball muttered.

"From this I think we can say that, as everyone here potentially had access to the murder weapon, we cannot use 'means' as a way to determine who might be innocent and who guilty," Vickery said. "And so we must turn to *motive* and *opportunity*. Motivation we all understand to be the reason or reasons why a person is driven to take a particular action. And by 'opportunity' we mean could a person have been in the location where the murder took place at the time it was committed. If a person can show that they were in a different place at the time, if they have an *alibi*, we can say that they lacked opportunity, and so cannot be guilty. Correct, Inspector?"

"Well, I think you've simplified things a bit, but I think you have the gist of it," the Inspector said.

Vickery gave the slightest of bows in the Inspector's direction, then continued.

"Most of the guests were watching Mr. Kimball's performance of *Hamlet* at midnight. Four people were absent: Leo Fulbright, Margot McCrae, Veronica Fulbright, and Artie Delancey. The rest of the guests could all see each other in the entrance hall at the time the murder is said to have taken place, so none of them can have committed the murder."

Those who had been exonerated looked at each other with a sense of relief, and avoided looking at the those who had not been.

Inspector Debney broke the silence.

"When he examined the body, Doctor Cole found this clasped in Miss Trenton's hand." Debney held up a short length of gold chain. "Could you tell us what this is, Mr. Fulbright?"

"It is a piece of watch chain," Fulbright said.

"From any particular pocket watch?" The Inspector asked.

Fulbright glared at him. "From *my* pocket watch," he finally admitted.

"Continuing with our account of what *seemed* to have happened, then," Vickery said. "Miss Trenton was stabbed with the sword, and as she fell backwards into the pond, she reached out and grabbed Mr. Fulbright's watch chain, tearing a piece from it. In his haste to flee the scene, Mr. Fulbright was apparently not aware that this damning piece of evidence had been left behind.

"Mr. Fulbright then hid the sword, and came out to the pond just after everyone else, and pretended to be as shocked as we were by what had happened."

Vickery paused for a moment and looked around the room. No one was looking in Leo Fulbright's direction. He sat with his arms crossed, staring up at Vickery from under knitted brows.

"Mr. Fulbright thought everything had gone perfectly, until he became aware that Artie Delancey knew something he shouldn't. Perhaps Artie saw Mr. Fulbright fleeing the scene, or perhaps he saw him hiding the bloodied sword. Whatever it was, Artie was now a threat to him, and to protect himself, Mr. Fulbright knew that Artie Delancey would have to be silenced. Forever."

"What about the attempt on Leo's life?" Bannister asked.

"It was faked," Inspector Debney said. "Mr. Fulbright had an accomplice fire the crossbow at him. He believed that this would make people think of him as an intended *victim,* in which case they would not think he could be Eleanor Trenton's murderer."

"And Leo's motive?" Margot asked.

"Eleanor Trenton had become an embarrassment to him," the Inspector said. "She had refused to become his lover, and she had proved herself a less than gifted actress when the cameras started rolling."

"It may not immediately be apparent, but Leo Fulbright benefits *financially* from the murder of Eleanor Trenton," Vickery said. "At first it would appear that her death is a terrible loss, perhaps the motion picture will not now be completed. But what if Eleanor's presence in the film had turned out to be a liability rather than an asset? Particularly when the much-anticipated romance between Mr. Fulbright and his new leading lady seemed to have fizzled even before filming was complete, taking with it all the much-desired publicity.

"To protect his film, his own reputation and future prosperity, perhaps Leo Fulbright felt he must remove this danger? His motivation was a mixture of personal gain, unrequited love, and self-protection."

"That's absolute rot!" Fulbright exclaimed, jumping to his feet. "I'm warning you, Vickery..."

"Warning me or threatening me, Mr. Fulbright?" Vickery asked.

Fulbright had the sense to realise that he wasn't helping his cause, and sat down.

"Eleanor Trenton had placed Mr. Fulbright in an embarrassing situation," Inspector Debney said. "As we are all now aware, he is a man with a violent temper, someone who must always have his own way, and so we can imagine how he might react if he felt Miss Trenton was making him look like a fool."

"Leo Fulbright *appears* to have all the prime requisites

of a murderer," Vickery said. "He had access to the means, a plausible motive, and—being absent from the rest of the group at midnight—the opportunity. He seems to fit the bill perfectly.

"I would say that it makes Leo Fulbright look like a clumsy murderer, and a fool for not establishing an alibi for himself for the time of the murder, but his guilt does seem plain enough."

"An untrained mind might accept all of this at face value," Inspector Debney said, without a trace of irony. "After all, this version of events seems to fit all of the available facts."

"Except that it doesn't," Vickery said. "There are facts that do not fit into this version of events. On the night of the murder, I saw Leo Fulbright pick something up from the mud near the pond." Vickery held up the red cloth-covered button. "Where did this come from?"

"It's from Eleanor's dress," Linette said.

"It is the same colour as her dress, but the dress she was wearing had no buttons on it. Mr. Malloy and I found another red dress in Miss Trenton's wardrobe, and this one *does* have a button missing from it. But how did the button get down to the edge of the pond? It can't have been torn off when Eleanor struggled with her murderer."

"And then there's the sack," Inspector Debney prompted.

Constable Brierly held up the hessian sack, which was now quite dry.

"Another of Mr. Malloy's discoveries," Vickery said. "I asked him to search the pond to see if the sword had been thrown in there. He did not find Excalibur, but he did find this potato sack. As you can see, the printing on the sack is quite legible: it had not been in the pond for very long before it was retrieved. Why was it there?"

"Then we have the dresses," Inspector Debney said.

"Yes, dear Artie Delancey had come down for the weekend

with two dresses and three pairs of shoes. Even if he had intended to appear *en femme*, why bring more than one outfit?"

"And why bring along red shoes if he didn't have a matching red dress?" The Inspector added.

"None of these things are explained by our account of what *seems* to have happened," Vickery said. "We cannot simply discard the facts that don't fit in with our theory, we must instead seek a theory that explains *all* of the facts."

"Then I am not guilty after all?" Fulbright asked.

"I did not go so far as to say that," Vickery said. "But I would say that the case against you is not as clear-cut as someone would like us to believe. For me, the thing that throws doubt on Mr. Fulbright's guilt is this piece of physical evidence."

Vickery held up the section of watch chain. The Inspector seemed surprised to see it in Vickery's hand, he patted his jacket pockets and scowled.

"A damning clue," Vickery said, "but a rather too obvious one. We are meant to believe that in a violent struggle, Leo Fulbright was not aware of this being torn from him. And further, that on undressing later he either did not see that the piece was missing, unlikely in a man whose vanity results in an obsessive interest in his own appearance. Or perhaps having stood in front of the mirror and noticed it, he was unconcerned about where this fragment might be found. No, I cannot believe this: a man who kills for reasons of self-preservation does not make such a careless mistake.

"One further fact: the ends of this piece of chain have been neatly cut, there is no sign of the stretching that would occur if it had been pulled free. This chain was placed in the victim's hand deliberately, to focus our attention on Mr. Fulbright, and away from clues which might identify the real murderer. In planting this clue, our villain has over-egged the pudding, so to speak."

"You're saying that a clue that points to Fulbright's guilt actually proves him innocent?" Garvin asked.

"It is not proof of his innocence, but it does rather steer our inquiry onto another track," Vickery said. "The planting of the broken chain becomes a clue of another kind. It tells us that the murderer wanted Eleanor Trenton dead, and also wished to see Leo Fulbright accused of her murder, and perhaps hanged for it. Our next question becomes: Who might wish to see both Mr. Fulbright and Miss Trenton punished?"

"Me, of course," Margot said.

Vickery nodded. "We do not take that as an admission of guilt, but as a new hypothesis which must be tested.

"Margot McCrae is Fulbright's long-suffering wife, and until recently his leading lady in a number of successful theatre productions. But now she finds herself replaced, both in the spotlight and, it would appear, in her husband's affections. Who could fail to feel scorned and angry in such circumstances? Who would not wish to punish both the betraying husband and the new-found object of his affections?"

"I won't pretend that I haven't wished them both dead," Margot said, "and I have said it out loud more than once."

"That is so," Vickery said. "You have made no secret of your feelings, to have done so would have been disingenuous, and might have drawn more attention than would giving vent to them.

"We have personal and professional jealousy, then, and also a financial motive, perhaps, with Leo Fulbright seeking to risk your joint finances in the making of a moving picture."

"I wasn't stupid enough to let him risk my money," Margot said, "only his own."

"But you did tell him that you might provide funding to allow him to finish the film—on one condition?" Vickery said.

"On a number of conditions, actually," Margot said. "But one specifically."

"Which was?"

"Leo must get rid of Eleanor Trenton and allow me to play Guinevere."

"Did he agree to this when you first suggested it?"

"No, he did not."

"Did you tell Miss Trenton that you intended to replace her as the queen?"

"I did."

"What was her reaction?" Vickery asked.

"She said: *Over my dead body!*"

Chapter 21

"Those were her exact words?" Vickery asked.

"You overheard them, you know they were. Dickie heard them too, I believe."

Dickie Bannister blushed.

"Did you kill Eleanor Trenton?" Vickery asked.

"Did I kill her because I wanted a role in a second-rate motion picture, and because Leo was having one of his brief flings with her? I did not."

"No, I do not believe you would kill her for those reasons," Vickery said. "Tell us about your riding accident, please."

"Now? What has that got to—"

"Indulge me, if you would."

"I don't see how—"

"Please," Vickery insisted.

Margot sighed. "I've told this story a hundred times or more, I'm sure everyone has heard it."

"I think some here are more familiar with the circumstances than others," Vickery said.

Margot McCrae seemed uncharacteristically reluctant to be the centre of attention, perhaps because the story she was being asked to tell was an uncomfortable one, both physically and figuratively.

"It happened in late November," Margot began.

"That would be eighteen months ago?" Vickery prompted.

"About that, yes. I had gone out to Whitestoke, we stable the horses there, for the weekend. I wanted to get away from the city for a while."

"Did Leo accompany you that weekend?"

"No. Leo is only ever a fair-weather rider. And he was one of the things I wanted to get away from."

"You had quarrelled?"

"We *always* quarrelled, Benjamin, you know that."

"This time you had quarrelled about Eleanor Trenton?"

"I didn't know that was her name. But I knew Leo had started pursuing someone. I wasn't sure how far this new dalliance had progressed, didn't want to know. I just needed a break from it. Horses are so much more dependable than people."

"But they can be dangerous," Vickery said.

"I don't blame poor Hector for what happened. He was spooked by someone. He had to be—put down after the accident, he injured himself terribly trying to leap a stone wall."

"Had Hector ever bolted before, or thrown you?"

"Never. He was a beautiful, placid creature, no temper at all. I'd had him a few years, he and I were quite used to each other. But as I am sure I told you, he was startled when that old woman appeared on the path in front of us. Hector reared up—I couldn't control him—and the sound he made, it was like a scream of fear."

"Or of pain?" Vickery suggested.

"Possibly, but she didn't strike him. She just loomed up out of the undergrowth, dressed in black rags, waving her arms about like a big old bat."

"Or one of the witches from the Scottish play?" Vickery asked.

"Yes, exactly like that. Crazy or drunk. Or both."

"Had you ever seen her before?"

"No. And she just disappeared. The police tried to find her, to talk to her, but she was just gone."

"Did it ever strike you that her sudden appearance at that moment, in that remote spot, was a trifle melodramatic? Like something from a play or a novel?"

"At the time, I couldn't think of anything. The pain in my spine was crippling."

"But afterwards, did you form any suspicions?"

"No, I—" She cast a glance sideways towards Fulbright. "Well, I did wonder, at one point, if it had really been an accident. Or whether someone had planned it, to get me out of the way."

"By 'someone' you mean Leo, or perhaps his new lover?"

"Well, yes. It's ridiculous, I know. It was probably just the medication, making me delirious. I know Leo would never—"

"And the old woman, you didn't recognise her at the time, or since?"

"No. It happened so suddenly, and she was more of a looming shadow than a person. If she was sitting here now, I'm sure I wouldn't recognise her," Margot said. "You don't think the 'old woman' was Eleanor Trenton?"

"I do not," Vickery said. "I think it is as you said, Leo was in London attempting to woo Eleanor Trenton, while she sought to persuade him to cast her as the queen in the motion picture he was in the early stages of casting."

"Then the old woman—?"

"I believe her presence was no accident. She was, I think, someone we know. Her costume was just that, something chosen from the theatre wardrobe."

"Then someone wanted to kill *me*?"

"They wanted you out of the way, certainly."

"I can't believe that anyone could deliberately—" Margot

shuddered. "They killed poor Hector."

"Your horse wasn't the target."

"Is there any evidence to support what you are suggesting?" Fulbright asked.

"Heresay and only what the police will call circumstantial evidence," Vickery admitted. "But it has been enough to convince someone that *you* were behind this staged accident."

"Me? What makes you—"

"The letters," Linette said.

"The letters," Vickery confirmed.

"That's prep—"

"You have deliberately concealed from everyone, including your own wife, the complete texts of the letters you have received," Vickery said.

"That's not—"

"Yes, it is. The letters warn that you will be punished for 'what you have done.' But you have carefully kept from us what the letter-writer believes you to be guilty of."

"I'm not *guilty* of anything!"

"Then why seek to keep the accusation secret?"

"The last thing I need is some crazy rumour circulating that I tried to—that I—"

"That you tried to do away with your wife by staging a riding accident," Vickery said.

"*Leo!*" Margot gasped.

"I didn't do it," Fulbright protested.

"But someone *believed* that you did," Vickery said.

"Either that, or they wanted everyone else to believe that daddy did it," Linette suggested.

"That is another possibility," Vickery said.

"This is all getting very confusing," Bannister said. "We have poor Miss Trenton murdered, and then poor Artie. We've had an attempt on Fulbright's life, and now you're suggesting that someone tried to kill Margot!"

"You are right, it is time that we brought an end to the confusion. I propose that we begin by explaining the poison pen letters. Why did you send them, Mr. Bannister?"

A hush fell on the room.

"I—I—I sent them." It wasn't a protest or a denial, but a quiet admission.

"You believe that Margot McCrae's riding accident was deliberately staged?" Vickery asked.

"I don't believe it, I *know* it!" Bannister said. "I know who the old woman was."

For the second time in as many minutes, Bannister had everyone holding their breath in anticipation.

"It was Artie," Bannister said. "Artie Delancey dressed up as an old woman and scared Margot's horse." Bannister sounded as though he regretted having to reveal a friend's guilty secret, and at the same time to speak ill of the dead.

"Artie told you this?" Vickery asked gently.

Bannister shook his head.

"You saw him take the witch costume?" Vickery asked.

Again a shake of the head. "I saw him put it back."

"Did you ask him what he was doing with it?"

"At the time, I made a joke of it, told him they'd shoot him for using theatre costumes for his own act."

"You thought he'd worn it as part of his night-club act?"

"What else would I think? You know how he used to dress up at that club, singing *A Little of What You Fancy* and *All the Nice Girls Love a Sailor* and what have you. I just thought he'd dressed up as a witch for something. I didn't know at the time what had happened to poor Margot."

"But you found out later."

"We heard about the accident, but it was a couple of days before we knew what had actually happened. At first I didn't make the connection, why would I? They just said the horse had been spooked by a mad old woman."

"Why did you become suspicious?"

"Artie just wasn't himself, he seemed really down in the dumps. He'd been arrested a few weeks before, and that upset him, but that all seemed to blow over. He got a slap on the wrist, or whatever, and he cheered up for a while. But then he got to really moping around, and I said to him, Whatever's the matter, dear? But he didn't want to talk about it.

"I thought perhaps it was romantic troubles, so I didn't push him, thought it would pass. But then I noticed he was being a bit shifty, and he looked pale and unwell. He seemed especially upset whenever Margot's name was mentioned, like he couldn't bear to hear about her. That's when I remembered the witch's costume."

"Did you ask him about it?"

"I mentioned it, just the once. I said, Artie, that night when I saw you back stage with that frock, the one from the Scottish play... Well, I thought he was going to drop down and die at my feet. Never seen anyone so pale, he was like a half-glass of milk. And shaking. I said, Whatever's the matter, love? And he just made me promise, *never* to mention the dress or anything. And I didn't."

"You never asked him why he'd worn the dress? Or if he'd gone off to the country to spook Margot McCrae's horse?"

"I didn't dare. You never saw how sick it made him look when I mentioned it that one time. But I started to put two and two together. I knew Artie would never have done anything to harm Margot, he had no reason to. Someone must have put him up to it. And I'm sure he never thought she'd get really hurt by it, I'm sure she was just meant to fall off the horse and sprain her ankle or something. He wouldn't have done it otherwise. That's why he was so sickened by what he'd done, I reckon."

"And when you put two and two together?"

"Did I say that Artie had been arrested?"

"You did."

"Police picked him up for, well, for being Artie. If we aren't too blatant, they usually turn a blind eye, but Artie thought the rules didn't apply to him, silly boy. They kept him locked up all night, threatened to have him up in front of a magistrate, and he was worried what his poor old mum would think, having her only son in prison. But anyway, I found out that Leo Fulbright sorted it all out for him, provided him with an alibi, said he'd pay for a good solicitor, or whatever was necessary, so the police just gave Artie a slap on the wrist and that was the end of it. Or so you'd hope."

"It wasn't the end of it?"

"I don't think it was. I think Fulbright told Artie he wanted something in return. I think he wanted Margot out of the way. So he had Artie dress up and go out to the country and jump up in front of her horse. He could have been kicked in the head and killed, but I don't suppose Fulbright cared about that."

"This is just nonsense. You can't believe— ?" Fulbright could hardly contain his temper.

"What I believe doesn't concern us at this point," Vickery said. "Mr. Bannister believed you were behind Margot's accident, and so he sent you an anonymous letter."

"It wasn't right, what he made Artie do. Threatening to tell the police the truth if he didn't do it. And then poor Margot, what it had done to her—" Bannister was moved almost to tears by this point. "I had to do *something*. I couldn't go to the police, of course. And Margot wasn't well enough to deal with it. I got an old typewriter out of the props cupboard, and I typed out the letter."

"What did you think it would achieve?" Vickery asked.

"I wanted Leo to realise that his secret was known, that

someone knew what he'd done. I hoped this would make him do the right thing, admit to Margot what he'd done, and seek her forgiveness," Bannister said. "They belong together those two. I just wanted to make it right again. Make him see that he was making a mistake chasing after that slip of a girl."

"What did Fulbright do after you sent the first letter?"

"Absolutely nothing! He kept it hidden, burnt it for all I know, and pretended he'd never received it. I couldn't believe it."

"I thought it was from some crackpot. It was nonsense!" Fulbright said.

"I typed a second letter, made sure I left it somewhere public, so other people would be around when he found it. He couldn't ignore it then." There was a note of triumph in Bannister's voice.

"But even that didn't produce the desired effect," Vickery said. "You sent a third letter, then a fourth."

"I wasn't going to let him get away with it," Bannister said. "I wasn't about to back off, even when he hired you, Mr. Vickery, to find out who was sending them."

"If Mr. Bannister is telling us the truth, he may just have provided us with Margot McCrae's motive for murdering both Eleanor Trenton and Artie Delancey," Inspector Debney said.

"I *didn't!*" Bannister seemed horrified.

"Margot wanted Miss Trenton out of the way because of the bitter rivalry between them, and she wanted Artie dead because he was responsible for her accident, and for the death of her favourite horse," Debney said.

"No, wait," Bannister said. "Margot didn't do it. *I did!*"

"You want us to believe that you are the murderer?" Vickery asked.

"I did it," Bannister insisted. "Margot had nothing to do with it. I couldn't bear to see her career end, just because Leo was besotted with that woman. She was making him act like a fool. I had to put a stop to it, anyway I could.

"And when I learned what Artie had done to Margot, I couldn't let that go unpunished, I had to deal with him as well. Please forgive me, Margot, and don't worry about me: I'm an old man, I'm at the end of my life. I'm just sorry I won't get to see you up on that silver screen. You will be fabulous!"

Chapter 22

"No, no, that really won't do at all," Vickery said. "Mr. Bannister is *not* guilty of murder. He has confessed only in order to protect Margot McCrae. But there was really no need."

"Dickie, darling, it really is sweet of you to take the blame for me. But I didn't do it. Perhaps I should have, but—" Margot shrugged. "I'm sorry to disappoint you."

"You didn't do it? Oh, Margot, I'm so sorry, I never meant to suggest that you were guilty. I only wanted to—"

"Protect me, I know. But I wouldn't have wasted my time murdering that sparrow-legged little chorus girl," Margot said. "If I was going to murder someone, it would have been my husband."

"I love you too, my dear," Fulbright said, teeth gritted.

"Margot had no reason to want Eleanor Trenton dead," Vickery said.

"But the motion picture. Guinevere. And Eleanor stealing her husband," Sir Geoffrey protested.

"Your niece was no match for me," Margot said. "You of all people should know that, Geoffrey. Leo never leaves me. He may stray from the path occasionally, but he's never really off the leash. And as for poor little Eleanor being an actress, well, perhaps we'll never know now. But she certainly wasn't ready to be Guinevere. I've seen the footage, and at the very least she would need to be dubbed so the audience could hear her."

"You've seen it?" Fulbright asked.

"Who do you *think* took the film, darling? I had to see it before the rest of them did. I needed to know whether she was going to be a serious rival."

"She could never rival you, Margot," Bannister said. "It was a huge mistake casting her instead of you."

"I agree," Margot said.

"As do I," said Fulbright. "I'm sorry, Geoffrey, but your niece would never have finished the film. Perhaps it is better that she left us without knowing that her dream was going to end. I'd already asked Margot to replace her, before Eleanor was—"

"I don't believe this," Sir Geoffrey said. "You two are in this together somehow. You both—"

"No, they didn't," Vickery said. "Margot had no reason to kill Eleanor Trenton: she had already defeated her in every way that mattered. Leo and Margot are not murderers, either separately or collectively. And the only thing Mr. Bannister is guilty of is sending the poison pen letters."

"What an old fool I am," Bannister said, shaking his head.

"You didn't tell Artie Delancey you were sending the letters, did you?" Vickery asked.

"I didn't tell anyone. Artie would have tried to stop me," Bannister said.

"He would probably have told you the truth," Vickery said. "That would have stopped you, I'm sure."

"I don't understand."

"Leo Fulbright didn't blackmail Artie. He didn't make him dress up in the witch costume, because Artie wasn't the one who wore it."

"But I saw him—"

"You saw him *return* the costume. He did that to protect someone else. The person who *did* wear it."

"Then the letters—"

"You sent them to the wrong person," Vickery said.

Bannister seemed to deflate as he accepted this. "What have I done?"

"Bloody old fool!" Fulbright said.

"Mr. Bannister acted from the best of motives," Vickery said. "He felt his friend was being misused. And he was devoted to Margot McCrae, he was distraught over the 'accident' that appeared to have ended her career. I think we might forgive him his actions this once."

"Dear Dickie," Margot said.

"Well, that's the mystery of the poison pen letters solved," Linette said, in an attempt to brighten the mood.

"Except for the fact that they were sent to the wrong person," Garvin said. "Who should they have gone to, Mr. Vickery?"

"Yes, who caused mummy's accident if it wasn't Artie?" Linette asked. "Do you know?"

"I do," Vickery said. "The person who attempted to kill your mother is the person who did kill Eleanor Trenton."

"If Leo and Margot are innocent, that leaves only one more suspect," Bannister said.

"Veronica Fulbright," Inspector Dabney said, to prove that he was keeping up with things.

"My sister did *not* kill Eleanor Trenton," Leo Fulbright said.

"Thank you, Leo," Veronica said.

"Aunt Veronica is the only one left who was out of the room when the murder took place," Linette said.

"We stated that there appeared to be three potential suspects," Vickery said, "and, as you say, Veronica Fulbright is the last of these. But I believe there is a fourth suspect who should be added to the list: George Starling."

"*George?*" Veronica tried to sound surprised, but the flush of her cheeks gave away her guilt.

"He is close enough to be included as a suspect," Vickery said, "both physically and metaphorically."

"He's *here?*" Fulbright breathed.

Veronica refused to acknowledge her brother's question, and looked instead towards Vickery.

"He's staying at the inn in the village," she said. "He came down with me on the train. I've been meeting with him for a couple of months. At first I wasn't sure I wanted to see him again, I thought it might be too painful. For me. And for him. I thought I might have changed too much for him to still—" She looked down at the drawing room carpet, but when she looked up there could be no doubt how well her reunion with George had gone. "I don't know why, but he does—"

"I think you underestimate yourself, Miss Fulbright," Vickery said.

"Yes, we should never underestimate my dear sister," Fulbright said. "Not when we know what she's capable of."

"Mr. Fulbright is referring to the fact that his sister once made an attempt upon his life with a bow and arrow, and as a result he had her committed to a private sanatorium," Vickery said.

Veronica Fulbright's face had drained of colour, though whether she was acutely embarrassed or angry beyond words it was impossible to tell. It took a visible effort on her part to overcome her feelings.

"You don't really think George played any part in Eleanor Trenton's death, do you, Mr. Vickery?" Veronica asked. "I'm sure he isn't the type. I know he threatened to kill my brother when he found out what had happened to me, but..."

"But *everyone* has wanted to kill Leo at some point," Margot said.

"But few of us have actually tried to," Veronica said.

"Yes, there is that to take into account," Vickery said. "Leo Fulbright took from you the person that you truly loved, and did the same to George. Perhaps one or both of you decided to do the same in return, taking Eleanor Trenton from him."

"Leo didn't *love* Eleanor," Veronica said. "She was just another one of his—what did Margot call them? —*dalliances*. He never genuinely cared for her. If I had really wanted to take away the only person Leo Fulbright ever truly loved, I'd have taken that sword to—"

"Me?" Margot suggested.

"Leo Fulbright," Veronica said.

Margot frowned, then laughed out loud. "She's right, you know."

"Discounting the revenge motive, then, we must consider whether Veronica Fulbright hoped to benefit *financially* as a result of Eleanor Trenton's death," Inspector Debney said.

"How could I?" Veronica asked.

"Having had you declared mentally incompetent, Leo Fulbright seized control of your father's estate: his half and your half. And then he set about using that money to fund a motion picture starring his latest 'dalliance.' You must have found that particularly galling. He was frittering your money away on a vanity project. Didn't that make you angry?" Vickery asked.

"Yes, it did," Veronica said.

"Angry enough to resort to desperate measures? To murder Eleanor Trenton to stop your money flooding into 'Fulbright's Folly'?"

"Fulbright's Folly?" Fulbright said.

"It's what people are calling your picture, dear," Margot said brightly.

"If I had thought of killing someone for money, my brother would have been the first choice," Veronica said. "With him out of the way, I could gain control of the whole estate. Margot might have challenged me for his half, but it would still be a better bet than trying to stop the film by topping the leading lady."

"There seems to be nothing wrong with your reasoning, Miss Fulbright," Vickery said.

"Haven't heard that in a long time!" Veronica grinned.

"Again you underestimate yourself: out of habit, I suppose. Hasn't the solicitor you have consulted confirmed that he believes you mentally competent? And provided you with a reference to a doctor who will be able to determine that fact to the satisfaction of a judge?"

"More mind-reading tricks?" Veronica asked, apparently concerned that her secrets were known. "Or lucky guesses?"

"Neither," Vickery said. "I sent Mr. Malloy to have a pint with George at the inn in the village. He confirmed what I had already surmised."

"He didn't tell me."

"I asked him not to. I hope you will forgive him: we persuaded him that it would be in your interests to wait until I could disclose the facts to your best advantage."

"It was you that talked him out of coming up here and confronting Leo?" Veronica said to Malloy.

"I helped George talk himself out of it," Malloy said.

"He was never fully persuaded that an attempt to appeal to Leo Fulbright's better nature would succeed," Vickery said. "When we presented an alternative, I think he was rather relieved."

"I *warned* him to stay away," Fulbright said.

Margot put her hand on his arm, quieting him.

"Let her have this, Leo."

"But the—"

"It's too late. Geoffrey's money is gone, it's never going to happen. Even with Veronica's half of the estate, it wouldn't be enough."

"Then what do we do?"

"We finish *Arthur and Guinevere,* and on the back of that, well... I've heard that California has a lovely climate. Getting away from the damp and the cold will do my back wonders, I am sure."

"Hollywood, Margot?"

"Hollywood, Leo!"

"Veronica Fulbright has an alibi for the night of Eleanor Trenton's murder," Inspector Debney said. "My officers have taken statements at the inn. Witnesses confirm that she arrived at the inn a little before ten o'clock, and that she was there until closing time. Then as George Starling's guest, she stayed for the traditional public house 'lock-in' that we in the constabulary admit to knowing nothing about. She did not leave the inn until after one o'clock, and Mr. Starling walked with her back up to the keep."

Veronica Fulbright sat back and smiled. Perhaps because she found herself proved innocent of murder, or perhaps because she no longer had to keep her reunion with George Starling a secret.

"You seem to have exonerated all of your main suspects, Vickery." Fulbright sounded less than impressed.

"We do rather, don't we," Vickery said. "That is because none of them were guilty."

"But Leo, Margot, and Veronica were the only people who were out of the room at the time of the murder. You said so yourself," Bannister said.

"They are the only ones who were absent at midnight," Vickery conceded. "But other people were in and out of the room before that."

"But we know that the murder occurred just after midnight,"

Bannister said. "We all heard the scream. And we saw Eleanor at the top of the stairs before Teddy did his mock *Hamlet*."

"That would certainly *appear* to be the case," Inspector Debney said, with a rather unattractive smirk. He seemed pleased to know something that the others did not. "I can assure you that the murderer is in this room, but it is not one of the three people we all suspected initially."

The guests all eyed each other nervously again.

"But how?" Bannister asked.

"Before we explain *how*, I should like to explore *why,*" Vickery said.

"You have worked out who did it, haven't you, Mr. Vickery?" Linette said.

"I have *a* solution to the problem," Vickery said. "A version of what *really* happened that fits *all* of the facts: I should like to present it to everyone, so that we might test it for flaws."

"Why do you have to turn it into a bloody game?" Fulbright said. "Just tell us and be done with it."

"Do you not remember your school days, Mr. Fulbright? Always we must show our workings out. We must demonstrate the steps which lead to our solution. We must be sure of those steps in our own minds."

"I think you should do it properly, Mr. Vickery, like they do in the novels," Linette said.

"Thank you my dear."

"He has to take each of us in turn," Linette explained. "Show how we might have done it, and why, and then explain why we are innocent. All of us except the murderer, who did do it."

"I shall do my best to uphold that tradition," Vickery said with a little bow.

"*Humph!*" Fulbright said, and muttered something under his breath about a waste of bloody time.

"If none of those three did it, who *did?*" Sir Geoffrey

demanded. "Who else could have had a reason for wanting Eleanor dead?"

"In these situations, we seem to find that everyone has a motive, Sir Geoffrey. The trick lies in finding out who was sufficiently motivated to act on theirs," Vickery said.

"I can assure you that *I* had no motive," Sir Geoffrey said. "I could never have hurt her, she was my niece. I *loved* her."

"Yes, I believe you did. Though I suspect your actions towards her might not always have been in her best interest," Vickery said.

"What are you implying?"

"You said Eleanor reminded you of her mother, your sister?"

"Yes, very much so. It was—sometimes it was difficult to remember that they weren't—that—"

"You and your sister were very close?" Vickery asked.

"As children, yes, we were. After she married that—after she married, we were less close. Her husband did not—wouldn't—"

"You saw little of your niece when she was a child?"

"I attended her christening, then I did not see her for many years. She was almost grown when I saw her next. A woman."

"Eleanor lost both of her parents?"

"Her father left when she was fifteen, just after Timothy was born. I don't know where he went. I imagine that he drank himself to death, though that may just be wishful thinking. Her mother passed away. An accident."

"You became her guardian?"

"Eleanor and Timothy's, yes," Sir Geoffrey said. "I was her godparent, it is what I was supposed to do. I have no family of my own—" Sir Geoffrey glanced sideways, not quite looking at Margot McCrae.

"You intended that your estate should pass to your god-children?"

"Yes," Sir Geoffrey said. "It was to be divided equally."

"Now Timothy is your sole heir?"

"Yes, I suppose so. I haven't thought about that. We haven't even had a funeral yet..."

"Eleanor's relationship with her father was a difficult one?"

"Difficult is one word for it. He didn't appreciate what a beautiful child he had. Or what a beautiful wife. He didn't know how to treat them."

"Your brother-in-law was a violent man?"

"I believe that... yes, he was. Towards my sister. And towards Eleanor too, I think."

"How did that make you feel?"

"What sort of question is that? I didn't know. Didn't find out until after he had left them."

"Your sister was happier without her husband?"

"She should have been. But I don't believe she was. She loved him. He was the father of her children, no matter what else he did to her. She thought she needed him. Perhaps she even thought that she deserved him. I can't explain it."

"Sometimes people are drawn to partners who are not suitable for them. They escape one unpleasant relationship, only to enter another equally unwise," Vickery said.

"I think that was true of my sister."

"And of Eleanor?"

"We either become the opposite of our parents, or we become them, isn't that what they say?" Sir Geoffrey said.

"You said Eleanor was like her mother."

"In more than just looks, yes."

"She sought out men like her father?"

Sir Geoffrey glanced towards Kimball and then Fulbright. "I would say so, yes."

"Strong men with violent tempers?"

"I say!" Kimball protested.

"What the—?" Fulbright said.

"She deserved better. Someone who really cared for her. I tried to show her that, but—" Sir Geoffrey shrugged.

"But she pushed you away?"

Sir Geoffrey's voice was a whisper: "Yes."

Vickery let Sir Geoffrey stare at the carpet in silence, knowing he would speak again in his own time.

"I would have done anything for her," Sir Geoffrey said. "She knew that. This motion picture thing—"

"She would come to you and tell you what she wanted?" Vickery asked.

"She could wrap me round her little finger."

"And when she had what she wanted, she would turn her back on you again?"

"No—yes, I suppose so."

"How did you feel when you realised she had manipulated you to get what she wanted?"

"That was just how she was."

"Did it make you angry?"

"No, Mr. Vickery. It made me unhappy. If I had been another sort of man, someone who needs power over others, then I'm sure it would have done. But I am not. I never laid a hand on her. I did not—"

"—kill your niece. I know that," Vickery said. "But I needed to *show* why I believed you to be innocent."

Sir Geoffrey looked at him and, after a moment, nodded.

"Sir Geoffrey had no motive for killing his niece," Inspector Debney said. "But others in this room did."

"There are really only four possible motives for murder," Vickery said. "The first is *personal gain*, usually for money, but sometimes for prestige, to gain a position of power or some other form of recognition. Secondly there is *revenge*, to punish someone for a wrong suffered, either by the murderer themselves, or someone the murderer cares about. Thirdly comes love, the *crime passionnel* as the little Belgian might put it: to remove an obstacle to love. Or, returning to the theme of revenge, to 'punish' someone for a love betrayed or a love unrequited. And finally we have the murder motivated by *fear*, committed in order to protect oneself: from a fear of exposure, perhaps, or a fear of being harmed, even killed, oneself."

"Let's return to our examination of potential suspects, shall we?" Inspector Debney said. "What about Mr. Kimball, the jilted lover?"

"*Me?*" Kimball seemed shocked at the suggestion. "I *couldn't* have killed Eleanor."

"Let's leave aside whether you *could* have murdered her, and explore whether you might have *wanted* to," Inspector Debney said, with just a hint of malice.

"Did Mr. Kimball have any of these motivations? Had he a reason to kill Miss Trenton?" Vickery asked.

"I would have thought his motivation was bloody obvious," Fulbright said. "Eleanor had just broken off her relationship with him, made him look like a damned fool."

"*Leo!*" Margot admonished.

"No, it's true, she had ended it," Kimball conceded. "But she didn't make me look like a fool: I did that myself."

"But she did rather rub your nose in it," Bannister said. "Parading around on Fulbright's arm this weekend."

"It was nothing worse than I deserved," Kimball said. "I have to take responsibility for the consequences of my own actions."

"That's easy enough to say," Fulbright said. "But I still say that it gives you ample reason for wanting her dead."

"Rather than throwing around accusations, I think we should restrict ourselves to examining the facts," Vickery said. "We have established that Mr. Kimball *did* have a *motive*, a desire for revenge on the woman who jilted him. And so now we must move on and establish whether he also had the *opportunity* to murder her. We must test his alibi."

"Let's see how the worm thinks he can wriggle out of it," Fulbright said.

"The death of Eleanor Trenton occurred at a few minutes after midnight," Vickery said. "How have we determined this fact?"

"The scream," Linette said, "and we all heard her fall into the water."

"And the time?" Vickery asked.

"The clock on the main staircase had just chimed midnight, it had just interrupted—" Garvin broke off.

"Interrupted what, Mr. Garvin?" Vickery asked.

"Mr. Kimball," Garvin said. "He was standing on the first landing near the clock, using it as a stage. He was—"

"He was doing his impression of daddy," Linette said. "Reading that ridiculous poem."

"Then we all agree that Mr. Kimball was standing on the stairs as the clock struck midnight?"

"Yes, he cursed the clock for interrupting him," Garvin said.

"And in the silence that followed the striking of the clock, we heard the scream and the sound of something falling into the water?" Vickery said.

This was answered by nodding from most of those present.

"If Mr. Kimball was standing on the stairs in front of us," Vickery said. "Could he also have been outside murdering Eleanor Trenton?"

"No," Linette said.

There was quiet in the room as everyone considered this.

"Mr. Kimball had the motive but not, it appears, the opportunity," Inspector Debney said.

"What about an accomplice?" Fulbright suggested. "While he was on the stairs making an ass of himself pretending to be me, he could have had someone outside murdering Eleanor."

"But who?" Bannister asked. "We've already excluded all the people who were out of the room at the time."

"Oh," Fulbright said.

Oliver Garvin and Linnie Fulbright exchanged nervous glances.

"Did *you* do it?" Garvin whispered.

"No! Did you?" Linnie said.

"No!"

"But we are the only two left," Linnie whispered.

"What about Timothy?"

"Don't be ridiculous, he's a *child!"*

"Er, Mr. Vickery," Garvin said. "I'm afraid something might have gone wrong with your investigation—"

"Oh?"

"You see, me and—Linnie and I are the only ones left, and we didn't murder Eleanor Trenton."

"Or Artie," Linnie quickly clarified.

"You didn't?" Vickery asked.

"No, sir," Garvin said.

"Explain," Vickery challenged him.

Chapter 23

"Explain?" Oliver Garvin seemed stumped.

"Yes, tell us why it couldn't possibly have been you and Linette that murdered our two victims," Vickery said. "Please bear in mind that it is not enough that you each provide an alibi for the other: as a couple, no one is going to believe you. You could have plotted the whole thing together. Take all the time you need."

"Er—well—" Garvin floundered.

"Means, motive, and opportunity," Linette prompted.

"I *know*, thank you, I was just getting my thoughts in order."

"Sorry."

"Means," Garvin said. "The murder weapon."

"Excalibur," Linette added.

"Are you going to keep interrupting?"

"I'm *helping*, it's my neck in the noose as well, you know."

"All right, but don't keep putting me off my stride."

"Sorry, dear."

"Excalibur," Garvin said. "It was in that prop stone thing: I didn't know how to get it out."

"I did!" Linette said brightly.

Paul Tomlinson

"Not helping."

"We have to tell the truth!"

"We had access to the *means,*" Garvin reluctantly admitted.

"*Opportunity,* then," Linette said, "access to the victim. Or victims."

"We were both here," Garvin said, "for the party on Friday night, and for the dinner on Saturday evening. I was supposed to be gone, Mr. Fulbright threw me out on Saturday afternoon, after he hit me with that rifle."

"Musket," Linette said. "What? We need to be accurate."

"After Mr. Fulbright hit me over the head with the *musket,*" Garvin said pointedly. "But I had to stay because Mr. Kimball took an axe to Mabel."

"His car," Linette said.

"My car," Garvin said. "Like everyone else, we had the opportunity to murder Miss Trenton."

"And Mr. Delancey," Linette said. Garvin glowered at her. "*Motive,* then!" She said.

"We don't have one," Garvin said.

"We must have, everyone else did."

"We had a motive to kill your father," Garvin said, "more than one."

"But he's not dead, is he?" Linette said.

"Live in hope," Garvin muttered.

"Perhaps we killed Eleanor because we wanted to hurt my father," Linette suggested. "Because he was an obstacle to our happiness."

"But like your aunt said, the only person Leo Fulbright cares about is Leo Fulbright."

"We didn't *know* that then," Linette said.

"Oh, *I* knew," Garvin said.

"What about a financial motive, then?"

"Again, a reason to murder your father, but how would we

profit from Eleanor Trenton's death?"

"Father was spending my inheritance on that stupid motion picture that Eleanor's acting was ruining. Not meaning to speak ill of the dead, but she was a little wooden."

"A *little*? If she'd been any more wooden, your father would have splinters in his—er—lips."

"But like Aunt Veronica said, if we were going to murder for money, we would have been better off killing my father."

"Actually, if your father's almost broke, we'd have been better off killing your mother."

"*Ollie!*"

"I was just *saying.*"

"I could never kill my mother," Linette protested. "Or my father," she quickly added.

"Where is this getting us?" Garvin asked.

"Ever-deeper water," Linette said. "Even *I'm* beginning to wonder if we didn't murder them."

"Perhaps it's time we wrapped this up," Garvin said. He glanced towards Vickery, who nodded encouragingly and smiled. "We didn't kill them. There's no evidence that we did. We don't really have a motive. And we're sorry that they are dead."

Linette applauded him silently, smiling.

"You seem to have eliminated all of the suspects, Vickery," Fulbright said. "Not much of an investigation. I hope the Inspector can make a better fist of it."

"Perhaps Benjamin still has a trick up his sleeve," Margot suggested hopefully.

"Not really," Vickery said. "I fear that there is something important that I have overlooked. Some important question I have failed to ask."

"You *did* solve the mystery of the poison pen letters," Linette said, by way of consolation.

"Except—" Garvin began, but was stopped by Linette elbowing in the ribs.

"Except what, my boy?" Vickery said.

"You said Mr. Fulbright played no part in staging his wife's accident, and therefore Mr. Bannister had sent his letters to the wrong person."

"I said that," Vickery acknowledged.

"Then who *should* he have sent the letters to?" Garvin asked.

"Did I not say?" Vickery asked. "Margot's accident was caused by Ted Kimball. It was he who dressed up in the witch costume and leaped out to startle the horse. Artie Delancey found out about it, and to protect Kimball, who was his friend, Artie offered to return the offending costume to the theatre. That is why Mr. Bannister saw Artie *returning* the costume."

Everyone was staring at Kimball. He shifted uncomfortably.

"You have no proof," he said. "You're guessing."

"Teddy?" Margot said. "Why?"

"Did you not have a brief 'dalliance' with Mr. Kimball at some point?" He asked Margot.

"That is not exactly a secret, Benjamin. It lasted all of a week. I was angry with Leo, I don't even remember why. I wanted to give him a taste of his own medicine. I didn't find it particularly satisfactory."

"Do you believe that Mr. Kimball was aware that he was merely functioning as 'medicine'?" Vickery asked.

"Of course he did. Didn't you?" She looked to Kimball for confirmation. He didn't seem able to provide it. "Teddy?"

"But that was years ago," Fulbright said. "Bloody long time to bear a grudge and do nothing about it. Why wait six years?"

"When you met Eleanor Trenton, were you aware that she and Mr. Kimball were courting?" Vickery asked.

"I don't—that is—"

"Of course he knew," Margot said, "that was why he pursued

her. Teddy had cuckolded him, and Leo wanted his revenge. You can just imagine the conversation, can't you? Why are you wasting your time with that drunken loser, come and play the queen in my new motion picture."

"That's not how it was," Fulbright said. "She came to me and asked for my advice. She had an audition, and wanted me to help her prepare."

"Do you honestly expect me to believe *that*?" Margot asked.

"He's telling the truth," Kimball said. "She went to him. Mr. Vickery was right, Eleanor knew how to get what she wanted from men. Especially older men." He glanced towards Sir Geoffrey.

"Mr. Kimball," the Inspector said, "I should warn you at this point that you do not need to say anything more. And that anything you do say may be set down in evidence to be used against you."

"I want to *finish* this," Kimball said firmly, glancing towards Vickery. Vickery thought about this for a moment, and then nodded his assent.

"You think that Eleanor *used* you, and then moved on?" Vickery asked Kimball.

"It was even worse than that," Kimball said. "She found that she had *no use* for me. Not then."

"Eleanor left you because Leo Fulbright offered a better prospect. What did you do?"

"I did what I always do. I got drunk. And then I went to see Margot."

"And you discovered that she had no use for you either?"

"That's when I found out that she had just used me before, to try and get even with Leo."

"Teddy, I'm sorry," Margot said, "I never meant to—"

Kimball shook his head, not wanting to hear.

"You wanted to hurt Margot?" Vickery asked. "And Leo?"

"I thought if Margot got hurt, Leo would go running back to her, filled with guilt and contrition, like he always did. And then Eleanor and I would stand some chance of—" He shrugged. "Hopelessly naïve."

"When Artie Delancey found out what you had done, what happened?" Vickery asked.

"Margot was in the hospital, nobody knew how badly she'd been hurt. Artie was afraid that she would die. I didn't care what happened to me, but Artie did. He really was my friend, probably my only real friend. He put the costume back in the theatre wardrobe, and he promised he would never tell anyone what I'd done."

"Were you afraid that Artie might try and blackmail you?" Vickery asked.

"Artie? He would never have done that. He loved me. He would do anything for me."

"And you exploited that fact, didn't you?" Vickery said. "When you murdered Eleanor Trenton?"

"I never meant for Artie to get hurt," Kimball said. "No matter what else you think about me, I want you to know that I did care about him. He was like my little brother."

"I think Artie knew that," Vickery said.

"You said there was a question you'd forgotten to ask," Kimball said. "You meant the photographer?"

"I did," Vickery said. "It occurred to me on Friday when I first heard the story, but then other things got in the way."

"What about the photographer?" Fulbright asked.

"On the night that Artie took Mr. Kimball to the *Pink Gardenia*, there were *two* photographers waiting outside."

"So?" Fulbright asked.

"Who sent the second one?" Vickery said. "Everyone assumed that you sent them both, but why would you send *two* photographers?"

"I didn't," Fulbright said. "I sent Garvin. He'd been hanging around the set trying to take pictures: I didn't know at the time he was also trying to take my daughter."

"Leo." Margot laid a hand on his arm again, as if to stem the rising of his blood pressure.

"Who sent the second photographer?" Vickery repeated. "No one in this room."

He looked round. People looked questioningly at each other, then back at Vickery.

"It was Eleanor," Kimball said. "She was spying on me. I thought at first that *he* had put her up to it," he nodded towards Fulbright. "But I think he got the idea from her."

"Why was she having you followed?" Vickery asked.

"I had been right about Leo going back to Margot after the accident. And I went back to Eleanor. I thought things were good between us. But I think she just wanted to keep her options open, in case Leo didn't come back to her when Margot recovered. She was stringing me along, and I was too stupid to see it. After about a year, I had become a habit with her, something she was used to.

"I had asked her to marry me, more than once. She had turned me down. I want to think that she was seriously considering my latest proposal, she hadn't said *no* straight away this time. You've already heard about her father: she didn't want to spend her life with another drunk. She wanted me to stop drinking. To prove that I wasn't like her father. And I was going to do it: I wanted to be with her so much, I would have done anything."

"You didn't make a very good job of it," Fulbright said. "A drunken brawl in the street outside a poofter bar."

"It was a mistake," Kimball acknowledged. "I wanted to go out on one final all-night drinking spree. And then the next day I was due to check into the clinic Artie had booked me into. With their help, I'd be cured. I'd never touch a drop again."

"But the photographers were waiting for you outside the bar," Vickery said.

"Seeing him standing there with that camera, with the big reflector thing, like a huge eye that missed nothing, captured everything. Winking at me and telling me that I had failed. Showing me that Eleanor didn't trust me. I was angry with myself, but it was easier to hit him.

"Perhaps if I hadn't attacked the photographer, Eleanor might have forgiven me. Given me another chance. But once she heard what I'd done, to her, I was just like her father. He hadn't been able to change, and she thought I couldn't either. I'd like to take a drink now, if I may?"

Vickery nodded to Malloy, who went to the sideboard and poured whisky into a glass. He handed it to Kimball.

"And so we come, finally, to what *really* happened on the night of the murder," Vickery said. "Would you like to explain it, Inspector?"

"Er—I think that you would tell the story far better than a mere policeman," Debney said.

"If you're sure?" Vickery said.

"Just get on with it, Vickery," Fulbright said. "We all know who solved this thing."

"On the night that Eleanor Trenton was murdered, a scream was heard and something that sounded like a person falling into the pond. We know this happened just after midnight, and so we believed this to be the time of the murder."

"You don't need to be Sherlock Holmes to figure that out: it's obvious!" Fulbright said.

"Perhaps it is *too* obvious," Vickery said.

"Don't talk in riddles, man," Fulbright said.

"We *assume* that the time of Eleanor Trenton's death was the time when the scream was heard."

"She certainly didn't scream *after* she was dead, did she?"

Fulbright said.

"There I think you are wrong," Vickery said.

"But the doctor confirmed the time of death," Linette said. "Didn't he?"

"Not exactly. He said that his findings were *consistent* with the murder having occurred at midnight. But there is a margin of error in such a calculation, particularly when the body has been submerged in cold water. Miss Trenton *could* have been killed at any time between ten o'clock and midnight."

"But the scream?" Linette said.

"Proves only that *someone* screamed just after midnight. We have nothing to prove that it was Eleanor Trenton," Inspector Debney said.

"Then who?" Linette asked.

"Eleanor couldn't have been killed at ten o'clock, or even eleven o'clock: we all saw her at the top of the stairs well after eleven," Bannister said.

"Did you speak to her?" Inspector Debney asked.

"Perhaps it was her *ghost?*" Kimball said: the whiskey seemed to have had an immediate effect.

"Don't be a bloody fool. She was still alive then, she was killed at midnight. There's no other explanation," Fulbright said.

"That is what the murderer wished us to believe." Vickery glanced towards Kimball, who raised his glass in salute. "The person people saw at the top of the stairs in the red dress was Artie Delancey."

"Ridiculous!" Fulbright said.

"Is it?" Vickery said. "Wasn't he of similar build to Miss Trenton, enough for him to be able to substitute for her in the horse-riding scenes in your motion picture?"

"Yes, but—"

"Artie did look good in a dress," Bannister said.

"The dresses!" Malloy said. "We wondered why Artie had more than one: he brought several colours because he didn't know which one Eleanor would be wearing that night."

"Correct," Vickery said. "And after the murder, Artie hid the red dress he had worn in Eleanor's wardrobe to throw us off the scent. He couldn't leave the shoes, because his were several sizes larger than Eleanor's, which we might have noticed."

"But Artie *couldn't* have stabbed her," Bannister insisted.

"He didn't," Vickery said. "Ted Kimball did, soon after dinner. He put her body in the pond. It was dark and he knew no one would find it there. Until he was ready."

"It was Artie who screamed at midnight!" Linette said.

"What about the sound of the body falling in the water at midnight?" Margot asked.

"The sack Mr. Malloy found in the pond," Vickery said. "It had been filled with blocks of ice, from the caterers the previous evening. Artie tossed it in the pond to make the sound."

"By the time I found the sack, the ice had melted," Malloy said.

"The red button was from Artie's dress," Fulbright said. "I thought it was Eleanor's, I was going to keep it..."

"I do not believe Mr. Kimball intended to kill Artie as well, at least not at first. But when it became apparent that Artie wasn't going to be able to handle the situation calmly..."

"Poor Artie," Bannister said. "He deserved better than that."

"So did Eleanor Trenton," Ted Kimball said bitterly. "I killed her because I didn't have the guts to murder Leo Fulbright. I wanted him to suffer for taking her away from me. I wanted everyone to think he had done it. I wanted to see the police take him away in handcuffs."

"They will be taking you away in a few minutes," Fulbright gloated. "Off to dance for the hangman."

"I'm afraid I'm going to have to disappoint you again,"

Kimball said. "I'll be gone before they get the handcuffs on."

"You're not going anywhere," Fulbright said.

"Always with the literal mind, Leo. No poetry in your soul," Kimball said.

"What is he wittering on about?" Fulbright asked.

"Mr. Kimball has, I believe, taken a fatal dose of barbiturates with his whisky," Vickery said.

"You let him *kill* himself?" Inspector Debney asked, shocked.

"I did not prevent it," Vickery said.

"But you *knew?*" The Inspector insisted.

"I suspected, but I had no proof."

Kimball slumped. Malloy, poised ready, caught him. Garvin and Linette rose so that Malloy could lay Kimball on the chesterfield.

"Three dead," Vickery said, "quite the weekend party, Mr. Fulbright."

"How the world will mourn the loss," Fulbright said, "two second-rate actors and a sexual deviant."

Malloy bounded across the room and swung a right-hook at Fulbright. It knocked the older man off his feet: he landed on his buttocks on the carpet with a startled *oof!*

Recovering himself, his face turning purple-red, Fulbright shouted up at Malloy, spittle flying.

"That was the biggest mistake of your life, boy! Hitting me in front of witnesses." Fulbright looked around the room, triumphant in is expectation of support.

Vickery turned his back on Fulbright and walked from the room. Dickie Bannister followed his example. Then Sir Geoffrey. Veronica Fulbright looked down at her brother, shook her head, turned and exited. Oliver Garvin took Linette's hand, and the two of them hurried out, not looking at Fulbright. The police constables and Inspector Debney also left the room. Malloy looked down at Fulbright, tugged his forelock, and followed the others out.

Only Margot McCrae remained.

"You might have done something," Fulbright said.

"I did: I'm here, aren't I?"

Chapter 24

Malloy came down the stairs carrying Vickery's suitcase. Vickery was standing in the entrance hall talking to Inspector Debney. Debney looked like a man who had just been handed a rotten fish.

"I took the liberty of packing for you, sir," Malloy said, interrupting whatever the Inspector had been saying. "Shall I bring the car round?"

"Thank you, Malloy. I think we are finished here, aren't we Inspector?"

With the greatest of reluctance, Inspector Debney nodded. He closed his notebook and wandered over to where Doctor Cole was standing, having examined his third corpse of the weekend.

"Are all the cars now in running order?" Vickery asked, as they stepped out from the shadow of the gatehouse onto the drive. They paused for a moment and looked in the direction of the pond.

"They're all working again, with the exception of Garvin's MG," Malloy said. "That needs a magician rather than a mechanic."

"Don't look at me, I'm retired," Vickery said. "I gave Garvin the keys to Ted Kimball's car."

"And he gave them to you in exchange for a lethal dose of barbiturates." Malloy said. It wasn't a question. "Did you get the pills from the doctor?"

"No, I've been carrying them with me for some time. But I recently found that I had no desire to keep them. I'm glad they did not go to waste."

"There's still one thing I don't understand," Malloy said.

"Only one?" Vickery said.

"Why did Kimball fire the crossbow at Fulbright the other night?"

"He didn't."

"Then who did?"

"Fulbright's sister, Veronica."

Malloy laughed. "Leo Fulbright had better watch out in future! Do you think he knows?"

"I am sure he suspects."

"And the police?" Malloy asked.

"I did not tell the Inspector. It is not in Miss Fulbright's interest that the police are aware of her second attempt on her brother's life. If someone asks, Dickie Bannister has agreed to accept the blame for it. But I doubt anyone will even mention it." Vickery nodded towards Malloy's swollen right hand. "Do you need ice for that?"

"I'm rather enjoying the pain." Malloy grinned.

"You shouldn't have hit him. But I'm rather glad you did."

"I felt sure Leo Fulbright would be the one killed this weekend," Malloy said.

"But then we would have had a dozen murderers, all lined up with their daggers, *n'est-ce pas, mon ami?*" Vickery said, curling an imaginary Belgian moustache.

"Which reminds me, when I asked you about *your* accent—"

"I told you I was born in Grimsby."

"You said Halifax," Malloy said.

"Grimsby is a small town *near* Halifax."

"When you say *near...?*"

"It didn't seem far when I took t'train."

"Was that a Yorkshire accent? Or Welsh? I thought detectives were supposed to be masters of disguise."

"Being who I am is disguise enough," Vickery said.

"Then why the accent?"

"I might ask you the same question."

"I'm Irish."

"Since when? It takes more than a couple of glasses of stout."

"I have an Irish birth certificate," Malloy insisted.

"And I have a tin sheriff's badge, but that doesn't mean I'll be chasing after Robin Hood any time soon."

"Douglas Fairbanks not your type then?"

"I much prefer a man in trousers rather than stockings."

"I shall restock my wardrobe accordingly."

Malloy loaded Vickery's case into the boot of the car.

"What will you do now?" Vickery asked.

"Time for a new position," Malloy said.

"Are you likely to punch your new employer?"

"That depends on how he behaves."

"I shall bear that in mind," Vickery said. He handed Malloy the keys to the Alvis. "We are not going to be undignified. At least not today."

Malloy opened the rear door of the car and stood straight, saluting. Vickery climbed into the back seat.

Malloy started the car, and with a last look back at Silberman's Keep, they headed off down the drive.

Author's Afterword:
'How to Not Write a Whodunit'

I didn't intend to write a whodunit, it sort of happened by accident. I wrote *The Sword in the Stone-Dead* in January, February and March of 2015: from first idea to complete 65,000-word draft in a little under twelve weeks. I had never written a novel-length story in such a short space of time, and those twelve weeks had included a couple of substantial rewrites. And it was all done in my spare time, because I had a full-time job at that point. I'm not saying 'look how wonderful I am,' I'm saying that sometimes a writer gets lucky, and the muse pays a visit; everything comes together and magical things happen.

Actually, I'm not saying that at all. I don't believe in the muse, in luck, or in magic. What really happened in those early months of 2015 was that I was *prepared* to write a novel, I'd figured out how to do it, and I sat down to prove to myself that I really could do it.

Up to that point, I'd written ten novel-length manuscripts and a couple of feature-length screenplays, and they were all rubbish. No matter how many times I rewrote them and polished them, I knew—in my heart of hearts—that they didn't really work. There was something missing. There were some good ideas in there, some humour, some decent dialogue, but each whole added up to less than the sum of its parts. I sent some of them out to agents and publishers, but none of them really satisfied me, so it was no surprise when they were returned with a 'thanks, but no thanks.'

For a while I thought that what I was missing was *character*. Good writing had good characters, so I needed to find out about character. I thought character had to be the problem, because I was pretty sure I had plot nailed. I'd read all the great screenwriting books, I'd attended sessions on how to write for television, I had plot sorted.

You read mystery novels, so you can probably already work out how this is going to end, but stick with me anyway…

I'd learned about three-act structure, and the eight-sequence breakdown used in screenplays: what I needed—or so I thought—was the equivalent of the three-act-eight-sequence model for creating characters. I searched around for a decent model I could use, but couldn't find one. Everything I read was just too complicated.

I spent three or four years developing my own model for creating characters. Three master archetypes, three hybrids. I wrote myself a manual—because that's what I do. I worked for over ten years implementing different library acquisitions software systems in a university library, learning how to use the software, and then developing in-house manuals that could be used for training people. Whenever I try and do something new, I write myself a user-guide. Having written 'the character book,' I put it to the test and wrote a new novel.

And it pretty much stunk like all the earlier ones. This new 'curate's egg' included characters as one of its relatively good parts, but the whole still didn't work.

Having worked for book suppliers and in libraries for most of my adult life, I've handled a lot of books. At one point I think

I'd probably read every 'how to write' guide out there, and had even been tracking down out-of-print ones on AbeBooks. I spent more time reading about how-to-write than actually sitting down and writing. It's how I used to procrastinate before YouTube. These days, with the availability of ebooks and print-on-demand, there are even more books on how-to-write. Occasionally I'll dip into one, for old times' sake but, in my heart of hearts, I know I'm unlikely to learn anything new. Flick through a 21st century how-to-write-screenplays book, and you'll find a lot of the same advice you can find in the how-to-write-photoplays books of the early to mid-1900s.

Where I did learn something new was in academic texts. The joys of working in a university library. I picked up John G. Cawelti's *Adventure, Mystery, and Romance*. It has the subtitle *Formula Stories as Art and Popular Culture.* This wasn't some sniffy professor looking down his nose at genre fiction and saying it wasn't 'proper' literature, this was an examination of how and why genre fiction worked. It wasn't a how-to book by a genre author, it was an outsider's view of the mechanics of it all.

Among my unsuccessful early novels was a fantasy trilogy about a thief and an actor. I wrote the middle book first, when I was in college, got hooked by the thief character and went back and wrote a book about him facing off against a dragon (because everyone has to write at least one dragon book), and then the third book was meant to have my actor and thief involved in a plot that was based on the traditional English country house murder mystery. I thought this one was going to be a breeze to write, because those Agatha Christie-type books were all based on a standard 'formula,' and all I would have to do was plug in my characters and location, turn the handle, and out would pop a novel.

Again, you can probably figure out how that one ended.

Like many of my other would-be novels, I got to about twenty-thousand words or so and the thing shriveled up and died. Same thing with my next project: I tried to write a contemporary crime thriller based on what I understood as the crime-thriller formula. It, too, stunk up the place.

It was at this point that I had one of those epiphany-things:

The problem with formula fiction is that no-one will tell you what the bloody formula is!

I don't believe in conspiracy theories any more than I believe in magic or muses, but for a while I did wonder if there was actually a secret plot to keep genre plots secret. You won't get the details from any of those how-to-write books. Of course, it is not a conspiracy, it's a matter of perspective.

John G. Cawelti's book looks at what these formulas contain, and why these things, in this combination and this sequence, appeal to audiences. His chapters on the 'classical detective story' gave me more insight into the 'formula' than any of the how-to-write books had ever done. At some point during my reading, I figured out that if you wanted to write a contemporary detective novel, you needed to have an understanding of how a 'classical' murder mystery worked and how a traditional 'man-on-the-run' thriller worked, because the modern detective thriller combines elements of both.

I decided to write myself a manual. Did you see that coming? I read, or reread, a stack of Agatha Christie novels. Why Dame Agatha? Because if you go into a high-street book store today, it will have a section that contains her books: not a few titles on a shelf, but virtually her whole back-catalogue. They're still popular. Edgar Allan Poe invented the classical detective story with a couple of short stories; Arthur Conan Doyle perfected and popularised the genre with his Sherlock Holmes short stories; but it was Agatha Christie that perfected the detective mystery at novel length.

Reading her novels, and Earl F. Bargainnier's *The Gentle Art of Murder: The Detective Fiction of Agatha Christie*, I learned three things. First, some of her novels aren't 'classical detective mysteries,' but are actually modern detective thrillers: she reflected the change in taste of her reading public. Secondly, if you read her novels in sequence, they provide a picture of the way British life changed between the 1930s and the 1950s, as the Empire faded. And thirdly, and most importantly for my purposes, there *is* a 'formula' plot for the whodunit that has, for all intents and purposes, two variations: (i) the body is discovered in Act I, as in *Murder at the Vicarage*, and (ii) the body is discovered at the midpoint, as in *Death on the Nile*. In these variations, the constituent parts are pretty much the same, they're just put together in a different order.

It's not clear from Agatha Christie's published notebooks to what extent she considered the structure of the whodunit to be a 'formula,' but I think it's fair to say that she did mess with her readers' heads by 'cheating' with the formula: *Murder on the Orient Express* and *Who Killed Roger Ackroyd* being famous examples. Maybe she just did this to stop herself getting bored with this type of story. She does acknowledge that writing a carefully plotted whodunit is harder than writing a thriller-type story.

If you're suspicious of 'deconstructionist' theories, have a look at Umberto Eco's essay 'The Narrative Structure in Fleming' in *The Bond Affair* (1966): he lists nine situations that occur in the James Bond novels and shows how they are presented in different sequences in different novels. It's hard to deny that he's on to something. And you'll occasionally see interviews with successful authors who admit that they learned how to structure a novel by (sometimes literally) taking apart an earlier author's work.

As I said, I didn't actually intend to write a traditional murder mystery novel: my 'handbook' was just a tool to clarify my understanding of the genre. I intended to go on and look at the thriller genre, and then put what I had learned together so that I could write my contemporary detective thriller. But having spent a few months in the company of Hercule Poirot and Miss Marple, I felt an urge to put what I had learned to the test. I wanted to write one of these things as a sort of 'proof of concept.' To prove that I really did know what the formula was. And yes, I'll admit it: I'd got hooked by the genre all over again.

I effectively set myself an end of semester exam, and the exam question was pretty strict: I had to write a *real* traditional whodunit. I was allowed to include humour, but I couldn't write a parody. It had to be set in the 1930s—the 'golden age' of the murder mystery—and be as historically accurate as I could reasonably make it. I was allowed to use words that Dame Agatha would never have used, because I felt that real people would *use* such words, even if publishers in the 1930s couldn't publish them. And I could be more open about sexual relationships for the same reason.

Historical accuracy wasn't always easy: Agatha Christie was writing about her own time, so knew what cars and fashions and songs and slang phrases were current; I had to research this stuff. Originally I had decided that my story was set during the May bank holiday weekend in 1935. I did end up being slightly vague about this in the end, not specifying the actual year, because I wanted to include some references to the British film industry that were a little bit later. The cars were an early part of the research, and I fell in love with the hero's Alvis Speed 20—that's the car on the cover of the book. If ever I write a bestseller, I shall buy myself one of those. And a Victorian folly.

'Murder at Fulbright's Folly' wasn't the first idea I came up with, my first idea was set on an airship, and turned out to be some kind of steampunk thriller hybrid—more of a movie cliffhanger serial than a classic whodunit. I liked the idea, but understanding the 'formula' meant I knew it wasn't right for the genre. My second idea became *Who Killed the Lady in the Lake?* in its first draft, until I remembered that Raymond Chandler already had dibs on the *Lady*. Wracking my brains, I came up with *The Sword in the Sternum*, but a quick Google search showed this to be the name of someone's blog, so I didn't want to use that. *The Excalibur Murders* was also taken, so was *Murder at the Round Table.* Eventually, I settled on *The Sword in the Stone-Dead.* Technically, and historically, the title is a cheat: T. H. White's *The Sword in the Stone* wasn't published until 1938, three years after my story takes place. Call it poetic licence. Though the less said about the 'poetry' in this book the better. (Gluttons for punishment might find the whole of *The Tragedy of Hamlet, Prince of Limerick* on my website, unless I've taken it down in an attempt to deny its existence).

Twelve weeks after setting myself the task, I had created the book you hold in your hands. I have no idea if it is a good novel, or a good example of the genre, but having finished it, I—as a writer—felt a sense of satisfaction that I hadn't felt with any of my earlier novel-length stories. I felt that this met my expectations. Not an A+ but almost certainly a 'pass.'

Strictly speaking, the 'formula' isn't really a formula, it's more of a structure. It helps you figure out what should happen where for maximum effect. All stories are based on a simple structure —set-up, rising tension (or suspense), payoff (or release). A joke is structured this way, and so is a novel. It's often referred to as the 'three-act structure'. In a novel you just have to spin it out for sixty- to a hundred-thousand words or more. You can use an eight-sequence approach to help you map those three acts. And you can use a genre 'formula' to help you figure out what goes where in the eight sequences. What I learned about my own writing was that I was trying to pile too much into the first third of my novels—by the time I got to twenty- or thirty-thousand words, I'd run out of stuff. I didn't understand the importance of pacing, of the steady release of information to the reader, of the importance of strategically placing particular turning points in order to achieve maximum dramatic effect. I'd just keep trying to make up new stuff to get to the required word-count, and as a result my novels were the wrong shape and didn't look or feel right. Like a body-builder in a mankini. Not that I've ever *felt* a body-builder in a mankini. Honest.

For most genre authors, this understanding of structure comes to them by a process of osmosis, from the novels they have read throughout their lives. They absorb it without really knowing it, which is why they don't lay it out in their how-to-write books. To them it is probably too obvious. Also there's the fact that they're probably uncomfortable about acknowledging that there could be a 'formula.' I had to learn it the hard way, and feel no shame in admitting that I used it.

The other great thing about a structure or formula is that it allows you to compare what you've got—your initial idea—against what you *need* to have, so that you can develop the idea into a novel. Formulas help you assemble and evaluate the raw materials—and having all of those to hand makes the writing process much smoother. The formula is also a map of where you are going, and where you need to get to on each stage of the journey, and if you have that, you're less likely to end up in the dead-end that is writer's block.

I've already revealed myself to be a heretic, so I'll tell you one last thing I like about formulas: they're a real boon when you write stuff *out of sequence* like I do. If I'm stuck with a particular scene, or unhappy with what I've just written, I skip over to another part of the story and write something I feel more confident about. That way I can still use my writing time while my subconscious is noodling away on the bit I'm stuck on. It's the finished item that matters: it doesn't matter how you write, nobody's ever going to know. Unless you're stupid enough to mention it in an afterword.

I'm not going to write any more about how this book was written, or how I came to publish it: on the website I have a more detailed analysis of how I plotted and wrote this book— it is full of spoilers of the worst kind, so please read the novel first! I will also make available a free ebook that gives an introduction to the basics of the three-act, eight-sequence structure that I'm using as the basis for my own learning about genre plots. As I learn new things, I will put more articles, blog posts and mini-manuals up on the site.

You can get in touch with me via the *contact* page on the website, or let me know what you think about *The Sword in the Stone-Dead* by posting a review on Amazon: I will read them all —how could I not?— and I look forward to your feedback.

Thank you for reading.

www.paultomlinson.org

Acknowledgments

Dame Agatha Christie provided the 'secret formula' – her *Death on the Nile* is a near-perfect example of the genre.

John G. Cawelti's *Adventure, Mystery and Romance* and Earl F. Bargainnier's *The Gentle Art of Murder* helped me uncover the secret.

Susan Zappala acted as first reader and typo-spotter, and tried to keep me sane during the crazier months of my 'proper' job. Thanks for taking on a hopeless cause, Doctor Zee, and for organizing the best leaving do (and gifts) I ever had.

Ange Hart gave advice on cover design and how to make InDesign do what I wanted it to do, while Isobel and Edward made a noise in the background, and Mike didn't. Visit my sister at 'The Pig Shed' print workshop: www.angehart.co.uk

My brother Mark and his family – Keri, Jake, and Alex – who should all have their names in this book in case I never do another one!

Stanley Tomlinson, who is 'Bill' to most people but 'Grandad' to me, and in memory of Doris Tomlinson, Reggie Goodman and Lou Goodman – because our grandparents contribute a huge amount to the people we become.

And finally Dot and Bill – 'Mum and Dad' to me and 'that couple with the weird son' to everyone else – thank you for putting up with the weirdness. And for extra typo-spotting.

About the Author

Paul Tomlinson was born in Nottingham, England, in 1966. He began making stuff up at the age of eight, but never thought he could make money doing it—which is good, because he hasn't. His parents got him addicted to books at an early age, teaching him to read before he started school, and bought him his first typewriter at the age of 12: they cannot, therefore, plausibly deny culpability.

Science fiction and Sherlock Holmes dominated his teenage reading, and he puts his interest in the macabre down to a love of Alfred Hitchcock movies—though one therapist did suggest a much more disturbing root cause, which is why he ended up in a wood-chipper. A fascination with story structures has led to various experiments with genre novels and screenplays, and some of his experiments have escaped out into the world. Fortunately they are too weak to do much harm.

The Sword in the Stone-Dead is his first crime novel, and he is currently working on a follow-up featuring magician-turned-detective Benjamin Vickery, and a contemporary crime novel set in Mansfield, Nottinghamshire's answer to St. Mary Mead—if St. Mary Mead were to ask: Where's the least exciting place you could set a crime novel?

34573209R00172